SPARROW

The River Bend Series

TJ MAKKAI

BOOKS BY TJ MAKKAI

River Bend Series
Crow September 2020
Hawk October 2021
Pigeon 2022

Their Confessions and My Lies 2023

Go to www.tjmakkai.com for more information about up coming releases.

I dedicate this to my friend Kris.

Everyone should have a friend they're not allowed to sit next to during an important meeting or a class.

Thank you for your friendship.

CHAPTER ONE

Twenty minutes after breaking up with Aaron, I was standing in Aiden Miller's apartment. Twenty-two minutes after the breakup, I was in the stairwell that leads to the sidewalk separating Miller's place from Aaron's. I was telling myself I went with Miller to his place to win the bet, but I knew I wanted to settle my curiosity.

I had seen him a few times at Aaron's bar, and it was general knowledge Aaron and I had been dating, so Miller's invite in the hallway at one in the morning had been ballsy and the coolest invite I'd ever received.

When I didn't respond to his one-word offer of "Drink?", he'd followed up with "It's one a.m., and you're leaving your boyfriend's apartment. Either you got called into work, which from the slippers you're wearing, I highly doubt it. Someone was in an accident—doubt it since you're not in a rush. Or you probably could use a beer."

"I hope the beer is cold," I'd replied.

His loft was small and held the most basic needs. One couch, one television that could be seen from anywhere in the loft, a kitchen table with two chairs, a desk but no desk chair, and a bed. Sparse but clean. He grabbed two beers from the fridge and handed me one without speaking since the invite in the hallway. His phone rang, and before he could silence it, he answered it. I heard a woman's voice requesting a reply to her greeting.

I don't know if it was his phone call, the frantic text from Sherrie, or that I felt like I was ten years younger as an awkward teenager standing next to a rock star instead of two twentysomething, consenting adults that had me fleeing the scene.

Standing in Miller's kitchen, I read her text: *drama in front of Peach's.*

The café was currently Sherrie's place of employment and had been closed for hours. Yesterday, she'd thought her sweet coworker Maggie was stealing from the register.

This better be about more than ten missing dollars.

I pounded half the beer, set the can in the sink, gave half a wave to Miller, and left without interfering with his phone call.

I texted Sherrie I would be there in five. She asked if I could bring Aaron. I said I could bring AMMO, if she was really in trouble.

We'd been trying to come up with a nickname for Miller and had ignored the spiderweb tattoo on his neck for inspiration. Finally, we had gone with the socially incorrect AMMO: All-Mystery All-Male OHMYGODHEISHOT. Soon after he acquired the name, he became more intimidating, and we were too shy to reference him by any other name but his given name Miller.

Looking back now, inviting Miller would have answered some questions but still left someone pregnant, someone dead, and someone looking for a beer at one in the morning.

CHAPTER TWO

I had never feared walking around River Bend, even at one a.m., bar time on a Thursday night, but the slippers might have been a mistake.

The small Wisconsin college town sits on the banks of the Mississippi River and has little violent crime. Drunk college kids, shoplifting, and general stupidity are the highlights on the town's online Community Relations and Safety Report.

Thursdays had always been my favorite night of the week to go out when I was in college, and Thursday seemed to have the same vibe in River Bend. Mostly legal-age students were at the bars, and there were fewer house parties on a Thursday than on the weekends. It was the beginning of the weekend and the beginning of fresh hope of meeting cute guys.

On the walk over to Sherrie, I thought about what Aaron had said. He had done most of the talking with little resistance from me.

My relief had turned to a pity party for me. I hadn't wanted to admit he was right.

Even though they were his words, it had felt like a self-inflicted wound when, before he walked out, Aaron said, "I don't doubt your feelings for me. It's what you do with them that has put us here." He grabbed his keys and called for Rita, his golden retriever, to join him as he walked out.

I had seen the breakup coming. Well, I had seen the engagement ring and freaked out. I suddenly changed from *What are we doing this weekend* to *What are you doing this weekend* and *I just watched this show I think you'll like* instead of saving it for us to watch together. It happened one weekend when I sat alone in the apartment and did nothing—when he was just two hours away—that got Aaron rethinking our future.

We had only met and started dating last July after my college graduation. I intended to stay with my aunt EG for the summer, but things quickly changed. I got a job at a hotel that suddenly developed into a career.

EG invited/insisted I stay with her rent-free and even encouraged Sherrie to do grad school at Jameson College and insisted Sherrie take the third bedroom rent-free.

After four months on the job, my boss sent me on a temporary assignment to another hotel in the Twin Cities. That hotel was short on managers, and my boss thought it would be a great learning experience for me.

The temporary job assignment came shortly after Aaron asked me to move in with him. I was simultaneously flattered and freaked out by this offer. I never really accepted or declined his invitation. I had been given his key out of convenience in October. It was mostly so I could let myself in if Aaron was not ready to leave his bar when I got there or to feed Rita. The loft space comes with the lease on the bar below. The house out near the Douglas Farm, he bought several years ago as a fixer, but I think that might be his forever home.

I never did the whole key exchange thing with him. EG is generous with her home and heart and does not much believe in locking doors except for a short period when someone was stalking us. Staying rent-free at EG's house with Sherrie and EG does not allow me to distribute keys to a perpetually unlocked door.

During my short stint in Cities, I could have moved back with my parents in St. Paul, Minnesota, and done the thirty-minute commute to the hotel, but I found a cheap sublet from a student at the University of Minnesota. I had to sign a six-month lease, even though the job was for three months. The rent was very reasonable, and considering I have been rent-free since leaving college, this was a no-brainer. The girl I sublet from left everything behind when she opted for a last-minute study abroad program. Literally everything was there except for two suitcases' worth of stuff. After the first week, I threw out her toothbrush and toothpaste. I bought new bedding and lived out of my suitcase.

I don't know if Aaron had intended to breakup with me this very night when he returned to his loft after leaving the bar, but things had become clear when he asked what I had done when I got back in town. I said I'd had dinner at EG's.

"I thought she went to Chicago for the week," Aaron said.

"I thought she'd be back, so I stopped in before coming here to the loft. Sherrie was leaving to meet Kay and Jenna for drinks, so I threw in a frozen pizza and watched TV."

"Why didn't you do that here?"

"Because I was there."

"Don't be funny." The anger was building in his voice. "I mean, if we're actually living together, don't you think you would chill here on the couch?"

"You weren't here. You said you didn't know how long you would hang at the bar. What difference does it matter what couch I sat on?"

"Your hair is wet, and you're in sweats. Let me guess, you also took a shower at EG's. Maybe did a load of washing."

"What difference does it make?"

"I would think if we are a couple, living together, those would be things you'd do here."

"Are you really making a big deal out of where I relax? I have been—"

Aaron never shouted, but his voice became a growl. "Don't give me that spiel again about living like a gypsy. You have been done with that assignment for three weeks. You go visit Mia for two days, and your first thought when you return to River Bend is *I think I will sit at EG's by myself on a Friday night.*"

I stayed silent, not for some grand effect but for lack of response.

Aaron spoke again. "You stay here like you stay at your sublease. I am done being a provisional player with you. I was so happy for you when they offered you that assignment. You assumed I am forever planted here. Instead, I am just another stop on your tour through River Bend. There is nothing wrong with having a partner with your vagabond lifestyle, but I've come to realize we differ on that. I am done."

Aaron had left me standing in his loft. I didn't know if he and Rita had gone back to the bar or his house out in the sticks, and I really didn't seem to care. Relief had washed over me when he left, but I realized now those were selfish thoughts. Did I have to consider his feelings before mine? However, if I wasn't looking out for my feelings, then why should anyone else?

Aaron was a good guy. He did not make enemies, but being his newly appointed ex-girlfriend did not allow me twenty-four-hour access to him. Would I miss him? I was the one that had opened the void between us. What would it be like having him, an ex, in this town? My previous boyfriends had been losers. There was not much to lose when I became an ex-girlfriend. Having said that, Aaron's prior serious ex-girlfriend, who was pregnant, had been hanging around a lot.

Let's see how he deals with two exes being in town.

Some sadness crept in but was quickly replaced with horror when my slippered foot sank into a giant puddle.

Horror turned to panic when I turned the corner near the alley, one block from the café, and it was lit up in blue lights. The police car lights drew the attention of several people as did the ambulance pulling into the area. My heart was beating double-time with the wail of a siren. My anxiety level was on the rise with each emergency vehicle I counted.

Sometimes the lesson is not what is in front of you but who is behind you watching.

CHAPTER THREE

The police were cordoning off the alley one block from Peach's where Sherrie sometimes parked. My mind was buzzing so I couldn't remember if her car had been at the house when I left or if she walked. She was not answering my texts, so I had to call, but that went unanswered.

A squad car was at each end of the alley. An officer that I didn't know was keeping onlookers back.

"I'm looking for my friend Sherrie. Can you tell me if she's there? Is she hurt?"

"You need to remain behind the line, ma'am," the officer replied.

"I just need to know if my friend is ok."

The officer puffed out his chest and squared off his stance. "This is a crime scene. I need you to step back."

It was almost comical how much this officer was acting like every TV cop ever written for bad cop dramas. The panic was overriding any need to mock this character. My phone beeped and drew my frustration away from telling him he needed to get a clue.

The text read *Sherrie's not here but best you go.*

It was from another officer and a friend, Wyatt Baumann. I looked down the alley, and through the flashing lights, I saw him standing near the ambulance. Our eyes met, and I nodded that I had gotten his message. He turned away. I knew that was all I would get, at least for now.

I stepped back, and from the corner of my eye, I could tell the first officer was still watching me.

If Sherrie wasn't there but needed my help, where could she be?

The cold night air, the wet slipper, and my nerves had me shaking, and I dropped my car keys.

The officer jumped at me again. "You need to leave now, Miss."

"Yes, sir. I just dropped my keys."

When I reached for them, I spotted a travel mug lying next to the drainpipe. It had cash sticking out of the lid, which had been awkwardly jammed on. Without hesitation, I scooped up my keys, the ten bucks, and the mug. It was a tall silver thermal cup with a handle and a worn-off logo. No doubt it had been a one-time expensive drink container, but right now, the ten dollars was the only thing giving it any value. No rational person would have grabbed the dirty mug, but my thoughts were all over the place and common sense was lost in my fever to find Sherrie.

If she was not the victim, could she be the one police were looking for? *I don't know if I ever had a stupidier idea cross my mind. Is stupidier even a word? From a breakup, to Miller's loft, to the panicked text from Sherrie, to the cop, to one a.m., I can't know at this point or even care if stupidier is a word.* Wasting time reviewing the English language made me no closer to finding Sherrie.

The cold, damp April air crossed through my sweatshirt. I limped my way down the block, deciding if I should get my car and search the area or head back to EG's in case Sherrie had left the area without waiting for me.

"Why are you walking so funny?" Sherrie came bouncing up to me.

I hugged her, and when I released her, I punched her in the arm.

"What was that for?"

Sherrie was alive and alert with no sense of dread, so I felt worse about my earlier nanosecond thought she might be the one causing trouble.

"I thought you were hurt. From the no reply to my texts, cops and ambulance, and you were nowhere to be found, I got a little panicky only to find you having fun hanging out in the streets at bar time."

"I wouldn't call it fun. Well, not now. You should have come with us tonight, but yet again, you abandoned your roommate for your boyfriend who may or may not show up for one or two hours depending on how busy his bar was."

"You're right!" I stopped walking and let that last thought wash over me. "I did choose him tonight and not my friends. Maybe my stuff is at EG's, his loft, my trunk, and wherever, but I went to his place to sit and wait, not as early as he would have liked, but I still went."

"What are you babbling on about? Are you having an existential crisis, and I'm missing it because it's the middle of the night and we're standing under a busted streetlamp and I'm rethinking my statement?"

"Aaron and I broke up. He did the breaking, and I didn't fight for it, for us, or anything. I let him go."

"Wow, that's big. Do you need a hug? I promise not to hit you when I'm done hugging."

Sherrie reached for her shoulder where I slugged her earlier.

"I'm fine. Relieved, I guess." There was nothing else to say on the matter. "Now tell me why you beckoned me here at this ungodly hour. Wait, what did you say, statement? What statement?"

"The guy in the alley." Sherrie pivoted away from me.

"I figured that much out but could use more of an explanation."

"You got that right, Claud. How about we walk and talk. I'm cold. You gotta drive. My car is blocked."

"I'll drive. I managed to grab my keys. Now tell me what's going on."

"First, tell me why you're limping."

"Not limping. I stepped into a giant puddle and my slipper is soaking wet and I can feel every pebble and crevice on the sidewalk."

"Those things were getting kinda gross. You call them slippers, but you've left the house with them on more times than one should."

"Whatever, just tell me what's going on and why you didn't answer my texts."

"I thought it'd be in bad taste to text you while giving my statement to the police."

"Seriously?"

"I was coming from Broadway, and I saw the guy drop."

"Drop? Drunk?"

"He took a step or two, fell forward and then back. Justin, Vince, and . . ." Sherrie shivered and kept talking. "They rounded the corner in full drunken riot mode. I looked at them, and when I looked back, the guy was on the ground. Drunk Justin is not fun, and I had hoped to avoid them."

"So you opted to go in the alley by yourself with a drunk guy? How drunk are you?"

"Well, my car was there. Sober actually, I nursed one beer all night. It was obvious he wasn't moving, and he was alone. I hesitated, and the guys had caught up with me. When they saw the guy on the ground, they went running into the alley. Vince called 9-1-1, and Justin just started freaking out and repeating *holy shit* and squirreling around like Mia does when she sees a spider. He was flailing his arms around when he cut his hand from the metal sign on the wood fence. Vince was more cool and stayed on the phone with the 9-1-1 operator until the cops arrived. It was kind of funny, he couldn't give them an address besides saying it's one block over from the pastry shop. He said next to the dumpster, in the alley, not the pastry shop, one block from the one with all the sugar. He couldn't even come up with the name Peach's."

"What happened to the guy? Was he . . . was he breathing?"

"I don't know. There was lots of blood. I bent down to get a closer look, and Vince pulled me away and then he went to the street, looking for an address and to flag down the ambulance. For some reason, I went into nurse duty for Justin. I pulled off his sweatshirt. He started to get touchy, clingy, and gross, and I nearly decked him. Instead, I shifted a foot to the left and let him see the bloody face of the guy, and he nearly threw up. I wrapped his hand in the sweatshirt and walked him down the street and sat him down on the curb. He lasted twenty seconds before he started pacing around again."

Sherrie looked at me and stopped talking for a second before asking, "Are you ok?"

"Why? Do I look like crap?"

"You are speed-walking, hunched up like your shoulders are glued to your ears, and didn't even stop at that corner to look for cars."

"It's one thirty in the morning, and I thought you could have been hurt, my foot is soaking wet, I'm freezing, and just realized my car is not in the usual spot. We have to go over to the lot behind the courthouse. Why did you drive tonight?"

"I offered to drive because we were supposed to go see that band Sway Tribe over in Sterling, but Kay realized she got the dates mixed-up." Sherrie yanked my arm and pulled me into the doorway of a hair salon. "Give me your keys and wait here. It will be a lot faster if I run and get the car. That lot is all gravel, and it will take you forever to cross it. Here, you'll be out of the wind."

She had my keys and was gone before I could object. I wondered if I'd hit my low point for the week: freezing in a doorway at bar time, clutching a filthy mug with a ruined slipper and no boyfriend, and then I realized my low point was probably Sunday night when I had cleaned vomit from the hotel entryway after having stepped in it wearing a new pair of suede boots.

I sank into a crouching position to conserve heat. My butt was wet from sitting on my foot, but the wind being blocked was a definite improvement. I must've looked like a fat umbrella stand that no one pays attention to because Miller walked past and he gave no notice I was there. His phone call earlier must have gone well, and he was on his way to meet whoever had called. It made me think I had been a backup plan. Some nights I might be ok with that.

Sherrie pulled up seven minutes later, and I opened the back door.

Sherrie was quick to respond. "You're sitting in the front. This is no chauffeur ride."

"I'm just tossing in this mug I found when I dropped my keys in my search for you. You do remember not answering my texts when you were hiding so I thought maybe you were the one in the ambulance. So I if want to sit in the back and let my Sherrie-induced anxiety drop from me, I will! However, I will take the front and keep you company."

I shut the back door and hopped in front.

Sherrie nicely deflected my grandstanding on our friendship. "Don't play smug with me, the passenger side has the only working heat vent."

"Amen." We both laughed, and Sherrie corrected me again. "As I recall, I only said some drama is going on, and nothing about needing being rescued. I was not hiding but giving my statement to the police."

"Why did you want me to bring Aaron?"

"I thought he could sweet-talk the cops into letting me get my car. I had no idea how long that area will be sectioned off."

Sherrie drove off slowly, and we saw the crowd had dwindled down to a handful of students.

I kept my eye out for Miller. Maybe I could figure out who his late-night booty call was with.

"What are you looking for?" Sherrie asked.

"I saw Miller walking past, and I'm curious to know where he was headed."

"Earlier, you texted asking if you should bring Miller instead of Aaron, what was that all about?"

"I was in his loft."

Sherrie slammed on the brakes. She was only doing about twenty-five miles an hour through the small-town streets so the grand effect was not there, but it made her point.

The smile across my face said it all. "Five points for me. Keep driving."

"It *has* to be more than five points. The bet was five points to get in the apartment, two points for learning something new, and three points for learning something private about the man. Since we are both the only judges and the only players, we can flex the point system in the AMMO— Breaking Down the Mystery Game."

"I was in there less than two minutes, and he was on his phone the whole time. I guessed I learned he lives alone. So I get two points for a total of seven. Thanks for pointing that out Judge A."

Sherrie laughed. "I, Judge A, upon reviewing the tally for you, Judge One, it is now seven to two. I suspect I am about to make the great comeback. Five weeks until completion of the bet, and I am on it."

"Still banking on your one and only plan of arranging to study together. You don't even have a class together at Jameson. How are you going to arrange a library date? You saw him twice on campus and talked to him once so you think you have some connection because you have the same professor. You get two points for learning he is from Michigan. Keep driving, we're almost to EG's."

"I am not ready to surrender yet. Do you want to hear something weird?"

"It gets weirder?" I asked.

"Right when Vince and I walked past Peach's and could see across the street and down the alley with the body in front of our cars, I thought I saw someone watching us from the alley behind Peach's."

"Was it whoever attacked the person in the alley? Did you tell the police?"

"That's that odd part. He was not running away. Someone was standing near the dumpster and faded out of sight. I asked Vince if he saw someone, and he didn't know what I was talking about. There were maybe five people on the block when I saw Justin and Vince, but since the cops arrived with the blue lights, thirty people showed up out of curiosity and this guy just backed away?"

"Maybe he had seen enough and is wise enough to know it's time to be back home."

"Well, I haven't got to the weird part yet. I thought it could have been Miller, and now he's back out again."

"The timing might work with him getting back to the loft, but it could have been anyone looking at all the emergency vehicles."

"It was before any cops or the ambulance arrived and . . ." Sherrie said.

"Hmm, got no more insight left in me. Can we just get to EG's?"

We would later learn Miller was always watching, and I should always let Sherrie finish her sentences.

CHAPTER FOUR

It took me seventy-three seconds from the time we pulled into the driveway for my head to hit the pillow and another thirty-three seconds to fall asleep. No thoughts swirled in my head about the breakup, fear of Sherrie being hurt, Miller, or the body in the alley. The adrenaline dropped out of me as I walked up the stairs to my room. I crashed hard for five and a half hours, and when I woke at seven thirty, my mind refused to go back to sleep. The white sloping ceiling above my head offered no answers. I lacked the will and energy for a run, but I knew lying around would drop me into a funk.

I kept up the pretense of going for a run with cute jogging pants, but my thoughts were doing the only running. I left EG's with my earbuds in but no music playing. I didn't even activate my running watch. Only my thoughts pushed me forward: Aaron, to work, to living at EG's, to my life in River Bend, to Aaron, and finally, to no more Aaron and contentment.

It was eight a.m. when I turned on Main Street, and I was a block from Aaron's bar when I saw Mallory walk out. From my understanding, they had been broken up for some time before we started dating. I'd only met her last November and tolerated her the best I could. A few months ago at the age of twenty-seven, she moved back from Chicago, where she was writing for some newspaper or magazine.

She made a play to get Aaron back while we were dating. That alone is enough not to like her.

The sun was barely above the horizon, and her long brown hair was draped over her shoulders with perfect curls and bounce. She was sipping a bright-green smoothie that probably had more nutrients than I had consumed in the last three days. Some things just didn't need to be perfect this early in the day.

The five-month baby bump was sitting high, and she was carrying it with ease. Mallory had been tight-lipped on the baby daddy, and her intentions of moving back to River Bend had been vague at best. Some locals, mostly Sherrie and me, had doubts about the true due date, and that fueled the controversy of who the baby daddy could be. There was no option to avoid her. The only thing I could do was walk with purpose and hope she did try to engage with me.

"Morning, Claudia, envy the morning run. I'm slightly confined to just a little yoga these days." Mallory sipped her green breakfast. "Aaron is in the bar already this morning. Just letting you know to save you a trip up."

"Thanks." I said it with a smile and just kept walking. I had no intention of going into the bar or the loft but could not let her know that. The bar was strictly off-limits, so I punched in the door code to the loft, climbed the stairs, ran down the hall, and out back before Aaron, Miller, or Mallory would be any the wiser.

It was a clean escape.

Sherrie had started working at Peach's Café over the Christmas holiday. After moving here last July, she'd officially started her master's program in January. Last fall, she had only been taking classes to line herself up for the highly competitive master's program in psych, criminal behavior, or vocational rehab. One day, I will have to figure out what program she's in. She left her last job at C&C when the owner was arrested for murder. The place was still in business, but Sherrie wanted to distance herself from any association with that company and family.

Peach's was owned by Jan, Aaron's aunt,

and had the most amazing pastries with decent breakfast and lunch sandwiches. The only problem, everything is covered in powdered sugar, and it sticks with you long after leaving the café.

We were there one morning when the cashier, Donna, had gone into early labor, and Ellie, the food runner, had taken her to the hospital. The breakfast crowd was just picking up. I thought Jan was joking when, instead of taking our order, she instructed us to get behind the counter and start working. Before I could say anything, Sherrie was tying on an apron.

I was still standing at the counter waiting for someone to take our order when Jan declared she would run the food to the tables, I was on coffee-making duties, and Sherrie would take the orders. It was the same computer system Aaron had in the bar. One of many jobs Sherrie held while moving to River Bend was full-time bartender at Aaron's bar. She went to very part-time when she started dating a fellow bartender, Pete.

Five minutes later, I was removed from coffee-making duties to strictly bussing and stocking supplies. I said something about helping Freddie in the kitchen and got a sharp no from the usually easygoing Jan. After two hours of controlled chaos, I was the only one with powdered sugar all over me.

Since that day, Sherrie had been working

there two to four times a week. Sadly, I was in the Twin Cities for most of that time and could not benefit from anything Sherrie would bring home at the end of the day. Technically, I should have been "living" at Aaron's place and would not have shared a kitchen with Sherrie, but I would like to think somehow I would have access to more of that amazing pastry.

When I walked into Peach's, Sherrie pushed me into the corner booth while she went back to the kitchen and returned with coffee and breakfast sandwiches.

"I think I need a new job. Do you think Aaron will give me more hours now that Pete and I have long stopped dating, or will that be weird for you?"

"Why do you need a new job? Did you creep out your coworkers with nonstop talk about the guy in the alley?"

"I didn't even get to bring it up. First, Freddie snaps at me for pulling wrong dough racks out of the fridge yesterday, and that messed up some of the deliveries. Honestly, I don't even remember pulling the racks out. It was the first time I did closing duties by myself, and apparently, I screwed up big-time. When I went to ask Maggie what I could do to make it up to Freddie, I definitely saw her putting cash from the register in her pocket. I didn't mean to be a rat, but nobody should be stealing from Jan. I told Jan what I saw, and she said it probably was not what it looked like and I should drop it."

"She is probably right," I replied.

"Wipe the powdered sugar off your cheek. I love Jan, but that was an odd reaction from someone who makes a living off one pastry sale at a time. Jan is so frugal about everything at the café, understandably so. We have to bring in our own beverage cup each shift so we don't waste the paper cups or use time washing an extra cup. It gets stranger."

"Enlighten me."

The sun was breaking through the clouds and lighting up half the dining room while we sat in the shadows in the back booth.

"Seriously, wipe off the powder, and don't smear any more across your face." Sherrie sipped more coffee before continuing. "Later, Ellie apologizes to me about the dough racks and said it was her fault. She said she had forgotten something, came back, and saw the racks still needed to be pulled. I asked Ellie what time she was here in case she saw the guy in the alley." She stopped talking and just stared at me.

"Don't tell me I have more powdered sugar on me. At this point, it is not gonna get better until I see a mirror. I'm not getting the strange part of your story. You're looking at me like I should have the answers, but I don't know the question."

"She lied about the time. Why would she lie about the time?"

"Are you sure, and why is it a big deal?"

"Maggie and Ellie were talking about the grade school open house last night. Ellie was there for her brother and Maggie for her grandkids. I know the time is not a big deal so why lie about it?"

"I still got no answers for you. How is Ellie working this morning? I thought she was in high school."

"She is in school but is part of some program for seniors that if you have enough credits you can work after attending morning classes, and some days are a flex schedule or something like that. Oh, did you hear the big news in town?"

"Other than the guy in alley? Hard to beat that one, and thanks to you, I got a firsthand look at one thirty in the morning."

"You can also wipe the sarcasm off your face. A high school kid overdosed on fentanyl."

"That was the person in the alley?"

"No, not sure what happened to him. The kid OD'd with friends in someone's basement."

"That should have been your lead story, and I wouldn't feel like a schmuck. That's tragic and horrific. That beats your missing money and bring-your-own-mug-to-work stories."

"Whatever." Sherrie dismissed my

nonplussed attitude.

We finished our breakfast sandwiches, and Sherrie said, "I work with theft, a liar, and bad management. That's not a great combination. I need something new. I don't think Jan will miss me much."

"I guess nobody likes a rat, including the boss. Now on to my morning, it will be spent trying to figure out where all my clothes are these days. I don't know what's in my car, in the loft, at Aaron's house, or at the dry cleaners. I need something clean for work this afternoon. I really don't want to go to the loft and look for my stuff."

"I'll do it," Sherrie volunteered. "I got three minutes left of my break, but I'm off at two this afternoon."

I rolled my eyes. "I'm sure you would, and I would like to think it's because you are a kind, wonderful friend and not for the pure reason of hoping to run into Miller. I was already in the place, so I won the points. You'll need to wait a day or so until I can figure out what I'm missing and needs collecting. This is so childish, sending you in so I don't have to see him."

"Speaking of things you don't want to see. Mallory has been here since we opened, and you just missed her."

"I passed her on the way here. Why is she still in town? Wonder if she will go for Aaron again or, worse, try to cozy up to me as we're both on team ex-Aaron?"

"I wanted to warn you that she may be here awhile. I heard she got a book deal. She's writing about my former boss, Colette, the mob, and the roots to River Bend. She also does freelance writing, and with the body in the alley and kid overdosing, she'll have plenty to write about."

"I now have an ex and his ex in a town so small that I can't—"

The sound of coffee mugs shattering broke our conversation. We turned our attention to Ellie holding an empty tray surrounded by broken glasses and ceramic chunks and her attention on a guy walking out the door.

"Damn, I missed Hot Guy," Sherrie said.

"What hot guy, and why have I not heard about him before?"

"Easy, Claud. You just broke up with Aaron."

"Not for me. For you? It's been several months since you and Pete were together."

"Pete and I were never together together."

"Don't play semantics with me. Your last overnight guest was a week after you stopped seeing Pete. What was his name . . ."

"Yeah, we were together. However, you can't make fun of Too-Much-Hair-Gel Guy. Remember when you dated Mr.-I-Only-Wear-

Sweats." Sherrie held up her hand when I started to speak. "Don't say anything else. We could go at this all morning reviewing our treacherous dating history. We could get Mia in town and go all night on this topic, but let's save our dignity and talk about Hot Guy. I only just saw him yesterday. He has crystal-blue eyes and a sexy scar by his ear."

"If it's the guy I think it is, he is an ass, gorgeous but not worth it. Plus, I don't think he's from here. He tried checking in the hotel last month but only wanted to use cash. Before I finished explaining we can't take cash, he swore at me and took off."

"Bummer. One less guy in the dating pool. I gotta get back to work, Ellie needs serious help today. We'll talk through your breakup, plan out you having to live with Mallory being in town, and how to get your stuff back after you're done working tonight. I can blow off Jenna tonight if you just want to Aaron-bash, or you can meet us at the bar."

Before I could answer, Sherrie stood, looked at me, pausing before she spoke. "Actually, maybe it should be just the two of us 'cause I gotta ask—"

"I said before I don't care if you go work for Aaron again. Now wipe the powdered sugar off your sleeve and left leg."

Sherrie left without saying anything else or finishing her last thought. Shame on me for assuming it was all about me and Aaron.

I was left thinking that Mallory staying in town was probably not the biggest problem in the world considering what had happened to the guy in the alley and the kid overdosing.

Sitting there, I would never have imagined my life intertwining with them as it did.

CHAPTER FIVE

I stayed at work until just after midnight for the sole purpose of wanting to sleep when I got home. Sherrie and Jenna were out drinking and finally stopped asking me to join them at eleven. I had never thought this before, but I kinda hoped the third-shift person would call in sick, leaving me to work overnight, and into my next shift. Elliot, the third-shift front desk employee, was thrilled when I left his workstation to take a call from Sherrie.

"I need your help . . . am at—" The line went dead.

I called back and no answer. She hadn't texted, but had actually called. There was no reply to my text so I texted Jenna asking what was up. Jenna said she had gotten home twenty minutes ago, so if I wanted to find someone to drink with at bar time I was out of luck for the night.

Thankfully, she answered when I called, and I explained Sherrie's weird call. Jenna said she and Sherrie and a few others had said their goodbyes. Leigha was really drunk so Sherrie offered to walk her home. Leigha lived in the first set of townhomes just off the Jameson campus but was unsure of the unit number. Jenna offered to go with me, but I declined. There was no need for more than two of us to clean up after a drunk girl, but she should keep her phone on in case I changed my mind.

The ride to the town houses was eight minutes from the hotel, but I sat in the car for another three trying to figure out what unit Sherrie was in. Still no reply to my text. I watched two guys stagger towards the second building and thought about asking them, but common sense told me to wait safely inside my car. A minute later, I saw a couple walking into the parking lot holding hands, and I figured this might be my only chance.

Oh, the things you learn at bar time in a small college town. It turned out that Simon, a regular at Aaron's bar, was not going home tonight with his girlfriend, but with an unnamed girl who was very eager to talk to me.

Unnamed Girl pointed to the first unit on the corner that had all the lights out and even offered up an address of a late-night after-bar-hours party.

Simon was doing his best to stand behind the girl and was avoiding looking me. I told her I appreciate the party information, but I was really looking for my friend who I thought needed a ride and not really looking for Leigha.

"If that girl who used to bartend is your roommate, I saw her up near the Square not too long ago," Simon said.

I offered up a thanks and left out any judgmental looks towards him. He had given me solid information, and I figured I wouldn't ruin his night by mentioning his girlfriend.

The drive took me four minutes since I had to avoid the drunk college kids spilling out onto the streets at bar time. Panic was starting to set in when I realized it had been nearly thirty minutes since Sherrie's help call. She had called, not texted. She never called. The only people that called me were my parents and EG.

I turned the corner, and three girls were leaving the main square, stumbling a bit and laughing and one girl tugging at her short skirt. I was scared to look in the car mirror to see what kind of state my hair and makeup were in after ten hours at work. I needed to stop thinking about my appearance so I could find Sherrie and be at EG's in ten minutes.

Pondering who else I could call in the hunt for Sherrie, I realized most of our girlfriends were sleeping, drunk, or with their boyfriends. That left EG, Aaron, or Pete—well, that really just left EG. Sure the guys would come help even if they were our exes, but I wanted a level head and not someone who I owed something to. Although Pete and I always had each other's back. No questions asked, like when he got into a van with me that had a dead body in it, because I needed help or when I covered for him at the bar when he tried sliding over the bar to beat Sherrie to the radio controls and broke the Guinness beer tap. I thought about calling EG because I needed someone with common sense to help me find Sherrie when it hit me.

Sherrie was rational and levelheaded but also a spitfire wanting in on the action. Ugh, I didn't know if I had the energy to play detective with Sherrie as I was sure she was back in the alley trying to figure out what had happened to the guy last night. I parked my car on Broadway near Peach's and pushed the door shut with the force of someone who has little sleep and ten hours of work in them. I had to hip-check the driver's-side door twice before it clicked shut.

Panic began to set in again when she didn't answer my latest text, and my call went straight to voicemail. Instead of playing detective, I couldn't help but wonder if she had been attacked.

I stopped walking in the middle of the street and let the last twenty-four hours wash over me. I had been trying to be so cool about my breakup that I, too, had missed the big story. Some guy had been attacked in the alley just on the other side of the shoe repair store, and a fentanyl overdose was now in the lives of those living in River Bend.

I had come to think of River Bend and these streets as my happy place. When I started running six months ago, I found my secret love of roaming these streets in the early mornings before the sun was up. In college, I'd always been a night person, preferring to stay up late to get something done instead of waking up early. I had mastered registering for classes all starting after nine a.m., expect that damn chemistry lab. After my first early run back in September, something shifted, and the dark mornings became my friend.

Each early morning run made me love this town more: solitude runs without earbuds, running along the river and listening to the Mississippi rushing past to pull me forward; long runs through the side streets, learning what neighbors were up early to distract me from the new miles; fun runs to keep up with the guy delivering newspapers and seeing how many waves I get from the delivery drivers; and through Jameson College campus to see some kids doing the walk of shame and admire the old buildings.

Last night, I'd had no fear of walking alone to meet Sherrie, but now it was different. These streets were different, but what difference did five hours make? At five a.m., I felt safe running around, but now at midnight, my roommate could be in trouble. Sadness dropped from me while fear rose up. I sprinted towards the alley.

Could something have happened two nights in row?

CHAPTER SIX

Running in my suit at midnight, I looked as ridiculous as the drunk kids I'd just seen stumbling out of the bars two blocks away. I sweated through my rayon blouse that clung to me like a wet plastic bag. I turned the corner so fast, I smacked right into a guy I had not seen before. His friend caught me when I staggered back and nearly lost my balance. He looked familiar, but this was not the time to get to know anyone despite his attempt to ask if I was ok. When I finally caught my breath and waved them off, a hand touched my shoulder and sent me jumping back a foot.

"Where've you been?" Sherrie stood there, actually swaying, rosy cheeked and vividly alert yet not harmed, so I slugged her in the shoulder.

"Me? I have been looking for you. Why haven't you answered any calls or texts?"

I followed her staggering walk past the corner building down the same alley as last night.

"Phone died. I told you where I was."

"Your phone cut out before you gave me the details. I spent twenty minutes wandering around this town for you. Please don't tell me you're here playing detective about last night or that you're trying to plant a marked bill in the register to see if Maggie takes it."

"Nice sense of humor at this hour. Good idea about marking the bills. Anyways, we were having drinks at Draw Bar, and I was on my home and remembered my car was still here from last night so I went to grab my jacket because I was cold."

"Let me get this straight, you leave your car here last night because some guy was attacked in front of it. You walk to work, walk home, walk to the bars, remember your jacket, and think it's safe to go in the same alley for a coat you haven't worn in a month."

"Plenty of people around. No worries for me," Sherrie said and added a hiccup.

"Is there more to this story? Why the call?" I asked.

"I was worried about the dough racks and wanted to verify I did it right this time."

Sherrie stopped talking. After years of being roommates, I have Sherrie's tics memorized. She talked nonstop and bounced on her toes when she was flirty; rotated like a wobbly ballerina when conspiring; looked like a frozen statue while doing mental math and puzzle-solving; and stood like a nutcracker when pondering high-stake situations. This was nutcracker with twist. Well, either a lemon twist with her gin and tonic or a lime twist with her tequila shot. Sherrie was serious and tipsy, and that was not an equal match for my tiredness and sobriety.

"So you were saying you wanted to make sure you did it right this time?" I had to prompt her to get on with the problem.

"I double-checked racks and coolers and everything was good but—"

"Let me guess, you screwed up the alarm code, and you pissed off Chuck because you woke him up."

Chuck was Aaron's older brother by two years at twenty-nine, former army, current military contract worker or high surveillance guru for some out-of-state company. You would not get a straight answer about his occupation. Now, most importantly, he was the guy that installed the security system in the café, Aaron's bar, and several other places in town. Overall, Chuck was a great guy. Both Rhoimly boys were well loved in the community. Chuck would do anything for you, but a nonemergency alarm wake-up call might put you in his debt and you never know when he will want to collect.

"I got in ok, but when I left, there was a light on."

"Oh my god, I am standing here because you left a light on. I should be curled up on a couch mulling over my breakup or elbow deep in a tub of ice cream, and you have me here because you saw a light. How much did you have to drink tonight?"

"Enough to have fun and enough to know when something is not right." Sherrie finished that with a hiccup. I just rolled my eyes, and she continued. "You know the door code panel?"

"No, but let's pretend I do."

"There is a key panel outside and one inside. You have to hit the code on both panels. When I went in, I hit the code and saw everything was correct. Freddie probably didn't trust my memory and came back this evening, but anyway. You have to wait five minutes before resetting the alarm. I stood at the panel, and I thought nothing of it at first, but then—" Sherrie just stopped.

"Oh my god, just spit it out. Unless you stabbed a guy and robbed him, it can't be that bad. Oh, wait. Did you see a ghost?"

"I wish! That would be cool, but I think you have to go to the hill to see the Gray Lady. We need to do a séance one night."

"Absolutely, but can we get back on track here?" I thought the drinks were catching up to Sherrie.

"A light turned off, and I thought I heard someone. I called out. No one answered."

"Where was the light? Register, prep kitchen, or dining area?" I asked. "Jan or Chuck have some weird timers or something."

"I doubt it. I'm sure Jan would have explained it. The light was behind the control panel."

"What's on the other side of the wall? Storage?" I asked.

"No, or at least I don't think so. That was why I was hoping you would tell me if I should call Chuck or if it would be ok if I stop at Aaron's bar and ask him. He practically grew up in the café and would know."

"I would advise against calling Chuck at this hour. You don't need my permission to talk to Aaron. Just this morning, you asked if I would mind you working there."

"That was about work." Hiccup. Captain Morgan rum had been her drink of choice tonight, as it always gave her the hiccups, or she burbs up the rum. "Asking a question at his hour felt weird, don't ask me the difference because I don't think I can explain it."

"I get it. When I drove around looking for you, I avoided Main Street so I wouldn't see his bar or loft."

Sherrie's nutcracker dance stopped. She opened her arms, but I declined the hug.

"I have to say you are rather well composed, but let me guess, you are kinda relieved after seeing that ugly engagement ring," she said.

"It was not so much ugly as it was just not my style, but can we not go there right now? So tell me about the light. And are you sure it was not a security light? If you're so worried, call Jan or Chuck."

"It's one a.m., and I don't want to panic someone if there's no reason."

"So you don't know if the light was part of the café . . ."

"And noise. I saw noise, I mean, I saw the light and heard the noise." The drinks were definitely hitting her.

"You've been standing in the alley waiting for me. Did you see anyone come out or hear anything else?"

"Not really?"

"I'm getting tired. Can you just explain what that means?"

"I swear I saw Miller again, but it could have been the others, Kyle and Mackford."

"Who?"

"The guys you just ran into."

"How do you know everyone?" I asked.

"What do you think? From working at the bar. The best damn townie bar, BAR. What do you think?"

"Of what?" I was trying to follow drunk-Sherrie logic.

"The best damn townie bar, BAR, where you get to know your town and ies. I am trying out new slogans to pitch to Aaron when I ask for my job back. Gotta go back to seeing everyone I know."

"I guess that's how I know people are—from visiting you and Aaron at the bar. Are we going to be like EG in five years where we know everyone in town?"

"I don't know if that is a good thing or not," Sherrie said flatly.

"So no one has come out of the café's back door, and I am assuming there is little or no cash to steal, so I will say it's fine for tonight. You can ask Jan about it tomorrow. Before you protest about confessing to Jan about your late-night reentry, just remember you would rather tell her than ask Chuck to pull the security tapes."

"You are right. If something bad was going down, Chuck would have it on camera or some strange silent alarm would go off. Maybe I'll swing by his place tomorrow and ask him."

"Sounds like a plan. Can we now go back to EG's?"

When we walked away, Sherrie said, "I also wanted to see what I could see."

"See what you could see? Jeez, how much did you have to drink tonight?"

"I wanted to know what were shadows or if I saw someone last night."

"Let the police worry about that."

"They can't if I didn't tell them everything," Sherrie said and followed up with a burp. It was double rum and coke night.

"What! Again, you buried the lead story."

"It's just that—"

A car turned down the alley, and the headlights lit us up like a Broadway play. Officer Holton Patrick got out of the squad car with a direct approach. "What are you two doing here?"

"Hey, Ho . . . Holton," Sherrie said.

"I hope you weren't driving," he said.

"Claudia's driving."

"We are just grabbing her coat. My car is on the road."

"Are you safe driving that vehicle?" he asked.

"I'm almost done with it. I'm looking at one tomorrow over in Green Ridge."

"Can I walk you two to your car? We still have not figured out what happened here last night."

"So the guy died last night?" I asked.

"I am just saying we don't know what happened. Sherrie, are you solid with the statement you gave my partner? Anything else you remember? It was just Vince and Justin with you?"

"Yup," she replied and left it at that.

Thinking her memory needed a boost, I asked, "What about—"

"It was exactly how I said it was," Sherrie said as we rounded the corner and could see my car. "Thanks for the escort."

"Claudia, let me know if you want someone to go with you to look at cars. A second opinion might be helpful."

Holton said, "I didn't mean to imply women can't shop for cars by themselves. I was just thinking you might like the company."

"Appreciate the thought but I'm good. My dad did all the research. I just need to see if I like it. Have a good—" My voice rose an octave when Sherrie pinched by butt. "Have a good night."

Sherrie shouted goodbye to Holton, grabbed my arm, pulled me to my car, and ran around to the passenger side, laughing. Her sudden outburst of giddiness made me forget she had confessed to not telling the police everything.

"Why did you run like a maniac?" I asked.

"Turn on the car, I'm freezing." Sherrie rubbed her arms to warm up. "I ran because you had no idea Holton was beginning to flirt with you, and from that blank look on your face, I know I'm right. A guy does not offer another guy's girlfriend assistance when buying a car."

I was gobsmacked at the idea people knew about my breakup. It made it more real. As Debby—I had named my car after Debby Boone—moved away from the curb, I almost sideswiped Holton in his squad car. He stopped, essentially blocking me in, and rolled down his window. My car was on the brink of collapse, and once my window was rolled down, it wouldn't go back up without a two-person assist. I opened the door and stood up while Sherrie was making kissing noises.

Driving away, we laughed and tried calculating how many people knew about the breakup. Aaron was not one to broadcast it, and social media dating status was not in his vocabulary. Sherrie decided Holton may or may not know about my relationship status. He was just running through the list of women in River Bend. He had this need to find a wife to fit his preconceived ideas of what his wife is expected to be. He doesn't date as much as he interviews women.

We laughed at Holton going home to review this whiteboard with a list of women. Under our names in the negative column: roams the streets at one a.m. and does not need his opinion when buying a car.

For the rest of the ride home, we forgot about Sherrie's partial statement to the police and the light she saw or thought she saw, but it was the second night in a row Miller had been watching Sherrie and the light.

CHAPTER SEVEN

That Saturday morning, for the second day in a row, I woke up in EG's house in my old bed alone, staring at the blank ceiling that matched my mood. I was no longer the sleek twenty-three-year-old with a cool job assignment in the big city with a hot boyfriend. Living in EG's was cool at first because EG was cool and free rent was killer as a recent college grad, but now I was a sponge, working at a hotel in a small town with a tiny dating pool.

The midmorning manager shift at the hotel was highly coveted if everything went smoothly in housekeeping that morning. It allowed you to sleep in and avoid being the first point of contact for any overnight issues. If you did your job properly, you could control when you left in the evening. Some of the most underrated positions in a hotel included the overnight staff and housekeeping. Those employees could make or break your day. No morning phone calls from the hotel meant I was on a good track for the workday, but not so much for me personally. No texts with second thoughts from Aaron were on my phone, and I was more than fine with that.

I left the house and noticed EG's car in the driveway. She must have arrived after I had gotten home at one a.m. The house was empty when I left, so she must have been on a morning walk. I hoped to have her energy when I was past the age of forty. Some days I wish I had it now.

The most impressive thing was Sherrie's bike was gone. After a night of drinking and the forty-five-degree weather, Sherrie was out riding before nine a.m.

Those two inspired me to get in a run after work today to prove to myself my semi-new running hobby was something I was doing for me and not because Aaron was a runner. I was determined to run a marathon this year and had started off great but had gotten a little sidetracked with my job assignment in Minneapolis. I had kept up the running, but the miles had not added up to anything close to being ready for a marathon.

I wanted to claim my streets back. I wanted the calm mornings of hope. I was caught between early morning runner and after-work slouch.

Work sailed by smoothly, except for Sherrie's nonstop texts giving me a play-by-play of her morning. After her morning bike ride to clear her head of booze and process everything from Peach's in the last twenty-four hours, she sent:

Sherrie: *Ride fantastic. If you run, beware of ice patch in woods north of town.*

Sherrie: *Can't tell if Chuck is helpful or a little salty with his texts*

Sherrie: *He suggested I don't drink and return to the café especially late night*

Sherrie: *I am still stumped on why Maggie is skimming cash. Should I tell Maggie I saw her? I told Jan so why not her?*

Sherrie: *I need an answer to that last one.*

Sherrie: *After work I'm heading to the campus library.*

Sherrie: *I will bring home food.*

Sherrie: *I mean, I will bring us dinner.*

Sherrie: *I'm sure your breakup sucks, but nice to have a dinner companion again*

Sherrie: *House is full. EG is back.*

Sherrie: *Seriously, can you answer me about Maggie?*

Sherrie: *Pick up drinks for dinner*

Sherrie: *Assuming you are busy at work and just not blowing me off. See ya tonight.*

Since things were over with Pete in December, our former college roommate, Mia, and I were the recipients of all Sherrie's energy. They had started dating Thanksgiving weekend, but things stalled pretty quickly.

One night, Sherrie had gotten a call from her ex-boyfriend Hudson at bar time. She had been up waiting for Pete to come over, and she continued talking to Hudson after Pete got there. Pete fell asleep before she was off the phone. The two of them had a long conversation in the morning about her non-resolved feelings for her ex. That was the shortened version of what happened that morning. They had continued to date for another week, but she felt Pete pulling away. He told her he liked her but did not want to compete with an ex-boyfriend. Sherrie tried highlighting that it was her ex, but Pete was not buying it.

Sherrie kept me out of most of the dissolving relationship. I made the mistake once of taking Pete's side. Sherrie was venting and not looking for an opinion when I unknowingly stood up for Pete. She was not mad but knew I would not be a fair ear to vent to despite being best friends.

Pete and I had gone through some shit together. When I say some shit, I mean one night at the bar, a crazed lunatic attacked Pete, and to protect Pete, I shot and killed the guy. And if that was not enough, a few months later, Pete was kind enough to stick with Sherrie and me when we were stuck in a funeral home with bodies going missing and mobsters being after us. As I said before, we had each other's back.

Same thing with Sherrie. We were always there for the other person. She stood by me with my crazy family drama and I with her and her nutty former job. We don't keep a tally of who has done the most for the other person; we just keep the other person close.

It was a rare Saturday evening that the three of us were home for dinner.

"This is an impressive spread you got us," EG said.

Sherrie was delighted with the menu. "From Peach's, we got potato soup and bread, the Pad Thai and ribs are from the diner. I just ask that we don't count the calories."

"Amen," EG said and then not so silently cursed us for not having to take heartburn medicine as we ate.

Sherrie followed my lead and avoided conversation about my breakup. I wasn't torn up about it and didn't need to rehash it.

Sherrie focused on her own dilemma. "I want to preface the story by saying I want to be a good employee and loyal to Jan. Seeing Maggie take the cash is too much for me. I told Jan about it but it wasn't easy. Then the denial by Jan about

Maggie makes me feel like a gossipmonger. Then Ellie comes in to cover for me and makes me feel more guilty, about what, I don't know. I just don't feel right about it. Maggie is stealing and Ellie is lying and I feel bad."

"I can't imagine Maggie doing anything like that." EG was usually spot-on about someone's character.

Over the years, EG had studied human psychology and attended various law enforcement behavior studies classes to help with her writing career. Spending most of her life in River Bend gave EG a special insight into people. She also taught the occasional class at Jameson and moderated the high school book club. If someone applied for a job instead of asking for personal references, the new employer would just call EG for the background check. EG was no gossip, but a well-developed encyclopedia about the families of River Bend. She had lived most of her life in River Bend and was a folk hero who put River Bend on the map on a national level. EG and my mom had grown up here as did their mom and grandparents.

EG continued, "Maggie is recently retired after teaching for thirty-plus years. Her husband still works for the county. Their son is married and just had their second child, and the daughter moved to New Jersey after college for a job. She is not the type."

"How well do you really know someone?" I asked.

"Good point. You never really know a person, but there are clues." EG went on to explain. "Last summer, I stopped at the hardware store for something, and it was extremely busy. Phil was in the store by himself, and the line was four deep. You know Phil can handle helping ten customers find something all at the same time, but at the register, he is a mess. Maggie had purchased three gallons of deck stain. At seventy dollars a gallon, that is not cheap. She went out to her car and noticed Phil had only charged her for two. Maggie came back into the store, waited for everyone to check out, and explained to Phil that she owed him more money. So what I'm saying is if she is not taking a free gallon of paint, she is not skimming five dollar bills from the register."

"What if it's for the cheap thrill?" Sherrie asked.

"I still doubt it. Maggie is helping out until Donna is back from maternity leave as a favor to her old friend Jan. Is the register always even at the end of the day?"

"Jan never said anything. Most transactions are credit or debit cards. We mostly use the cash to pay out the tips at the end of the shift."

"If Jan never said anything, I think maybe you misread something you saw. How is Ellie working out at the café?"

"I can't figure her out. Nice enough, but hard to talk to and kinda jumpy. She did me that huge favor Friday and got kinda weird when I thanked her. She got all squirrelly and walked away. All I did was say thanks," Sherrie said.

"What do you know about her?" EG asked.

"Not much."

"Is she the small skinny one with dyed jet-black hair?" I asked.

Sherrie nodded. "She has not had it easy. She was caught shoplifting a few years ago, and no one would give her a job because of it."

"Totally makes sense," I said.

"Does it, Claudia? As you said earlier, how well do you really know a person? I tell you one thing about Ellie, and you think you have her figured out as some punk."

"She was caught stealing," Sherrie rebutted.

"Let me tell you the rest of the story, and then you can maybe start to know someone. Her mom is gone. She has a brother Adam who about seven maybe eight years older. There is a younger one, Ben."

Sherrie jumped in. "He is a cutie. Quiet. After school, he comes to Peach's and waits for Ellie."

"Is he the one you took the sock puppets to last week?" I asked, and Sherrie nodded again.

EG continued, "I don't know the family, but I believe the dad is absent a lot. I think he does construction work and generally is not a nice guy. He fell apart when his wife died. What most people don't know about the story is she got caught shoplifting peanut butter so Ben would have something to eat. Ellie is allergic to peanuts. She had just enough cash for school supplies for Ben but did not have enough for food for him. She used her food money on his school supplies. It was not a cheap thrill like she wanted a pretty lipstick. She did it to take care of Ben.

"It gets me worked up when people judge others without the whole story. I would like to see people in this town go just six hours without food and see what kind of decision they would make."

Sherrie got up from her seat, walked around the table, and gave EG a hug over her backside. "Thank you for that story and lesson. So much for my master's in psych."

I stayed where I was and left the last rib that EG had been eyeing.

"Anytime. I got suitcase full of stories that break most people in this town wide-open." EG half laughed. "What are you girls doing tonight? I'm reading a book about a hundred-year-old house, but I hope you're not living like you're a hundred. Are you going to hang with Aaron at the bar, or you playing wingman for Sherrie someplace else?"

Sherrie and I looked at each other and remained quiet.

"Talk about knowing people. What's with that look? I have been in Chicago for three weeks so I apparently missed some stuff."

"Claudia and Aaron are less than forty-eight hours off splitsville so the word is still out on how things will go down between them but I don't think we are thinking about going to his bar tonight."

We waited for a reaction from EG, maybe gather some empathy or suggest a fun night of burning some of the guy's belongs, a cleansing of sorts.

Her response was more stunning than Aaron breaking up with me. "Well, girls, you don't seem overly upset so that is a good thing. You are strong women that don't need a man just to have someone to call a boyfriend. You will be just fine. I'll miss knowing the boys will not be around. I felt better knowing Aaron might be here when I'm out of town. However, it is best to break it off early when it's not a right fit."

EG finished her wine, stood up, grabbed a blanket and book, and headed out towards the screened-in porch when she tossed this loaded bomb on us. "Besides I never thought they were best matches for you two in the long term. If you want the whole marriage thing, you would be better off swapping boyfriends. I thought the better pairing is you, Sherrie, with Aaron." EG turned from Sherrie to me and boondoggled me with "Pete is your best match, Claudia."

I laughed at the idea because logic dropped from my brain. Sherrie gave a forced laugh picked up the remnants of dinner and went to the sink. Her lack of a snappy reply spoke volumes. I just didn't know what she was saying at the time; I didn't recognize this tic.

CHAPTER EIGHT

Sherrie had made plans to go out with Kay, and she gave me what I call a half an invite. She was walking out the door and asked if I wanted to go yet heavily suggesting I let my breakup sink in. She reminded me about the time in college I had one date with a guy that tried ghosting me, and I was relentless in trying to find him just so I could have the last word. I didn't want a second date, but I didn't want him to think he broke up with me. It was a long week for Sherrie and Mia having to live with my obsessive need for closure.

I spent the night watching three movies but never seeing one of them from start to finish. Mostly scrolling through social media at things I would not remember ten minutes later. I was buried deep into the sofa in comfy sweats and a soft blanket but couldn't sit still.

I thought about not having Aaron around, and it only made me slightly sad. I thought about dating and what it meant. Was I dating with the aim of marriage and family? I knew I wanted a commitment from a guy, and I do believe in the whole marriage idea and saying vows to each other, so why was I freaked about moving in with Aaron?

It was like when I was accepted to college. I knew I wanted to go to college but didn't know what I wanted to study. A school wanted me, which was exciting, but it expected me to know what I wanted from them. I didn't know that until the end of my sophomore year. Moving in with Aaron and then seeing the engagement ring was like someone asking what my college major was when I still a junior in high school.

I had to balance my emptiness with knowing it was the right thing for me. If Aaron was supposed to be the one for me, I would know, right? I snapped off the TV and went upstairs to my room around eleven. I heard Sherrie come in not too long after, but I stayed quiet, staring at my ceiling, not wanting to engage in conversation. I felt better just knowing Sherrie and EG were home with me.

Up before the sun, and I knew I would be not able to fall back asleep, so a run would be the only way to start my day. Never have I hesitated before about the safety of the streets, but the guy in the alley had me second-guessing if I should be out before sunup, but then I remembered the pepper spray and alarm bracelet my dad had bought me when I was running in the city a few months ago.

I spent more time looking for the security gear than I did picking out my running clothes and brushing my teeth and hair combined. The weather was colder than expected, and I opted for music instead of my favorite true crime podcast. There was no need to be listening to those stories at this hour and in this town. I decided to stick to the main road that took me past the town square, away from campus and the river and towards the interstate and my hotel. I wanted a high-traffic area. There was no mile goal this morning, which was unusual so I didn't know when I should turn around. Suddenly, I understood how women get in trouble when alone. It was pitch-black out, and no one knew where I was or when I had left. It would be at least an hour before churchgoers would be out and about.

I was a mile past the hotels and interstate going downhill at a decent rate when the thought of going back up it became overwhelming. I slowed down and grabbed my phone and hoped Sherrie or

EG would be up. EG responded immediately that she already had plans for the morning and was headed out of town afterwards.

EG amazes me. It's six thirty in the morning, and she has plans on a Sunday. I was still holding out hope Sherrie would respond when a black truck slowed down after it passed me going in the opposite direction. It did a U-turn and was approaching me slowly. The choice was call 9-1-1 or the bear spray. I had pressed nine when the I heard the window roll down. I pressed the one, and my heart was beating triple-time. The song playing in my mind was classic '80s one-hit wonder by Rockwell, "Somebody's Watching Me."

"Claudia?"

Hearing my name made me lightheaded with relief. "Pete! What are you doing out here at his hour?"

"Me? Are you running? You don't look like you're going very fast."

"I was on decent run. So good I lost track of where I was and stopped to text Sherrie and EG to see if they wanted to meet at Towne's diner for breakfast. It's closer than running home."

"Hop in, and I can take you wherever you want to go," Pete offered.

"Cool." When I shut the truck door, Sherrie responded with "omelette and hash browns are needed for the bingo win." I was not sure what the bingo win was all about, but I knew what the order meant and directed Pete to Towne's and texted her to drive my car. "Sherrie is in for breakfast. It's got to be better than this pink bottle I see here. How bad is the hangover if you are up this early? Does this really help?"

"Hangover, no, but it does help with the acid reflux. It's been bad lately."

"Please join us. Warning, she is hungover. You two seem cool hanging out together, right?"

All I got was a "sure" from Pete, and so I pressed him for some information, "So, we know I was running but what are you doing up at this hour? Walk of shame or stride of pride?"

"There is never shame in my life," Pete said, and we both laughed. "Seager—my buddy, you know him from the bar—he had a bonfire last night and then the plan was to get up and go fishing. We are crashed at his place and two of the guys had no interest in getting up this morning so I bailed before Bucknall woke up."

"Let me guess, you didn't want to listen to him while fishing."

"Nice enough, but the guy never stops talking."

"I'm serious about the breakfast invite," I said when Pete pulled up to the front door of the truck stop diner.

"Can't refuse a second offer."

Pete and I walked in and he went to greet some older gentlemen sitting at the counter. I should have been more shocked to see EG than I was. She caught my eye and glanced at Pete and back to me. She was seated in the back booth talking with someone I couldn't see until it was too late. I was struck with disappointment about her breakfast companion. Anyone would have been better than Mallory. I would rather have it be Aaron or even my ex before him.

EG said, "I didn't think you would take me so seriously or move so fast." Her eyes flashed towards Pete.

I flashed back to her comment about Sherrie and me flipping boyfriends. All I could do was laugh and just say, "Things are not always what they seem to be."

Thankfully, Mallory was in no position to turn and follow EG's glance, and EG did not elaborate.

Mallory piped in with, "Another morning run. You're making me wish I was more mobile these days."

Any decent person would have asked how the pregnancy was going, but I did not have it in me.

With an awkward moment of silence between us, Mallory continued, "EG has been wonderful in helping me with my book. You are lucky to have such a wonderful aunt."

I looked down at the egg whites and orange juice and thought about the greasy breakfast I had earned while running and just smiled to myself. "Yeah, I am lucky, but in this town, she kinda belongs to everyone so I learned to share." I couldn't let Mallory think she had a piece of EG that no one else did. Maybe I was hungry, or maybe I just didn't like her. "Well, I'll let you two get back to work." My resentment grew when I admitted only to myself that she looked adorable in the wool newsboy hat.

I found us a booth and tried ordering a double espresso just because I knew Mallory couldn't have any caffeine, but Joanie asked if I wanted creamer or milk with my coffee. Pete came to the table with coffee mug in hand. He ordered pancakes, sausage, hash browns, one egg, and a side of fruit.

When I was done ordering, Joanie informed me I didn't have to match Pete's appetite, but I told her my roommate was on the way, and I would be splitting the food.

I turned to Pete and said, "No judgment."

Pete was quick to respond. "This is my breakfast and lunch, so you can . . ."

"Can what?" I asked. "Don't hold back because I'm a girl. Bring it on."

"Holding back not because you are a girl but because I am a gentleman."

"Well played."

I looked out the window and saw Sherrie parking. A twinge of panic shot through me, I should have told her sooner that the invite now included Pete. Things were cool with them, but that didn't mean she needed to be smacked in the face with seeing him at 7 a.m. on a Sunday.

Sherrie slid into the booth, and we surprisingly had an easy breakfast without an awkward moment until I excused myself. I remembered the ten bucks in the travel mug and went to claim it, leaving those two alone. I got a sideways glance from Sherrie that Pete caught. I made it back in under two minutes, so it could not have been so bad.

I volunteered to pay for everyone's breakfast, not with the found ten dollars but the multiple found ten-dollar bills.

"What's with the generosity? It is because you smell and coaxed us here at seven a.m.?" Sherrie asked.

"You're welcome for the breakfast invite. Not sorry about the body odor, it was a hard run. Remember the ten bucks I found two nights ago? Turns out it was a whole lot more."

"Seriously! How much more, like, do you have to find the owner?" Sherrie said with a bright smile.

"I don't know. It was in that mug rolling around in the back of my car. I only first looked at it now, and I was freezing out there so I grabbed five bills. It's four tens and ten ones, and there is some more stuffed in there but not a ton. Guessing about ten bills, but I don't know the denominations."

Sherrie and Pete both looked at me without saying anything, and the lack of words produced a pit of guilt in my stomach.

"I found the mug on the sidewalk in the middle of the night. What am I supposed to do with it? When I get home if I find any type of identification I will search the person out."

"That's fair," Pete said. "I'll leave the tip so we have good karma."

We said our goodbyes to Pete and went to EG's. The shower felt as invigorating as the long run and as comforting as a big breakfast. Sherrie left for the campus café to get some studying done before the library opened at ten. She was quiet on the ride and said few words before she departed. Something had shifted with her, and I couldn't figure it out.

After a morning run, I built up energy, and it was great for a day full of work but it was a damp gray day in April. The only thing on my list to do was to look at cars. Sunday morning television offered nothing, the house was clean, and laundry was done. The only thing left was to gather my stuff from Aaron's, but that would have to wait until I knew he was at the bar. I decided to head down to Green Ridge early and see if any cute shops were open.

Backing out of the driveway, I was blocked by the same truck that had rescued me in the dark this morning. "What's up, Pete?"

"You left this in here this morning, and I figured you should probably have it with all the weird stuff going on in town." I grabbed the pepper spray from him and he asked, "Headed to work?"

"Nope, something worse, car shopping in Green Ridge."

"What are you looking at? Want a truck? I'm looking to get rid of this thing."

"There are several cars my dad researched online that look fine for me. I don't know much about trucks, but this looks pretty good to me. Why do you want to get rid of it?"

"Have you ever seen me drive this before?" I shook my head, and Pete continued, "In three years, I helped twenty-three people move, and I didn't even know all of them. Owning a truck is the biggest charity work I do. I drive it as little as possible as not to be seen in a truck. Seager's brother, Guy, is trying to sell me something. If you're headed to Green Ridge Motors and haven't made contact with a salesman, ask for Guy."

"Wanna come with me, and we both can check out cars?" I had no idea where that invite had come from, but I thought it would be nice to have someone with me.

Sherrie came riding up on her bike and quietly half smiled at us. "I forgot my laptop charger."

She was in the house and out in under a minute, and I needed to explain why Pete was there.

"Pete returned my pepper spray and alarm I left in his truck. Hey, if you're riding around, you take the pepper spray today, and I'llwill get some more when I'm in Green Ridge."

She took it and was gone with no more words.

I turned to Pete. "Are you my car shopping buddy?"

"Aaron at the bar today?" Pete asked.

I hopped in the truck and must have given him a funny look because his next word was "oh."

"We broke up, but apparently Aaron told only some people. I can't imagine Aaron getting chatty with Holton."

Pete looked at me, confused.

"You can't follow my train of thought. Last night, Sherrie was convinced Holton was hitting on me."

"Detective Holton is not your type?"

"I thought he was police and not a detective."

"He is aiming to be a detective, and I hear sometimes he crosses the line. Watch yourself around him," Pete warned. "He has his own ideas on how things should be."

Those last words of being careful went over my head, and Sherrie was too far gone to hear them.

Four hours later, I got a text from her. *I think I did something stupid.*

CHAPTER NINE

I laughed at Sherrie's text since it could mean anything. The only reply I could give her was *I did something fun or maybe crazy. You tell first.*

Sherrie: *Where r u*

Me: *Almost home. Car shopping*

Sherrie: *When you're home just use the word Jellyroll*

Me: *I have nothing to say about that. Give me more.*

Sherrie: *How long will EG be gone?*

Me: *Maybe Wednesday, gone to see my mom. What's up*

Sherrie: *. . .*

Me: *OMG did you hook up with someone*

Sherrie: *No but we have a guest*

Me: *Oh shit did you score points? Is Miller there*

Sherrie: . . .

There was no final reply.

I didn't know if I was nervous or excited to walk in the door when Pete dropped me off. We'd spent the morning trolling the car lot and test-driving some cars with multiple calls to my dad. Pete was semi-tolerant answering some questions from my dad since we had started looking at cars my dad had not researched. Pete walked away the last time I called my father as he had one more question I couldn't answer. Pete eventually took the phone, and I heard him laughing. Forty seconds later, he had a strange look on his face. I had apologized for my father hounding him with so many questions.

Pete replied, "It wasn't your dad. It was . . ."

I felt my face get flush. "Did my mother get on the phone?"

Pete was silent.

"What did she say?"

"Can we just skip it?"

He pulled into EG's driveway.

I hopped out. "Thanks for the afternoon. I can't believe my decision. I promise not to give my dad your number. He will probably come to town on Thursday when I finish the financing and pick up the keys, so you might want to hang low."

"Got it. He's not so bad. I just don't know as much as he does about cars. I don't want to be held responsible for your choice," Pete said before he backed out.

I looked up and saw Sherrie watching us.

I walked in through the screened-in front porch to the front door only to find it locked. It really got me thinking what stupid thing Sherrie had done to warrant a locked door. She was downstairs, unhooking the security chain on the door before I could knock.

Before I asked my hundred questions, Sherrie said, "You've been car shopping with Pete this whole time?"

I whispered my answer. "Are you asking about car shopping or about Pete?"

Sherrie hesitated, and before answering, someone called her name.

I couldn't place the voice. It seemed to be twenty years too young to be Miller.

She grabbed my hand, reminded me to say *jellyroll*, to be cool then pulled me upstairs while shouting, "I'm on my way, and I'm bringing my roommate."

Each stair I climbed added ten more questions I wanted to ask. I followed Sherrie into her room and saw the sleeper couch pulled open. A bedsheet hung from a single nail in the ceiling, creating a canopy over the pulled-out bed with two little feet sticking out.

Sherrie spoke to the little feet. "Remember I

told you I live with two ladies. The older lady will not be here for a few days. The one in the photo with the purple shirt. This is Claudia."

I walked around to the end of the pull-out bed and spied a blond boy around the age of seven or eight with shaggy hair, round eyes, and a towel draped over his shoulders. Sherrie looked at me with wide eyes and nodded in my direction as if I knew the next line.

I went with the game and said, "I'm Claudia, but some call me Jellyroll."

The boy gave me a smile. His hand dropped from the blanket he was holding, and he gave me a wave.

"You and Sherrie have been hanging out today?" I said.

"That's right," Sherrie answered. "Maggie, the other Jellyroll, was watching Ben but needed to go somewhere. Ben is here with us for the night."

"Cool, we don't get too many visitors. I like the canopy you guys made. What other fun activities have you done?"

Ben shrugged his shoulders and looked at Sherrie.

She said, "We went to a movie and made some drawings and watched some TV. Ben likes it best under the canopy. We're hoping you got some ideas."

"Of course, because why wouldn't I have

ideas on how to entertain someone of your size." I looked at Sherrie when I said it. I was pretty sure she understood my sarcasm, but I was up for the challenge. "Got it. Give me a sec."

I ran to my room and dug into three boxes before I found three pairs of fuzzy Christmas socks. I put on a pair and went sliding into Sherrie's room and pretended to crash into the wall and collapse. That produced a large albeit fake roar from Sherrie and a small smile from Ben.

"You think you can do better?" I asked.

Ben didn't move, but Sherrie put on the pair I tossed her and slid across her room pretending to slip and fall on her butt. Ben giggled at Sherrie when she flailed her arms and kicked up her legs.

I slid back and forth like a speed skater only not moving forward and managed to get a bigger smile this time from Ben. Sherrie did more slides across the long length of the room. Ben moved out of the canopy, lay on a his belly, and laughed each time we pretended to crash into something.

"It looks like someone with a cape could do much better," Sherrie said.

Ben sat up and let Sherrie put the fuzzy socks on him. I found two elastic hair ties and pulled them up on his calves so the socks stayed up.

We whooped and hollered while Ben skated across the floor. The laughter, even fake laughter, felt good. I looked at my watch and was surprised only nine minutes had passed.

Sherrie was going to have a long night on her hands. I wanted us to binge some reality TV, but most of it was not suitable for youngsters.

I excused myself and went downstairs for some salty snacks and to plan out my night. A minute later, Sherrie followed.

I managed to squeak out one question before she ran back up with scissors and brown paper grocery store bags. "How'd you get roped into this?"

She returned a minute later, slipping on the last wooden step. Watching her hold back non-little-kid-approved language was kinda funny.

She sat on the step, tore off the fuzzy socks, and leaned against the side wall. "I am freakin' exhausted."

"How did you get roped into this, and when was the last time you babysat?" I asked.

"Probably six years ago, maybe when I was a junior in high school. Maggie from work called in a panic asking if I could watch Ben. I guess he hangs out at her house a lot, but something happened and he couldn't stay there."

"So he's not Maggie's grandson?" I asked.

"Ellie's brother. The one EG mentioned at dinner and who I made the sock puppets for."

"How long is he here?"

Sherrie stood up from the stair landing and

talked as she went into the kitchen. "Well, that's the stupid thing I mentioned. Actually, one of the stupid things. I'm not sure, was thinking it was for the evening but it could be overnight."

I let her get a drink before bombarding her with questions. "How do you not know? Where is Ellie? When or how are you supposed to find out? Overnight on a school night? Does he have clothes with him? How did Maggie get you into all this?"

She put her finger to her lips to quiet my voice and yelled up to Ben, "Keep working on the hats. I'll be up in a minute." Sherrie sat on the arm of the sofa and whispered to me, "After the library, I was napping on the couch when Maggie texted asking if I could help. I texted *sure* without really understanding what she meant and said something about calling myself Jellyroll. When I saw her, I said something like 'What's up with the jellyroll comment?' She said it's a stranger danger code word, like when an adult who isn't the kid's parent picks them up from school is suppose to know the code word or the kid is supposed to go running away. It's to make Ben feel safe."

"Does this happen so often with Ben that he needs a code word?"

"Not a clue."

"So if it's overnight do you take him to school? What school?"

Sherrie slunk onto the couch cushion and

sprawled out like a rag doll. "I have no idea. Maggie and Ellie are not responding to my texts."

"Looks like you got your hands full." I laughed.

"You should watch what you say." Sherrie smiled. "You can't stay at Aaron's, Kay is gone for the night, and Jenna's roommate annoys the piss out of you so you are stuck with me. Well, stuck with us unless you have more plans with Pete?"

"What are you making us for dinner?" I asked in defeat and acceptance of our dinner guest.

Again, I let the remark about Pete go. She was ok with having breakfast with him and maybe working with him again at the bar, but did she have issues with me being friends with him? I couldn't ask because we heard Ben calling Sherrie's name.

His call for Sherrie was to show off the paper hats he'd made. I guess the fuzzy sock slide game endured me to Ben because I was called up to collect mine.

My stomach rumbled, and despite the 4 p.m. hour, I declared it was time for dinner. Sherrie's car, for some reason, was still in the alley, so we piled into my car.

After Sherrie installed the booster seat, Ben insisted she sit in the back seat with him and was highly concerned about the one working seat belt. We headed to the Blue Daisy Diner, hoping there would be something on the menu that he would like.

The three of us walked into the diner, and Sherrie and I spied the only other guest in there. Together we mumbled, "Hell's bells."

As if the other diner was not troublesome enough, I got a call from EG's neighbor telling us someone had broken into her house. That sent us reeling.

CHAPTER TEN

Ben giggled. "You said a bad word."

"Rhyming words are not bad. Hell's bells is rhythmic poetry," Sherrie said, and she watched me roll my eyes.

The lone server at the restaurant misunderstood our wave to Mallory to mean we wanted to share the table with her. She placed the menus at the three open seats, and without being complete heels, we decided to accept our fate.

"Hey, nice to have company. Sherrie, I like that blue sweater." Mallory must have understood our hesitation. "I'm almost done, so I won't invade your party too long."

I took the seat next to Mallory, allowing Ben to sit opposite me and next to Sherrie. He suddenly shifted back to the quiet kid I'd met before the sock sliding uproar. Ben gave half a wave and kept his head down while he and Sherrie discussed the menu. Nothing appealed to him, but she kept trying.

"Burger, burger with cheese, chicken fingers, breaded chicken."

Each item was getting resistance.

"I bet they would do plain noodles for you," I said.

Sherrie tried again. "You can have anything. I'm paying, it's my treat."

His eyes widened, and she whispered something I couldn't understand. They agreed on a cheeseburger and fries.

Sherrie added, "To be honest, I'm not paying. Claudia won this money." She tossed three twenties on the table.

Ben grabbed one and said, "Just like Ellie. You take this from her safe I saw in the car?"

Sherrie and I exchanged looks.

Mallory's head swiveled between us with intense interest, and she turned to Ben. "I know Ellie—well, I know Adam. He's just a year younger than me."

Ben didn't respond to Mallory.

"What safe?" I asked.

"The metal rocket where we keep our secrets," Ben said.

This time Sherrie, Mallory, and I all

exchanged glances,

Ben continued, "Ellie put the blue dot on this money so we know when we can use it. Blue dot is emergency only so we shouldn't use those monies." He pointed to the other two bills lying on the table.

"Are you talking about the silver cup rolling around in the back seat of the car?" I said.

"I can show you." Ben stood up, grabbed Sherrie's hand, and walked her out of the restaurant.

The timing was perfect because the server brought over water for us, and I said I could order for the table. I gave her my order and Ben's and guessed at what Sherrie wanted.

When the server left the table, Mallory said, "You didn't have to order without Sherrie just so you wouldn't have to talk to me. I'm ok with awkward silence."

"Well, you're better at that than I am," I said, and drank some water. "It's not just that. On the way over here, I started to get one of those deep headaches, dull and throbbing behind the eye, and these bright lights are not helping."

There was a long semi-uncomfortable pause before Mallory said, "I know what people think of me, and with Aaron—"

"You know Aaron does not say anything bad about anyone."

"Yeah, that's kinda annoying."

I laughed and said, "Gossip and trash-talking are not in his wheelhouse. Both are fine by me."

"My career is based on it," Mallory said, and we both laughed.

The best part was watching Sherrie's reaction to Mallory and me seemingly getting along.

Ben ran in carrying the travel mug he called a safe. He sat back in the chair and waited for Sherrie to sit before he said, "Since I have this does that mean I get to see Ellie and we can go home?"

Sherrie looked at me, and I shrugged.

She said, "I don't think just yet."

Ben put his head down and hugged the metal mug like a security blanket.

The server brought over Mallory's food she had ordered before we arrived. The salad was no surprise, but the double order of fries was. Mallory pushed the salt and pepper and sugar away from the center of the table and moved the fries to the middle and said to Ben, "You can have some of my fries. Fries are the best when you aren't feeling happy."

Ben pulled on Sherrie's arm and whispered. The only word I could understand was *jellyroll*. Sherrie looked at Mallory and said to everyone at the table, "No, she is not but let's say just jelly friendly. You can have some fries."

"Please, everyone have some," Mallory said, and we all dug in.

Ben asked Mallory, "What are you not happy about?"

"Today these fries are not about happy or sad, it's just what I've been craving. The Blue Daisy Diner has the best fries," Mallory said, then she responded with honesty, "But since you asked, I didn't know I was sad until I was thinking about work and what I needed to improve on, and I have no idea how to do it."

I kept looking at the fries since I didn't know how to respond to that.

Mallory, uncomfortable with her own frankness, spoke again. "Ben, I love your shirt. I used to play basketball. Do you like to play?"

Ben patted the picture of the ball on his chest. "I like dribbling. Ain't no good at making it in the big basket."

Until our food arrived, we spent the next few minutes talking about sports we had played. The server set down the cheeseburger in front of Ben and tried placing the French dip in front of me, but Sherrie grabbed it, leaving me the second cheeseburger.

Before he started eating, Ben opened the mug and asked if he could return his cheeseburger.

"Is there something wrong?" I asked.

"There's only emergency money left in here,

and I don't think we have enough for this food."

Tears filled my eyes. I had no idea how that hit Sherrie and Mallory except for the weighted silence.

Sherrie said, "I'll treat, so you don't worry."

Mallory added, "Ever have onion rings? I'll treat. You have to try them. They make you happier than fries."

Sherrie jumped in, "I think that's a great idea. You can eat, Ben."

I had little time to react because I got a text from Jorge, EG's neighbor, asking if we were home and asking me to call him immediately so I stepped away from the table to make the call.

I returned to the table pale faced and did not touch my food.

"What's up?" Sherrie asked.

"Nothing." It was all I could say.

"I'm just about done, so I'll get the check and go, and you can talk," Mallory said.

"Oh, no. I appreciate that, but it's not you, not that, it's just . . . let's just eat."

Mallory raised her hand to catch the attention of the server, who was chatting with the cook. "I think we need a double order of onion rings for the table."

Ben knocked over the mug on the table, and the lid fell off. The contents went spilling out.

Mallory pulled the empty fry plate away

from the center, allowing Ben and Sherrie room to gather everything. He held onto the container while Sherrie collected and combined the bills, a key, and notepaper, and stuck it back in. Ben insisted on lifting each plate, making sure they had everything.

After he picked up Sherrie's plate for the third time, she said with a sharp voice, "We got it all."

He kept is head down and didn't say anything. Sherrie raised her plate, then Mallory and I did too.

He spoke in barely a whisper, "Mr. Harry can't see this."

"Who is Mr. Harry?" I asked.

Ben didn't answer.

I asked again, "Who is Mr. Harry?"

Ben held up his finger to his ear and drew an imaginary line down to his neck. "Just like Harry Potter, but Mr. Harry has a scar on his neck and not his forehead. That's how I know he's not the good guy. He keeps looking for his monies."

"You have the safe now, and we have you so we will protect you," Sherrie said.

"I want to see Ellie." Ben turned to Sherrie.

She had texted Ellie throughout the evening and had gotten no response. She said, "She's working right now, so you have to stay with us."

"If she's working, can I go to the room?" Ben asked.

Sherrie and I exchanged looks, and neither one of us had an answer.

Sherrie said, "We can take you back to the tent fort."

I jumped in fast. "Maybe not right now. Let's just eat." I looked at Ben and my phone, and Sherrie understood I wouldn't say anything in front of him.

We ate quickly and silently. Finally, Sherrie got up and went to talk to our server. She came back with three crayons, large coffee filters, and scissors. Mallory and I watched her take Ben's hand and whisper something that made him give me the safe. She led him to the far corner booth and showed him how to make snowflakes.

Sherrie joined us at the table. "I got him making snowflakes, and we have to judge them when he's done, so I don't know how much time we have. So spill it, Claud."

"That call was from Jorge. He just saw someone sneaking out of EG's house."

"Holy shit," Sherrie said.

"He walked out his back door and was headed to his garage when he saw the back door open and someone dressed in all black step out. He called after 'em, and the person took off. He called me to see if we were home, and then said he would call Wyatt and walk through the house together with him before we go back."

"Claudia, open that mug," Mallory said.

"Why?" I asked.

Mallory rolled her eyes. I was offended when Sherrie smiled with Mallory, who said, "Someone was just in your house, you have a kid from a known drug family, and that kid is carrying a mug he calls a safe with secrets."

Sherrie and I each got a text from Wyatt telling us to stay away from the house until he clears it.

"Hurry up and open it," Sherrie said. "I'm not sure how I can keep Ben occupied with snowflakes."

I pulled open the lid, removed the cash and the small key. Written on the paper was MBSR3D4. "What is it?" I asked.

Mallory and Sherrie had no answer.

Ben called Sherrie's name.

"Put that away, fast!" Sherrie grunted.

I shoved it all back in the mug just in time as Ben came to the table proudly carrying the coffee filter snowflakes.

"Those are great. Can I keep one?" I asked.

Ben nodded, and Mallory asked, "What if we put them in the safe to protect them?"

He shook his head. "No, that's for secrets only."

"Do you know what the secrets are inside there?" Mallory asked.

Ben didn't say anything, and Sherrie pulled

him over to her lap and looked at the snowflakes. Mallory didn't understand much about negotiating with a seven-year-old.

Sherrie asked, "You know the bills with dots are for emergencies. What about the other stuff? Is that for emergencies, or should we keep in the tent?"

"It all stays together. Ellie can tell you. She said this is a big week, and it will be the best vacation ever. We're going somewhere fun."

"Vacation?" Sherrie asked.

"We started at Maggie's house, and Ellie said we have to wait before our trip starts."

"Do you think the trip started with Maggie, and maybe I am the fun surprise?"

Ben just shrugged.

Our server delivered the onion rings, and Mallory munched on them while I joined the conversation.

"I'm sorry the vacation was kinda boring with Sherrie, but school will be fun with your friends tomorrow."

"Vacation. Ellie said vacation so I go to Maggie's this week."

Mallory piped in between munches. "There is no school in River Bend this week for spring break."

"Ben, can you make three more snowflakes for Ellie?" Sherrie said.

He ran back to the booth and out of earshot.

"No school! I didn't agree to all day and evening, much less overnight and tomorrow! I got class tomorrow," Sherrie said.

I thought for a second, then said, "Let's just drive to Maggie's?"

"Can't," Sherrie said.

"Why?" I asked.

"She didn't elaborate. She dropped him off and ran."

"Maggie Culpepper?" Mallory asked.

"Maggie from Peach's. Come to think of it, I don't know her last name," Sherrie answered.

"Early sixties, former teacher?"

Sherrie nodded in agreement.

Mallory continued. "I think it's her husband. I heard my mother talking about it. He's back in the hospital for some heart issues." She dipped an onion ring in ranch and gobbled it up.

Our server came over with the checks and said they were closing up in ten minutes.

Sherrie said, "Apparently Sunday evenings aren't big business for the Blue Daisy Diner."

Our server answered, "We are not normally open even this late, but I paid Joe ten bucks for the extra thirty minutes."

I looked around the empty dining room and couldn't help myself. "Why?"

"There's been this cute fellow that's been

coming in the last few nights. He's been a nice change of pace from the locals and truck drivers I usually get in here. But I guess he found what he's looking for, since I haven't seen him tonight."

"You sure he ain't local? Maybe I can help," Mallory said. "You're a Peterson, right? I lived a block over. I'm a Douglas."

"I thought you looked familiar. Previously, he came here about once a month with a rental car. No one seems to engage with him when he dines here so I figure he can't be from here."

Sherrie gave her the cash for our bill, and Mallory handed over her credit card and asked for a to-go box.

"Where are we going to go if we can't go back to EG's and Maggie's is a no-go. I can't believe I got us into this. How am I to handle Ben? I am exhausted, and it's only been a few hours. How do mothers do this all day every day?"

"You're right, where are we going to go?" I said.

The three of us sat there in silence listening to the hum of the fluorescent lights.

Sherrie broke the collective think tank when she instructed Ben to return the scissors and crayons to the counter and to wash up. He asked to finish one more snowflake for Ellie, and Sherrie gave him the thumbs-up.

"Seriously, where do I take him? Somehow I

could find Ellie's house and drop him off, but if she's not answering, I can't imagine that being a good idea."

"Probably not," Mallory said.

Sherrie looked her up and down and was about to say something when Mallory seemed to understand what Sherrie was thinking.

"My place won't work. I actually don't have a place."

Mallory stopped talking like that was the end of what she had to contribute, but we didn't take our eyes off her.

She knew she had to finish. "I'm living at home in my old bedroom. My parents' bungalow that barely fits the three of us."

"But at least Ben will be safe . . ." Sherrie didn't finish her own sentence as she was not even convincing herself that that was a proper solution.

Mallory said something more frightening than learning she was living at home. "The obvious place is the house."

That generic word *house* was enough to understand what she meant, but what it meant was monumental.

CHAPTER ELEVEN

"Mallory's right," Sherrie said.

I just nodded. Neither one of us moved.

Mallory picked up the to-go box and slid the five remaining onion rings in. "What's with you two?"

Again we were silent.

"How about we do something until Jorge and Wyatt walk through the house?" I said.

"Like what? I already took him to the movies. The library is not open on a Sunday night. I'm not an ace with kiddos," Sherrie said.

My phone rang. It was Jorge again.

He said, "While Wyatt and I were upstairs, two guys came to the door. They pounded on the screen, and when we didn't answer right away, they stepped onto the front porch and rang the bell.

When I stepped off the stair landing into the living room, all I could see were two male figures on the porch. They took off when they spotted me."

I finished up the call and relayed the information to the girls.

Sherrie received a text from Holton asking her to come in tomorrow and give her statement again. "They think I know something, and I am not telling them and—"

Ben came over, and we all stood up. He and Sherrie headed outside. Mallory was getting ready to leave and grabbed the onion rings.

I asked, "What about the salad, you hardly touched it?"

"I came here for the fries and quiet. My mother has the house stocked with her version of nutritional foods and has barred anything that has flavor. We compromised on the low-fat ranch dressing. She is so distraught about her single daughter having a baby on her own, she's controlling the one thing she can, which is the grocery list. My cravings for salt and fried food is off the charts." She looked to her belly. "The doc said I'm maintaining a healthy weight gain, so I sneak here to settle my cravings before I head back home for grilled chicken and broccoli without garlic bread."

In that moment, she almost seem likable, maybe not by me, but probably to someone.

"Hey, I think your friend is in trouble," our server shouted.

The cook flew out with a knife in his hand before Mallory and I were barely out of our seats. We had a hard time seeing outside because of the bright lights inside. When we got to the door, Sherrie came flying in with Ben. He was squeezing her hand and through his tears was crying for Ellie. Sherrie was panting, sweating, and a little shaky but still strong on her feet. We heard tires squealing, and ten seconds later, the cook came in, still holding the knife, red-faced and breathing heavily. He looked to the server, "I told you he was bad news. I stayed for ten bucks for that loser." He turned his attention to Sherrie, "You ok, Miss?"

Sherrie nodded and said, "Thanks for the help."

The cook did not hesitate to respond. "Everybody is fine, so everybody out."

He left us standing in the doorway stunned. Ben clung to Sherrie, who tried picking him up but temporarily lacked the coordination to. He let me hoist him up and sit him on the back of the booth so he could hug Sherrie and her him without having to hold his weight.

"What happened? Should I call the police?" I asked.

"And say what, some guy yelled at us?" Sherrie said.

"What did he say?" Mallory asked.

Sherrie looked at Ben, giving us the impression any replay of the incident would have to wait until Ben was out of earshot. "After we get settled I'll go to the station and make a report. Holton wants me there again anyways to review the other night."

Before our server walked away, she said, "I should've known sexy eyes, a badass scar, and a name like Ryder could only mean trouble."

"I'll get the car. You two can wait here and don't come out until I pull up," I said.

"We still don't know where we're going?" Sherrie said.

The throbbing behind my eye was getting worse. "I will go to the house and pretend to be ok with that, but you have to make the call," I said through gritted teeth.

Mallory spoke up. "I'm not sure where you guys are going, but I was suggesting Aaron's house."

In a matter of minutes, Mallory went from a lonely, honest River Bend local who knew everyone, typical pregnant woman, to not the most observant person.

I answered bluntly, "We know. We got it the first time."

I ignored her mumbled *oh* and turned back to Sherrie. "Please make the call."

The overhead lights turned off, leaving security lights on over the register and kitchen.

Our server let us know one of us left a scarf behind, and when Mallory left to fetch it, I turned to Sherrie and said, "Please figure out where we're going." I stood in the doorway to have a better view of the parking lot now that the overhead lights were out and scoped out a clear lot and made a dash to my car.

It took one turn of the key to know the night had gone from weird to scary to awkward.

CHAPTER TWELVE

I don't know if I was relieved or not that Mallory was still in the café. She was the logical and only choice for a ride.

I walked in carrying Ben's booster seat and backpack. Sherrie looked at me with dread.

"Debby died," I said.

Ben with his soft, shaky voice said, "Someone else died?"

"Oh no. I named my car Debby, and she won't start."

"Adam can do magic with cars," Ben said.

"No magic is going to help Debby."

"Sure just mix the wires," he answered.

I didn't think hot-wiring the car would make Debby come back to life, but I thought about it for a split second before I turned to Mallory and simply said, "We need a lift, and apparently you know the way."

We walked around to the side of the diner, Sherrie holding Ben's hand while taking two steps forward and one backwards, jumping in place, and repeating. Her silliness eventually produced a giggle from spooked little Ben.

The streets were void of traffic, but Mallory and I kept watch for any car or person that might come and give us more trouble.

Sherrie and Ben loaded into the back of Mallory's shiny SUV, and Mallory hoisted her belly up and into the driver's seat with a slight struggle.

When I opened the passenger-side door, Mallory grabbed a fast-food bag off the seat and tucked it under her seat. "Fries from yesterday," she said.

Country music popped from the radio, and Mallory was quick to change it.

"Sherrie loves country," I said, acknowledging the unexpected sounds.

"Really? I never would have guessed that," Mallory said.

From the back seat, Sherrie replied, "Why is that? Because most people who look like me are not showing up at the Country Music Awards?"

Mallory didn't answer.

Sherrie let her off the hook. "I like the old stuff, country-western stuff, my dad would listen to, like Charley Pride, Johnny Cash, Hank Williams, and anything that takes you to the blues. None of this poppy country music, besides Shania Twain. That woman can sing." Sherrie was doing just fine until she said, "At least I don't sing every tune my dad introduced me to any time something freaky happens."

Mallory was about to shift the car into drive when she looked at me and said, "Is that why you were mumbling that song from Warrant, when we ran to the front of the café to check on them outside?"

I didn't mind being called out on my singing because that happens all the time, I just didn't like Sherrie seemingly letting Mallory into our private lives, but then again, she was driving us to Aaron's house.

I clutched onto the travel mug and replied, "It was 'Jump' by Van Halen."

Ben settled quietly next to Sherrie, and I stewed in my seat thinking about heading to Aaron's house and was not sure what to expect.

I turned to look at Sherrie. "How about we drop you guys off, I go talk to Jorge about who's hanging around EG's house, and grab your car keys and car, so we're not stuck out there."

Reading my mind, Sherrie said, "Aaron's at the bar, and he said he would come out only if we needed him."

"We still need a ride back to town. We can't expect Mallory to play chauffeur for us."

"Fine, but first, come in and show me how the house works?"

Mallory and I exchanged looks and both smiled. It would have been a classic moment if someone other than Mallory was driving, but with no other choice but to share it with her, I conceded and laughed when I asked, "How the house works? Do you want a tutorial on the doors or chairs? Maybe Mallory can write a how-to book about houses."

Sherrie pulled herself to the edge of her seat, wedged her shoulders between the seats, and whispered through her teeth, "I hate lonely houses in the country. They're creepy and stuff of horror movies."

"Country?" Mallory said. Three blocks from the diner, she turned down a gravel road I had never noticed before. "We'll be there in under three minutes."

"Where are we?" I asked.

We were still so close to town before Mallory turned.

"Seriously?" Mallory said.

"We're headed to Aaron's house," I retorted and expected a sudden stop and U-turn.

"No shit," she replied. I let the swearing in front of Ben go, and she answered, "Let me guess,

112

Aaron never brought you this way. He had you go eight miles out of the way because he didn't want to use the shortcut through my Aunt Molly's land. Kettle Lake is just through the trees on the left. This gravel road is the property line to my aunt's land. There is a dirt lane cut through the trees that curves around to the beach and up to the hou . . . house." Her voice shot up as we bounced up and down on the not so smooth road.

Mallory slowed down to manageable speed that kept us in our seats.

Before Sherrie slid back, she warned us, "Couldn't you have gone the long way? This is how horror movies start. Unnamed roads on a dark night leading us to an ex's house."

Mallory and I laughed, but I refused to look at her to completely share the moment with her.

Twenty seconds later, Sherrie leaned forward again. "Claud, you know eighties music; I know horror movies from the seventies and on. The Black person always gets it first. I'm most at risk."

"You said it yourself, it's in the movies. This is real life, you're fine," I said without any conviction in my voice.

"Denial is where trouble begins." Sherrie huffed before sitting back.

She was not completely wrong about trouble beginning that night.

CHAPTER THIRTEEN

Mallory steered her SUV off a gravel road to a dirt road lined with trees and covered in last season's dead leaves, pine cones, and several large dips. She skirted around the beach and up the slope to Aaron's driveway. She remembered to swerve wide right to activate the motion sensor lights. We were lit up like Times Square.

The white house attached to the motion sensor sat dark. It was too early for the moon to be out, and the gloomy clouds suppressed any natural light.

Sherrie unhooked Ben from his seat, and he opened the door but waited for Sherrie before leaving the car. As she moved across the back seat, she said to Mallory, "We appreciate the ride."

Mallory looked at me and said, "If it's okay

with you, I need to use the bathroom again. Another great enjoyment of pregnancy is having to pee every five minutes. After that last pothole, my bladder has been busting at the seams."

"It's not for me to . . . of course, come in." I had no other option but to let her come in, but I could make it seem like a favor.

Sherrie and Ben stood close to the car as they waited for Mallory and me to exit. Mallory waited at the bottom of the five wooden steps that led to the small cement slab in front of the door. Most people would have walked up the stairs and waited by the front door, but she knew—because like me, she was Aaron's ex-girlfriend—the key to the house was under the second step.

I flipped up the step, pulled the key hanging from the hook, and bounced up the remaining steps. Mallory held Sherrie and Ben back until I tossed her the key, and she returned it to the proper place. It was intimate and creepy the routines we knew when coming to Aaron's house.

The side door entered into the kitchen, and I flipped on the lights while Mallory darted into the bathroom. Sherrie took Ben to the living room and turned on the television for him. I turned on the heat while waiting for Mallory.

Sherrie stopped me. "You are not going anywhere yet. You need to walk upstairs and turn on some lights."

116

"Want me to check under the beds too?" I asked.

"Don't make fun of me but yeah."

She followed me upstairs, and we checked out the first bedroom full of old furniture from the house. The closet door was open, and no one was hiding inside.

The second bedroom with a double bed and nightstand was also free of the boogeyman.

The first thing I noticed in the master was that the king bed was made with one side slightly neater than the other, giving me proof of no overnight guests. Aaron made his side of the bed loosely pulling up the sheets and comforter and the other side remained intact from the day the fresh bedding was put on the bed.

I waited at the top of the stairs while Sherrie checked out Aaron's closet and bathroom, leaving a trail of lights on in each room.

Walking down the stairs, Sherrie instructed me, "Hurry up. Don't stay in the house too long, better yet take Jorge with you. Gentle with the car brakes."

"I got it. This is not the first time I have driven your car or dealt with your crazy. Now just figure out how long he will be with us," I said.

We stepped out of the stairwell to find Mallory panting with her back to the kitchen door.

"Claudia, I got bad news. I was waiting in

the car for you and went to turn it around when I realized the shortcut through the woods was a mistake. I got a flat tire."

Without hesitating, Sherrie jumped in, "See this is how it all starts. Have you guys not seen one horror movie!" She didn't even take a breath. She might have been scared but, as always, was willing to charge forward. "Well, at least I'm fed and have decent clothes on. Mallory, you can sit with Ben, and we'll change your tire."

"We?" I loved Sherrie's ambition but seriously. I had barely processed the idea of a flat tire, and Sherrie had already whipped up a plan.

"Don't tell me you don't know how?" she answered.

"In theory, I guess I know how. My dad showed me once. All right, let's do this."

Mallory was shrugging off her coat and stopped us dead. "There is a bigger problem. I don't have a spare. I blew a tire about six months ago and put on the full-size spare then forgot about it."

Ben came into the kitchen with his coat on, asking, "Is it time to go to the room?"

"Like I said before, we can't take you home until Ellie says ok," Sherrie said.

"What about the room? It's . . ." Ben looked up and saw Mallory was in the kitchen and stopped talking.

Sherrie gestured towards the living room. "Why don't you watch some more TV while we talk in the kitchen?"

"Fine," Ben muttered.

Thanks to the old farmhouse, the small square kitchen was closed off from the family room. Aaron had started renovations in the basement and had not made his way up to the main level yet. Sherrie flicked on the overhead lights, illuminating the entire square kitchen, and I winced. She found the stove light and hallway light, which my headache could tolerate better, giving us enough light to see each other.

I put the travel mug on the table in the center of the room, and when Sherrie went to sit, she nicked the table leg, and the mug wobbled.

She grabbed it before it dropped to the floor. "Ewww, why is it wet?"

"I have been clutching it since the diner. Your talk of horror movies made me sweat a bit," I said.

Mallory smiled and said, "You mean it had nothing to do with sitting next to me while driving our to ex-boyfriend's house?"

I couldn't help but laugh. "Nah, sweaty palms are due to the talk of horror movies, but the sweaty pits are due to awkwardness."

Sherrie laughed and took control again. "Now that you two are friends, let's figure this out."

I kept my eyes diverted from both of them but spied Mallory on her phone.

"We are here for the night," Sherrie said. "Claud, talk to Jorge again and get more details about who he saw leaving the house and the two that were knocking on the door and took off when they saw him."

"I will have my cousin come get me. He can drop you off too, Claudia. If you don't want a ride, I can wait at my aunt's on the other side of the lake. I'd ask her for a ride, but Sunday evenings are usually a two-gummy night, and she's probably higher than the rooftop about now. Let me try my cousin."

Sherrie responded quickly. "Please don't share with anyone that we're here or why."

"Who do you think I am? I'm not blasting to the world you guys are hiding here. I'll go wait at my aunt's place."

I quickly jumped in. "No need to walk in the dark over to your aunt's. It's probably over a half mile to the house. Sorry, we didn't mean to imply anything."

"It's fine. I'll text my cousin to come here," Mallory said.

Sherrie's phone rang, and she couldn't answer it fast enough.

"Ellie, where are you? What is going on?"

. . .

"He is fine. He really wants to see you."

. . .

"Not until you tell me . . ."

Ben must have heard the phone and Sherrie yelling into it. He came running into the kitchen, and before she knew what was happening, he snatched the phone out of her hand and ran into the living room with it.

Sherrie and I chased after him. I think Mallory wanted to join us, but quickly getting up from the table with her belly was not an option at this point.

Ben was on the sofa, and we heard Ellie and him singing some song I didn't recognize. Then the singing promptly ended, and she said, "I love you," and the phone went silent. Ben closed his eyes, balled up in the corner of the couch, pulling a pillow to his face. I grabbed the blanket I had kept on the reclining chair, tossed it over the backside of the couch, making a mini tent. Sherrie sat by his feet and said he could stay under there as long as he wanted.

I stood there with them for a minute before I returned to the kitchen. The stuff from the mug was spread out on the table. "What the hell are you doing?" I arm-swept the money, note, and key into the corner of the table.

"Relax," Mallory said without apology.

"Some of the bills are marked. I took photos of several of them and sent them to somebody I know. They can tell us if the numbers on the bills are linked to any investigations."

"You think this is that big?" I leaned as far away as I could, while remaining in my chair, from the supposedly tainted drug money. I knew I looked stupid.

Sherrie came back in the kitchen and handed me the blanket she had been sitting on.

Mallory continued, "You never know. I have seen crazier stuff. You have marked bills, a key with the strange code of MBSR3D4, a somewhat-missing sister of that boy, both of which are related to Adam, who spent time in jail. It doesn't hurt to ask some questions about what we have here."

I jumped right in. "You recorded the numbers on the notes? Are you writing a story about this? Because if you are, I don't . . ."

"No. Well, not yet. Remember I just ran into you guys at the diner and didn't know a story even existed. An hour ago, I would have bet money that right now I would be sitting with my parents watching *60 Minutes*. But I'm always looking for a story. You have to admit, there is some type of story here. I don't write headlines; I do features. This story is not going to blow up overnight. Either I'm writing it, or someone else is going to write it. So let me have your portion of the story right."

"We're not the story and don't want to be part of any story," Sherrie said.

"Really? Let's not forget your run-in in the parking lot, Sherrie. What happened out there?"

Sherrie and I looked at each other and nodded together, silently agreeing to talk in front of Mallory.

Sherrie sat down. "No writing about this." She pushed back on the chair, balancing on the back two legs rocking slightly as she gave us the story. "Ben and I were twenty feet from the car when another car comes racing up to us. I don't know if he was watching us in the parking lot or if it was driving around and just spotted us. I wasn't paying attention. This guy with the beautiful eyes, the one I've seen at Peach's, starts talking to us, well, mostly to Ben. He was asking for Ellie and asking for what was his. He bent over and said something to Ben I couldn't understand. Ben kicked him in the shin and then the guy grabbed my arm and said something about money that was his and asked, 'Where is that little bitch?' Ben kicked him again. I'm not sure where that kick landed. That is pretty much when the cook came running out with the knife and the guy took off."

"Tell me about the car he was driving?" Mallory asked.

"A red four-door sedan, maybe a Ford or Toyota," Sherrie answered.

Mallory pressed for more. "Was there anyone else in the car?"

Sherrie wasn't enjoying the questions. "That's all I saw."

"There has to be more. There is always more," Mallory said.

"If she said that was it, then that's all," I answered for Sherrie.

Either Mallory didn't understand or wasn't easily offended. Either way, she didn't know better, and asked another question. "So he's not local but familiar with the diner and where to hang out on a Sunday. Is it random that he saw you guys or was he following you?"

Sherrie let her off easy. "As I said, I don't know. I wasn't keeping watch in the parking lot."

Mallory got up and went to the cookie cabinet and found some chocolate chip cookies. She held out the bag to us. I took one, and Sherrie declined.

She munched on the cookie and walked around the table, stretching her legs. I don't know what bothered me the most: that she still knew where the cookie cabinet was or that she was comfortable enough to just start eating Aaron's food.

As she walked around, she repeated everything that had happened since we met her in the diner. I shushed her to keep her mumbling to herself. This old farmhouse had closed-off rooms, and I was pretty sure Ben couldn't hear us, but better safe than sorry.

Mallory stood in the doorway peering into the living room and asked Ben if he wanted some cookies and disappeared. She returned shortly sans cookies.

Instantly, Sherrie snapped up on her feet and fumbled through two cabinets before she found a small bowl and went into the living room. She returned to the kitchen, tossing the cookie bag on the counter. "You can't leave him the bag."

Mallory slowly lowered herself down, and for the first time, I saw her rub her belly. She said something I couldn't understand.

"What did you say?" I asked.

She waved my question away. "It's nothing."

Sherrie figured it out before me and said, "You will get the hang of it. I'm sure you know more about being a mom than you think."

"I'm not sure about that, but at this point, I have no choice."

The subject of her impending motherhood came up, and I had several questions, and none of them were any of my business, but thought this might be my chance to ask them without looking catty.

I skipped the *who's the daddy* question and

eased into the conversation. "Are you planning on raising the baby here?" I said *here*, implying River Bend, but sitting in Aaron's kitchen, it felt like I was asking if she wanted Aaron back.

She must have felt the same awkwardness or was surprised about the personal question because a few beats passed before she answered flatly, "River Bend for now. I got a house and will be moving in shortly."

Damn, she is putting down roots.

I asked, "Did you find out the sex?"

"No." Mallory said nothing more.

That should have prompted a normal person to move on to a new subject, but I had nothing to lose at this point, so I asked, "Any names, or top contenders?"

"No, yes. I mean, I have some. I have ... Sorry, I'm a mess. This pregnancy has my hormones all crazy, and I'm so claustrophobic at home. I've got no space and get a thousand questions a day from my mother. She means well, but most days it's too much. I finally had to put her on a four question a day limit and threaten to find daycare if she doesn't let up. I know I should be grateful she wants to watch him, but all the questions wear me down. The only thing I can leverage with her is daycare.

"Truth be told, I don't think I could afford daycare. I could only get the house thanks to that book deal, but after that advance runs out, I am not sure of my next move. I know I'm fortunate at twenty-eight with only newsprint experience to have a book deal. I have been living off pathetically low journalism wages with periodic contract work. So to answer that question from earlier again, I'm always looking for a story and trying to get income."

Sherrie reached back behind herself for the bag of cookies and slid them over to Mallory, who had not taken a breath during that confessional.

I reached for a box of tissues so I wouldn't look insensitive to the situation and even got up to get her some water, but I led the conversation with, "Him?"

After taking a bite of cookie, Mallory asked what I said.

"Him. You said your mother is watching *him*."

She nodded. "You must think I'm shit. I do know the sex of the baby. It's something I wanted to keep for myself. Needed something private. I told one friend in Chicago, and she sent me some designer boy clothes that I have stuffed in the back of my car so my mother doesn't find out. You can't understand what it's like moving back to your childhood home. I texted my mother once from inside the house, and I got a ten-minute lecture on cell phone etiquette from someone who still has a landline."

Sherrie jumped in. "Yikes. Must be rough. I thought I had it rough living with Claudia who doesn't know how to soak a pan after making scrambled eggs."

"Aren't you funny. Mallory is sharing with us, and you're taking shots at me. If you want to talk about the difficulties of living with people, we could talk about me constantly tripping on your shoes left in the doorway. Not near the doorway but in front of the door so people have to work an obstacle course to get in and out of the house."

Mallory smiled while wiping a tear away. "That is what I miss. Watching the two of you together. My friends in Chicago text me about bars and what outfits look good. I don't have a close friend who has had a baby that I can ask questions."

"There are a ton of books," I said.

"It is just not the same. Plus, my mother has checked out every one of them from the library and put them on my nightstand. I didn't have the heart or energy to tell her I already downloaded them."

Sherrie jumped in before me again. "I know I'm a gem. Claud's a work in progress, and even putting us together, we got nothing to offer in the way of baby stuff, but for fried food at a diner, you can give us a call."

A smile came across Mallory's face and then a snarl as she stood up. "Another trip to the bathroom. I swear I pee three times what I put in my body these days."

When the bathroom door closed, I swung my head towards Sherrie.

She held up her hand and whispered, "Don't. I know what you're going to say—why was I making those dumb jokes—it's because I know you were working your way into asking about baby daddy. I want to know too, but she won't crack yet. Give it time."

She was right. We sat silently in the kitchen, and then I wasn't sure I even said the words out loud because Sherrie didn't reply until I repeated them, "What are we going to do?"

"I heard you the first time. It's just I don't have an answer."

"Let's start with what we know. Ellie knows we have Ben, and she is avoiding you," I said.

Mallory returned to her seat at the table.

"She's doing something dangerous and doesn't want to involve Ben. Think she's selling drugs?" Sherrie said, convincing no one including herself.

Mallory added her take. "There are so many angles you can take with this. Maybe she is a witness. Better yet, what did the guy say in the parking lot—he wants what is his. If this mug of money is hers, she might be in some serious stuff. Is there more money or drugs? What is he looking for? Marking the bills? Her idea or did they come that way? How are you guys connected?"

Sherrie and I said nothing.

Mallory must have realized how she sounded. "First off, despite the completely obvious different physical appearance you both have, you've got the same back-off-bitch look with the head tilt, one raised eyebrow, and a dead stare. Second of all, I am not saying you guys are involved in some hideous or nefarious crime, but remember someone was just in your house and two guys knocked, then ran away. Remember that is the reason we're sitting in his kitchen."

"I guess we just got schooled," Sherrie said.

Ben called Sherrie's name. She showed him where the bathroom was and found a movie for him to watch while Mallory and I sifted through the mug of cash, looking for the note, this time in a comfortable silence. Soon, that began to annoy me. I should have been able to not like her, but it was getting hard with her crying and her admiring my friendship with Sherrie.

If that was the only problem that night, I would have been ok with being tolerant of Mallory, unfortunately—or fortunately—it all led us somewhere else.

CHAPTER FOURTEEN

The three of us sat in the kitchen for another half hour trying to decipher the code. The headache that had started as a slow burn had picked up to a full-on throb. No amount of googling was going to answer all our questions. We moved to the living room and watched the end of some animated movie I couldn't focus on. Mallory spent the entire time on her phone anxiously typing. I understood her need for a story, but it irked me she was writing about something I was involved in.

She went to the spare bedroom on this floor for what I assumed was a private conversation. That room was empty except for the winter clothing and hunting gear in the closet, and that left a lot of echo in the room. We couldn't understand what was being said but could hear her voice raise with each comment. She returned to the living room and somberly asked if she could spend the night.

I didn't know if it was up to me or not as it was not my house, and I mumbled out "Of course," but it was more of a question.

"My cousin is such a . . ." Mallory caught herself and held back her language in front of Ben. "My cousin had a few drinks and showed up at my parents' house thinking I need a ride from there. I guess my mother yelled at him so much for drinking that he stormed off and left his car at the house. He probably only had one beer, but my mother's scorn is enough to make anyone want to bury their head in the sand before returning to the house. Before you ask if my mother or father will pick me up when I said I was here, she was so delighted that I was at his house she said it was too late for them to be driving. The driving in the dark excuse is pulled out when it is convenient for her. Besides playing nutritionist for me, her other full-time job is playing matchmaker."

"She will be crushed to find out that it's just us and Aaron is at the bar," I said.

"Telling her I'm with EG's niece, it could go either way. My mother is a book of contradictions. She loves knowing that EG's writing made River Bend famous, but for a lady to be in her forties and not married is not natural. If it wasn't for my Aunt

Molly, I don't know if I would have come out of River Bend with my sanity. The Douglas side of my family is a wild yet have common sense. My mother's side, the Pattersons, are a different bunch."

"Sorry, I couldn't be of help." I laughed.

"I don't know what's with me. I have overshared a lot this evening. That is usually not my style."

"It happens to the best of us. With all that being said, that means I'm not driving Sherrie's car back tonight so I'm going to bed so I will . . ."

"At eight thirty?" Mallory commented, missing my hesitation.

"The only thing to stop my headache from hitting complete full migraine stage is sleep and some medicine. I will probably be awake at four in the morning, but I will be headache-free so that's worth it."

"I'll text Jenna or Kay and see if they can get us in the morning."

"I think it's Ben's bedtime." Sherrie tapped Ben's knee. "I will read to you. Take your backpack, and the three of us will go upstairs. Mallory, I'm assuming you're ok with the couch?"

"I will stay in this recliner. It's better for my back. One of you can have the couch."

Thankfully, Sherrie answered. I might have been on friendly terms with Mallory now, but I was not sharing a room with her.

"I'll sit with Ben until he falls asleep, and Claud and I can share that big bed upstairs in case you want to stretch out."

Ben held Sherrie's hand, and she led him to the staircase between the kitchen and living room but paused on the first step.

She turned to me, pointed to the front door and kitchen door, and whispered, "Check the locks on the doors and windows." With Ben's back turned away from us, she did something truly comical. She swept her right hand across her throat and made squeaking noises when she raised her fist and made downward slashing gestures. All she was missing was the shower curtain from *Psycho*, but otherwise, her portrayal of slasher movies was spot-on.

I sent them on their way upstairs and checked the doors, took my migraine medicine, and left Mallory in the living room. Sherrie found a toothbrush in Ben's backpack and some pajamas for him. She managed to download a few kids books on her phone and put him in Aaron's bed.

After I found my old toothbrush in the bathroom, I walked into the spare room and eyed the double bed.

Sherrie walked in behind me. "I knew you would have issues being in Aaron's room, so don't complain about the small bed size. I get the side by the window since you'll probably have to pee during the night."

"I will be out cold in about ten minutes with this medicine. Nothing will wake me up. You only want the window side to be away from the doorway so when that fictional horror movie stalker shows up, I'm the first one they get when they come up the stairs. I know you better than you know me."

"Doubt that," Sherrie said flatly.

"There is no way you know me better."

"Maybe, but you don't know me as well as you think you do, or you just choose—" Sherrie stopped short and left a loaded thought hanging in the air.

"I was having fun here. Trying to lighten the horror movie vibe you got going on in your head. What are you talking about?"

"Nothing. I'm going to sit with Ben until he falls asleep." Sherrie turned to leave.

"Wait a minute. What are we, an old married couple? Dropping hints at something then walking away, giving the other person the silent treatment. For the last few days, you have been dropping little comments here and there. Just like in college back in the apartment with Mia when she didn't keep to the shared cleaning duties. Instead of just asking her, you would make a comment like, 'I think your backpack is next to the vacuum, that all upright thing that needs to be plugged in to work.' I had to say, 'Hey, Mia, Sherrie is trying to tell you to vacuum,' and it still took her two days but she did it. You made comments when I was with Pete. Are you mad the three of us had breakfast, or we went car shopping?"

My hands suddenly felt sweaty, and my heart was beating fast. We had never once fought, and while I was not angry, something was building up. I was scared.

Sherrie was quiet so I kept talking. "Right now, you have your right toes resting on top of your left foot like you are going to spring into a ballerina pose and that means you are conspiring. I just hope it's still with me and not against me."

"Not against you." Sherrie took a deep breath and raised her voice just a bit. "It's just . . ."

Ben came over and pulled Sherrie's arm. He wouldn't look at me when I said his name.

She bent down, listened to him whisper and said loud enough for me to hear, "It's ok. We are not fighting. It's just she thinks she know me better, and I choose to believe she doesn't. Otherwise, it means . . ."

Ben whispered again, and Sherrie got on her knees. I saw her say the words "I promise."

She stood up and said, "Let's get you back to bed. I bet Claudia will even read you a story."

"Absolutely. Just give us two minutes," I said.

"We can finish later. He has to get to sleep."

"Just two minutes. I will be out cold in ten. I just took the migraine medicine." I didn't want it to be a standoff between Ben and me, but I was on borrowed time.

She told Ben to hop back to the bedroom and see if he can make it in bed with one jump. I heard soft thumps and Sherrie applauding, and ten seconds later, she was back.

I wished it was the migraine medicine that was making my head swirl, but it was her words that left me dumbstruck.

CHAPTER FIFTEEN

Sherrie gently laid out what was bothering her. Me and Pete? She agrees with EG. When she was done, she paused but didn't wait for me to respond before she went to read to Ben. I think I sat on the bed but later couldn't remember feeling my body or my movements. Her words were heavy, not malicious; they weighed me down.

She must have read him a few stories and came back, handed me her phone with the reading app open, and said, "He's almost asleep, so if you read softly, he will be out. Just don't get him laughing, or we may never get him to sleep."

Ben was on the far side of the bed lying on his side with one foot over the blanket. He was wearing the socks from our slip-sliding game at EG's house. I took the spot I would refer to as the place next to Ben and not as Aaron's side of the bed. If I wasn't so befuddled by Sherrie's comments, I would have noticed how cathartic it was being here with Ben and Sherrie. It allowed me to move past the shared memories with Aaron.

I got through one story, and Ben was fighting to keep his eyes open. I knew if I got up he would stir, so I stayed where I was. After I said goodnight to the moon and all other things, Sherrie's words looped in my head. Did I really know her tics, and did I choose to ignore them for my benefit? The final blow that she had tossed my way was so baffling. Yet could they be right?

It couldn't be right; she thinks it's logical. But relationships are not logical. You can't control who you like. You can control how you react to those feeling and that logical. Attraction, fate, and soul mates is not something one can explain much less predict.

My brother often called me a dodo bird because it was something he could say in front of my parents without getting into trouble. I worked so hard at not being the dumb naive kid that got run over and run out that maybe I jumped over others and lost myself in the process. Thoughts skipped through my head in no particular order . . . them, house, us, home, him, her and all over again.

She had started big with how I'd skipped over the fact that she liked Aaron when she first met him. I did remember her nonstop talking and teased her. She didn't care I had gone out with him but that I did not acknowledge she had a thing for him too. Before I could ask if we had to call dibs on a guy, she reminded me about the time in college when Mia went out with Marcus, and I'd been flirting with him for a whole semester and how upset I was Mia didn't acknowledge all the hours I had put into my future nonexistent relationship with him.

Did Sherrie still have a thing for Aaron? She didn't go that far, but I couldn't help but wonder.

Sherrie admitted the second thing bothering her was something internal, but it spread out to me. She was beginning to settle into life in River Bend and knew she would be here several more years getting her master's and maybe PhD but was having a hard time completely feeling settled at EG's. She said I never called it home. It was always referred to as EG's and never our home.

She said when I returned from working in the Cities or even spending time at Aaron's that I would remind her about trash day or not to pack the top shelf of the fridge with too much stuff or it would freeze. EG never made her feel as a boarder but an equal roommate. I had failed to realize she had spent more days and nights in the house than I had yet still treat her as a guest.

The last thing was so startling I couldn't

understand how she got to that conclusion. Again, its not logical but does that matter? Did it make sense? Different perspectives make you see things differently as EG explained about Ellie shoplifting food to feed her brother. Did that make her a thief or a hero like Robin Hood? Was Sherrie's last point correct or just another perspective that wasn't on point this time? EG's opinion meant a lot to me, and then to top it off with Sherrie's perspective, did that make it more real?

Whatever perspective was right, I fell asleep minutes later with my last thought being a happy thought.

Several hours later in his sleep, Ben kicked me. I woke up in the sitting position with my neck craned to one side, still holding Sherrie's phone. I stumbled my way to the bathroom to get rid of the cotton mouth from the medicine.

Sherrie was asleep when I got to the guest room, and I found my phone charging and a second charger waiting. Sherrie always thought of everyone, and I guessed I could learn that lesson.

I woke up that Monday morning at five thirty, fresh and headache-free, and managed to find some of my clothes in Aaron's room and took a shower. When I made my way downstairs, Sherrie was drinking coffee and rooting around in the fridge.

"There is probably stuff in the freezer

downstairs," I said, but I wasn't sure what to expect from Sherrie.

Did I have to apologize for my actions that I barely processed? Was I in the wrong? Had she just needed to say it all out loud and was now over it all?

Was this the beginning of the end for us?

"Don't have time to bake anything. Jenna will be here in twenty to pick us up." Now she was rooting through the cabinets looking for something and not at me.

"Everyone else up?" I asked.

"Ben got up at six a.m. and is eating cereal in the living room watching television. Mallory went downstairs for something." She stopped pulling open drawers and looked at me for the first time.

"I just want to talk about what you said last night," I said.

Before I got another word in, she said, "We got problems."

Frozen in my tracks, I couldn't help feeling lost. Losing this friendship would crush me. My cheeks got flushed, and my hands started to sweat.

She waved her hand in front of my face. "Hey, Claud, are you in there? You are zoning out. We got problems." She lowered her voice even more. "She never texted her cousin last night or anyone to pick her up, and some of the stuff from the mug is gone?"

"What are you talking about?" I asked, still confused but slowly realizing she did not mean she and I have problems, but as a team, we are facing new issues.

"Last night when you went to bed at eight, I was still up like a normal person and sat watching TV with Mallory. She dozed off some time after nine, and her phone slid off her lap. I went to pick it up and put it back in her lap, but she got a message from a friend and I read it."

"Oh, and?"

"Well, that message was nothing interesting. I don't know what over came me, but I scrolled through her old texts. The previous text was from two twenty and the previous one was nine thirty. She lied about texting her cousin for help with the car."

"That bitch . . ."

Sherrie's eyes got big, and her head tilted sideways. I heard a spoon rolling around the edge of the bowl and knew Ben was behind me.

It wasn't smooth, but I tried to recover. "That beach witch."

"You said a bad word again," Ben said.

"I was finding words to rhyme with witch in the ditch and did not do a good job," I said.

Sherrie took his cereal bowl and handed it to me. "Take care of this. I got to get him dressed. Find a garbage bag or something and gather up all your

144

stuff from here so you don't have to do it later, and you can just clean out the loft."

"Already with a plan. I haven't even had some coffee yet."

"I had about three more hours of being functional last night while you were sleeping off your migraine. I don't know about staying at EG's yet, still working on all that, but I figured we can't overstay our welcome here."

The basement door hinge creaked as it opened. Mallory was there with her hair pulled back and fresh makeup on. I would have loved to know what else she was carrying in her purse and if there was something to make me look less zombie-like. At least she had bags under her eyes.

I turned back to Sherrie. "What else did you find out?"

"A lot. We're on a time frame here. Jenna has to be on time for work. Now let me get him dressed and ready."

I had a hundred questions about us, Mallory's phone, and what else she had figured out last night. Sherrie tapped her watch, reminding me we were on a time crunch.

Mallory walked around me carrying a canister of coffee grounds. She poured the remaining coffee out of the carafe into two mugs and made a fresh pot, mixing a small portion of the regular grounds with the decaf grounds she'd brought up from the basement freezer. Aaron kept the decaf grounds for when his grandma visited.

I took the decaf canister and said I would return it to the basement. I think it was the intimacy of her knowing about the decaf grounds over the betrayal of lying to us about not texting her cousin that annoyed me most. Walking down the steps, I realized I had no more right than she did as we were both exes.

I wanted to do something truly childish and leave something of mine behind so the next girlfriend will know I was there before her. On the last step, I teetered for a second when the thought of what if Sherrie was the next girlfriend crossed my mind. A burst of laughter came from an unknown place.

My pockets were empty, and I had nothing on me to spare that I could leave behind in the basement. Besides, Aaron was done with the drywall, and most of the new flooring was in so he would do a thorough clean sweep of the place. I had to think of somewhere else.

The heavy duty garbage bags were on the workbench. I only grabbed one and did a quick sweep of the basement and knew nothing of mine was here. Back upstairs, I decided to leave the large throw blanket I'd bought. His mother had used it so I knew he would keep it.

Mallory was drinking her coffee from the

souvenir mug Aaron and I had gotten from the annual Alien UFO festival/baseball tournament weekend from an even smaller town north of here. That too could stay.

Upstairs, I found some underwear, socks, one shirt, and mascara. Leaving underwear would be tacky and something Aaron would just dispose of. Mascara was too pricey, so I had to think of something else and fast.

In the meantime, Sherrie stripped the bedding off the guest bed and Aaron's bed and had the washing machine going while still humming the same song as last night. Ben was on Sherrie's heels as she kept a wild pace restoring Aaron's place as it was before we had arrived. He was asking when he was going to see Ellie and if he could talk to her again.

Our phones dinged with a message from Jenna. She was here and didn't want to come to the door because the gravel driveway would mess up her shoes. I stood in the kitchen holding a garbage bag of my stuff, dazed from tabulating my feelings about everything Sherrie had laid out last night, Mallory's lies, and Ben's nonstop talking.

Mallory finally spoke. "Wow, that kid has energy this early."

"I had a cousin from the ages of five through ten wake up every day at six, and suddenly, one day everything changed and it took a freight train to get him out of bed. Just appreciate the early bedtime while you can," I said.

"Mallory, are you coming with us? Jenna can drop you off if it's in town, or are you still waiting on your cousin to come get you?" Sherrie asked.

"I'll take the ride and deal with my car this afternoon." She was munching on cold leftover onion rings like it was her last meal ever. She used her middle finger to pick up the last two crumbs before tossing the container in the garbage.

Sherrie rolled her eyes because she had already taken out the garbage, but didn't say anything.

Mallory poured the coffee down the sink and hesitated before leaving the mug in the sink and not washing it out. I had a feeling that was the equivalent of me leaving a piece of clothing behind. Aaron was not one to leave something in the sink.

The skies were gray, and the temp was hovering in the mid sixties. You couldn't ask for anything better than April in River Bend.

I made sure the door was locked, and Sherrie loudly reminded me and others in earshot, "You know we'll have to come back, put the stuff in the dryer, and make the beds."

There was no response from Mallory, but I really couldn't put the fault on her for not volunteering to help. It was because of us she was here and had slept in a chair. Sherrie pulled Ben's car seat from Mallory's car and got him settled in back. We climbed in on either side of him and let Mallory ride shotgun. Jenna gave no reaction to her strange mix of passengers, so Sherrie must have filled her in on some stuff.

Before Jenna had the car in reverse, Mallory said, "That suit jacket looks great on you. You're looking sharp this early."

I jumped in to save Jenna from a dull exchange of false affirmations. "Mallory, where can we drop you off?"

"Meb's Juice and Java."

"Where are we going? I want to see Ellie. This is not the way home," Ben said.

"We're taking a different route. It's longer but better for the car. The bumpy road ruined Mallory's car."

"This is not the way home." Ben was getting feisty.

"In a few minutes, you'll see," Sherrie said.

"Are we going to our vacation spot?" he asked.

"We're going to get breakfast."

"Ellie brings home breakfast stuff all the time. So will we see her now?"

"I wish Sherrie would bring more stuff home. It's all good stuff from Peach's," I said.

Mallory kept her head in her phone, and Jenna kept quietly driving.

Sherrie started diverting Ben's attention away from the missing Ellie whining. "I spy trees with new leaves. I spy a yellow sign. I spy . . ."

"I never thought I would have to explain I-spy-with-my-little-eye to someone of your age. If I had to guess, I bet Ben knows how to play, so I'll start us off. With my little eye, I spy something furry."

"Squirrel!" Ben said with delight. "My turn. My turn. With my little eye, I spy lots of brown."

"That's the wall at the gas station," Sherrie said.

"Nope. It's the bottom of the trees. I go again. With my little eye, I spy secrets."

"That's not a clue. All I see are boring garage doors behind a metal fence and an empty lot," Sherrie said.

"But Ellie said that's where our fun will start."

From the front seat, Jenna popped in with, "Before you guys spy more stuff, where am I taking you all back there?"

"Take us to Peach's, and I'll buy everyone breakfast, and we can finally get my car that's a block away."

Three minutes later, Jenna pulled onto the side street just past the alley and to the side of Peach's. The three of us fumbled out of the back seat of the car. Ben ran inside with Jenna. Mallory still had her head in her phone.

"Hey, we're buying breakfast for everyone, and that includes you." I got no response so I tried again. "It probably won't be as healthy as a smoothie, but it will taste better."

"Sorry, I'm slow. I got a reply about the serial numbers."

We waited for Mallory to hoist herself from the front seat, shift her maternity top over her belly, pull up her pants, and walk past us, going inside.

"Did she really just leave us hanging?" I asked.

Ben jumped back out of the café, whining, "Ellie's not there."

Sherrie grabbed his hand. "We're having breakfast now. Hopefully later, we can see Ellie."

Ben ran back in without another word.

Jenna and Mallory were waiting for us at the counter, and Jenna said, "Do you mind if I take mine to-go? I want to get some work done."

"Absolutely, order whatever you want. We appreciate the early morning ride from the boonies," Sherrie said. "Mallory, you as well, order whatever you like. Claud, take my card, and order me the breakfast sandwich of the day and a double latte. Let me find Ben and figure out if he wants something to eat."

Jenna said, "Ben went around the corner, probably sitting on the sofas. Thanks for the food. I will keep you posted if I hear anything." She went the the counter to order before leaving for her job.

She worked for a judge in the courthouse that was attached to the police station. Some people tended to overshare, and others didn't realize the faux barriers between the benches were meant to filter the sun, not noise. Conversations could be overheard while having a smoke. Jenna was professional and conservative with what she passed on but would help out a friend when needed.

Sherrie walked out to grab her coat from Jenna's car, and Mallory and I ordered. Then we found Ben clutching his backpack sitting on the oversized throne-like chair. Thankfully, he had not opened his bag because Sherrie removed the mug with all the money, the code, and the keys that Ben had insisted he have. He kept repeating, "It's the start of our vacation."

Mallory and I sat on opposing couches with the coffee table between us, and Ben was still in the big chair at the head of the table.

"I got you a donut and a hot chocolate," I said.

"Where are the marshmallows? Ellie always puts lots of marshmallows in it." Ben grabbed his cup and marched around the corner to the register counter like a seasoned café customer.

I wanted to jump on Mallory for lying about

texting her cousin, but I was not sure how much time I had before Ben returned. I didn't want her explanation interrupted, so I made a run at another conversation. "You said something about the serial number on the bills you sent to a friend."

"He didn't answer me directly. He wanted to know how I came to possess those marked bills. So I am only implying they might be part of some investigation."

"There's no way he'll tell you more if you talk to him?"

"Not up front. It's a 'this for that' type of conversation, and I got nothing . . ."

Sherrie returned. "I wouldn't say nothing, it looks like you got a good breakfast and without powdered sugar. Let me fix that." Without missing a beat, she swiped her finger across my scone and down Mallory's sleeve.

Much to my surprise, Mallory left the powdered sugar where it was and drank her green tea. She had only eaten half her bagel with light cream cheese before she pushed it away. Her only reply was to me. "You are doing it now." Seeing my blank expression, she said, "You are mindlessly singing that same song Sherrie has been since last night. It's like you two are one person."

"Well, at least I can say I am singing along with this background music."

"I appreciate breakfast. I'm going to head

home to shower and get fresh clothes," Mallory said.

Minus the bags under her eyes, it was truly amazing how fresh she looked despite sleeping in her clothes and in a chair all night.

"Let me give you my number in case you get more information you can share with us," I said.

As we exchanged information, Mallory asked a question, and my answer made her go pale.

"If you guys can't go home tonight, are you going back to Aaron's?" she asked.

"We haven't really discussed it yet. Sherrie has to give her statement again to police about what she saw in the alley the other night. Maybe we'll run it by the cops and have them cruise our street. I will see what Jorge has to say. I don't know if we can go back to Aaron's. It will depend on if we still have Ben. Jenna's or Kay's might be an option. Worse case scenario, we'll call Chuck," I said.

I had never seen someone recoil so fast when mentioning a hot dude's name.

"Ok, bye. I'll call if I find out anything." She stepped back, paused, took another half step back before she added, "You can call me if . . . if you want to get a . . . if you have anything to share with me." With that, Mallory turned and left without looking back.

Sherrie took the seat next to me on the couch, and in a whisper asked, "Was she just really asking to be your friend?"

"Who knows. Did you see the way she reacted when I mentioned Chuck's name? She has less aversion to Aaron than she does to Chuck."

"You don't think he is the baby daddy, do you?" Sherrie asked.

"Remember that night with Jenna and Kay when we did the backwards math and listed the men that might be baby daddy. Chuck was not in town, and we don't think she was in River Bend around that time besides the weekend we were trapped in the funeral home."

"You can always fudge a due date by a few weeks, and Chuck travels more than he is here in River Bend and is always very dodgy about his whereabouts. They could have met up in Chicago. Speaking of hot guys, I just saw Miller," Sherrie said. "Where is Ben?"

"He went to get marshmallows," I said.

Sherrie shot up and went around the corner and came back without him. "Freddie gave him marshmallows before Jan scooted him from behind the counter."

She ran to the restrooms, and I scanned all the tables and booths, both the seats and underneath.

Seven years ago, after losing a kid I'd babysat for twenty minutes, I learned to look under the table. A small kid can easily hide with all the chair legs.

We abandoned our breakfast and ran out the café door. Sherrie went right towards Broadway. I went left towards the alley. The area behind Peach's was clear.

The view across the side street and into the alley where Sherrie's car was still parked was void of people but had many blind spots between other parked cars and dumpsters, so I ran down the alley and still came up empty.

This was a lot to process this morning. My head was still rattling from Sherrie's bombshell last night, a budding friendship with Mallory, and a missing seven-year-old all before breakfast.

Sherrie rounded the corner empty-handed and wide-eyed. I shook my head but it was obvious Ben was not with me.

"Did anyone see anything?" I asked.

"The shops are not open. There was one old lady walking but couldn't be bothered to answer much of anything. A few cars drove past. All the other cafés are several blocks away. Mallory was rounding the corner two blocks up. Can you text her if she has seen anything?"

"If we weren't so worried about Ben you would have some enjoyment with me having to deal with Mallory."

"Just text her." Sherrie was in no mood for me to crack jokes.

This wasn't a funny situation but humor was my first defense when I was scared. I texted and her reply was instant. She had not seen Ben or anything funny and asked us to let her know what we need her to do.

"You said you had seen Miller. Was he on the street or in the alley, by himself or . . . ?"

Sherrie held up her hand to stop me. "He was in the other alley behind you. Halfway down from Peach's, walking away slowly. No coffee in hand or backpack. The same cars are there now as there was ten minutes ago."

"Did he see you?" I asked.

"Not sure. He didn't acknowledge me."

"Should we call the police?"

Sherrie didn't answer me and was on her phone texting.

"Police. Should we call them?" I repeated.

"I just sent Ellie and Maggie a message saying Ben ran away. We should go to the police, but I was told not to call them. However, is this different because Ben is missing? Who's to say Ellie and Maggie are the good ones here? Just because Ellie took care of Ben doesn't mean she is all good. Who abandons their brother with a coworker who is so unreliable that she pawns the kid off on me?"

Sherrie was firing off a lot of questions, and I didn't have answers for any of them. Not even a funny, not funny satire on our situation. She looked at her phone praying for a reply, and when nothing came up, we locked eyes and together we chorused, "Hell's bells."

CHAPTER SIXTEEN

"You know who we have to call?" Sherrie asked.

My first thought was Pete. I didn't know what Pete would do for us, but it would be nice to see him. I wasn't sure if I really believed myself or if Sherrie had put it in my head last night. After she had gently unburdened herself, telling me she too had liked Aaron, she pointed out that I hadn't given it a second thought before I'd gone after him. Although to be fair, he had made the moves on me before I had even known what was happening.

Her second point was she was right. I had never called EG's house where I had been living as my home. I had always referred to it as EG's house, and EG had made every effort for Sherrie and me to consider it our house and home. Whether I called it home or not should not reflect how Sherrie felt about it.

The third topic was the same conversation I'd had with Mia in college. I had not necessarily told them over and over again it was their turn to take the garbage out, but more so, I was telling myself it was not my turn. Maybe I could have done less verbalizing of other people's task. I gave her a half a point for bringing that to my attention.

Lastly, she said my connection to Pete was more than friendship. I had always said we shared a bond after we had a near-death experience in the bar one night. Long story short, Pete was knocked unconscious, and I was a foot away from him when I shot and killed a guy and refused to leave Pete's side.

Sherrie delicately pointed out that Aaron was twenty feet away locked away in a walk-in cooler. We were broken up then, but he was still part of the emotional roller coaster that evening. I often read stories about people in perilous situations that form a tight bond, and thought that was me and Pete. Maybe I didn't include Aaron in that circle because we had already established a bond, or had something else pulled me closer to Pete?

EG thought Aaron and Sherrie were a better fit as were Pete and I. Not sure I was buying their viewpoints, but I knew, last night my last thought before a deep slumber was sitting with Pete in my new car. I had been thinking ahead, and it made me happy.

Funny thing was even if I was, or might be or could or would be interested in Pete, that is not to say he has any interest in me. We spent the time car shopping avoiding the subject of Sherrie and Aaron. I knew he had dated at least one person since he and Sherrie had broken up. It could have been more, and I just didn't know it. As a good looking bartender, he had no shortage of girls ready to date him.

A car drove past and snapped me from my deep spiral of thoughts. Sherrie was thirty feet ahead, and I last recalled her saying something about calling someone or asking if she saw something. I had to run to catch up to her and was a little nervous to ask her to repeat herself. Ben was missing, and all I could do was think about me.

We jogged several blocks over, and she entered the back staircase to the rear entrance of the hallway that led to Aaron's loft over the bar.

Hell, I missed a lot when I zoned out back there.

I was out of breath, but managed to stop her before she pulled the heavy door open to the hallway. "Explain this again."

"You mean explain it. Don't have time to ask where your mind went to back there. You are usually pretty good at coming up with a plan in crisis mode, but I figure we'll try this before we call the police."

"What is *this* you're referring to?" I asked, having no idea what I hoped it could be.

"Follow me." Sherrie swung open the back door, and we swiftly walked past Aaron's door, the first loft on the floor. He was probably out for a run at this hour, but no telling when he would be back. We passed several other doors and the central staircase leading down to Main Street. "If Ben is just running around, he'll go back to Peach's since he knows we're there and that that's the best chance of seeing Ellie." She whispered and under her breath came, "I hope."

"So what are we doing here?" I clung to her as we tiptoed down the hall.

"Remember I said I saw Miller when I went to get my coat? We're here to ask if he saw anyone lurking around."

"Why are we whispering?"

"What if it's him? If he's got Ben?"

"So we're going to barge in there?"

Sherrie didn't answer. She put her ear to the door and knocked. When no reply came, she reached for the doorknob but stopped. Her eyes narrowed on the doorjamb. "Look, it's not pulled tight. I don't think it latched."

I reached for her arm. "Are you crazy?"

She ignored me and knocked hard, pushing the door, and it swung open. She called out, "Hello.

Anyone here?"

I wasn't sure if I was relieved or disappointed the loft was empty. Sherrie repeated her hello and took a step inside. We scanned the loft and saw no evidence of Ben being there. Nothing was out of order; nothing was different than when I was there a few nights ago.

"We shouldn't be here," I said.

"If he comes back, we will just be honest."

"Honest?" My voice raised several octaves, and suddenly, my throat was dry.

Sherrie high-stepped her way towards the bathroom like a cartoon character. "No one in there," she said twenty seconds later and looked under the bed.

I finally worked up the courage and walked over to the old rolltop desk that had probably come with the rental. After doing another look across the loft, I figured most of this stuff had probably come with the place. Probably left behind by former college kids not able to take any large furniture with them when they packed up their cars for the last time. Landlord probably got tired of hauling away stuff and turned it into a furnished rental.

It was odd that there was not one personal item in the room. He was too sexy for tacky posters of hot babes riding motorcycles, but maybe let there be one piece of something. The desk had more power cables than notebooks. The only thing identifying that this might be Miller's apartment was the binder full of football plays for the local high school where he was assistant varsity coach.

My eyes were darting around his desk looking for . . . oh, I didn't know what I was looking for. I jumped five feet when Sherrie pulled my arm. We headed for the door without incident but our luck soon fell short.

CHAPTER SEVENTEEN

We stepped into the hallway and shut the door when Miller stepped up from the center stairs.

This moment was why I know Sherrie and I will be friends for life despite her unhappy venting last night. I too can take action when needed. We had each other's back. I knocked on the door we had just shut, shouted hello into the peephole like it was a microphone, and feigned surprise when recognizing the man walking down the hall. Sherrie was frozen like an ice sculpture.

I said, "Hey. We came by to see if you were home and to ask if you saw anything this morning."

"I saw lots of stuff this morning." Miller's voice was even and held restraint as if he suspected us of coming out of his apartment.

"Sense of humor. I could appreciate it if I

wasn't worried about a kid that's missing," I said.

"You sure are interesting." Miller stopped walking twenty feet from us. "A boy is missing?"

"Sherrie said she saw you in the alley this morning, and we were wondering if you saw something that could help us find him. We were on our way to his house when we passed your place and thought to ask if you saw anything."

"If I were a boy running away, I probably wouldn't run away to home. Not if you two gals were watching me."

I instantly felt my face flush. Miller stepped closer to his door and to Sherrie and me. We shuffled towards the door opposite Miller's.

He put his key in the lock, jiggled the knob, and pushed open the door. "If it's only been a few minutes, I wouldn't worry too much. My kid brother would disappear and pop back up all the time."

It was not the time for it, but I couldn't help myself. I nudged Sherrie with my elbow as we had just learned something personal about Miller. It could have been a bag of bullshit, but for now, I would take the point.

Before he closed the door, he said, "If he doesn't pop up, come back, and I can help search."

Miller shut the door, and the dead bolt clicked into place. We walked at a moderate pace back down the hallway past Aaron's loft and bolted

166

down the metal stairs into the alley.

"Hell's bells," we said together again.

Sherrie pointed out, "That's too many hell's bells in a twenty-four-hour period."

"You said a bad word," I said.

That got a half a smile from Sherrie.

I continued, "I'm sweating and will need a second shower soon. Where could he have gone? Should we check his house?"

"I don't know where he lives. Maybe Jan or someone else at the café will know. For all we know, he's still there and we missed him. He could be freaking out, thinking we abandoned him." Sherrie raised her hand to show me she was trembling.

I knew it was from concern about Ben and not about us narrowly getting caught by Miller. When under pressure about herself, Sherrie was calm and cool, but her compassion for others hit her hard.

We speed-walked our way back to Peach's. Sherrie was laser focused, head scanning the left side while directing me to concentrate on the right. Traffic had definitely increased in the last ten minutes, but foot traffic was minimal.

Peach's business had picked up as well. The register area and coffee station were packed, and most of the tables were full. Sherrie headed behind the counter, and I headed to where our half-eaten breakfast sat. I had no desire for lukewarm coffee.

A minute later, Sherrie stood near the coffee station and waved me forward, and I followed her out the door.

"I got Ellie's address and more issues," she said.

"Do I really have to prompt you to go on with your story, or are you pausing for dramatic effect?"

"Someone was in here looking for me. Didn't leave their name. Jan has no time or patience to be drilled by me. She didn't seem too concerned about Ben and said he runs around all the time. I just think this is different."

"I agree. I have little experience with little kids, but he seemed to really like you, and the only thing that would draw him away would be Ellie, unless someone yanked him away. Let's swing by their house to be sure."

We were back outside heading towards Sherrie's car when we had a moment to rethink our plan. The trash company had two large trucks in the alley and from what I could guess, they were switching out dumpsters.

"You are never going to get your car back. Before you took off for Miller's loft, you said something about calling someone."

"Good idea. I guess we got at least ten minutes before I can get to my car. Chuck's place is a three-block walk."

"Why not look at the security camera in the café?"

"All Jan has is a laptop, and I can't interrupt her during peak hours. You have seen Chuck's computer system. The guy has four screens with sharper image quality than NASA. We'll be able to see which way Ben went and if someone was hanging around."

"We can also figure out who's asking about you," I said.

"We'll swing by Ellie's home and then give her a ten-minute warning that I'm going to the police. I can't believe I haven't called them yet. Wait, screw the warning from Maggie. I've got a missing kid. Calling police now," Sherrie said.

It was as if someone was listening. Sherrie's phone beeped with a message from an unknown caller, and it sent a chill down my spine.

Ben is fine.

There was no comfort in those words. We looked at each other and knew this was too big for a *hell's bells.*

Who is this? Let me talk to Ben.

Sherrie received a photo of Ben smiling. *Why should I believe you?*

Next was a photo of Ellie and Ben together, both smiling with a message. *Appreciate the help.*

Why shouldn't I go to the police?

Jellyroll.

Why are people after me?

Don't know. Erase these messages.

Sherrie tried calling the number and instantly got a recorded message. "The person you are trying to reach is unavailable."

We did the only thing we knew to do and took off running. "It's not even seven thirty in the morning—you better give Chuck a heads-up that we're on the way."

A block later, my phone beeped.

It was Mallory. *I think I figured out the message.*

"Does she need me to beg for the information?" I asked Sherrie.

"If she's still at that greenie weenie juice place, it's around the corner. I hate to say it, but she might recognize more people on the security footage than we will," Sherrie said.

"You might be right, and with Chuck being gone so much, I don't know who he knows around here any more. Are you sure he's home?"

"He replied to my text of us coming over with *Door is open.* I think he got back last week after being gone for two months."

We walked over one blocked and saw Mallory at the window counter seat scrolling through her phone, slurping up the last of a smoothie. Sherrie tapped on the window and motioned for her to join us. She was slow but efficient with her movements. I couldn't imagine giving up caffeine when pregnant. Alcohol would not be a problem like caffeine, which I was currently lacking.

Sherrie wasted no time when Mallory walked out. "We need your help. Do you have time to come with us?"

She just started walking, and Mallory and I followed a half step behind.

"I have time, but you gotta slow down," Mallory said.

You couldn't really fault her for that with the extra weight and lack of good sleep. Just then I realized I judged everything that women did. I felt ashamed and justified at the same time.

"Someone is still looking for me, and Ben ran off," Sherrie said.

"Ran away or playing a game?" Mallory asked.

Sherrie stopped hard, pivoted, and looked directly at Mallory. "Do I look like I am playing a game?"

I suddenly felt the need to defend Mallory and spoke up. "She's trying to get a handle on the situation. The last time she saw him, you guys were knee-deep in an I-Spy game." I turned to Mallory. "Ran off but supposedly is okay. We just need to verify it."

We came upon Chuck's house. A simple three-bedroom, one-bathroom ranch-style house built in the '60s. Without having been in the house since Sherrie and I crashed there for several weeks while EG's house was being repaired nearly eight months ago, I still knew exactly what I would see. Everything in its place, sparse, clean, with everything one needed to live on without any extras besides an outrageous television/speaker setup and one bedroom with high-tech gear. Any homey touches had been placed there by Lesley, Chuck and Aaron's mom.

Curtains covered the large front window, and Sherrie didn't even bother with a knock. She pulled open the screen door and had her hand on the doorknob when she noticed Mallory had stopped frozen, pale and unwilling to move from the sidewalk to the walkway up to the house.

"You ok?" Sherrie asked.

"Ah, sure. I just didn't realize this is where we're going." She mumbled something under her breath.

She took slow steps towards the front door, and I followed behind. Sherrie looked over Mallory's shoulder to me and raised her eyebrow. All I could answer was with a shrug of the shoulders. This was the second time she'd flinched when Chuck was mentioned in a conversation, and

I had no idea what her hesitation with him was about, and I couldn't wait to find out.

CHAPTER EIGHTEEN

The front door opened to the living room, and the smell of fresh-brewed coffee hit me like a warm hug. Sherrie walked through the living room and turned left down the hall. I went to the kitchen and poured two coffees. I was pleased to see Chuck still had some of our favorite coffee. He even may have restocked with his own fresh supply. The buffet of sugar varieties we'd left behind remained at their supply level. I poured three various colored packets of sugar into Sherrie's and left mine as dark as possible.

I grabbed the two mugs in one hand and the carafe of coffee in the other and walked past the kitchen table and Mallory. I gave her a head nod for her to follow me. The guest bedroom door was open, and the bed was neatly made with a handmade knitted blanket lying squarely folded at the end. The master bedroom door was shut. In the second guest room/office, I found Sherrie next to Chuck, who was in front of several monitors. The smell of Irish Spring soap settled over the coffee.

Sherrie took our mugs from me while I refilled Chuck's. I kept my eye on him to gauge his reaction when Mallory, who was still taking her time, followed me in. I was pleasantly delighted when Chuck froze if only ever so slightly when Mallory rounded the corner, but it was his look when he saw her belly that had me unnerved.

I didn't know Chuck well enough to know what he was thinking, but I felt a sudden shift in the room.

I was offered a *thanks* from him for refilling his cup, and Mallory received no acknowledgment. Sherrie remained seated in a kitchen chair that she must of have pulled into the room. Chuck stood from his desk chair and raised the center laptop workstation to a stand-up position. He kicked the chair back towards Mallory and me. I left to return the coffee carafe to the kitchen.

Mallory was sitting near the door in the vacated seat, and Sherrie was standing next to Chuck. He was explaining to Sherrie how to pull up the different camera images.

She asked, "All you have are these three views?"

"I don't know what you were expecting, but this is not a spy operation. Jan just wanted something by the back door so she could see what vendor was causing all the damage to her doors. I had to convince her to put in a real camera over the register. The previous camera was nailed to the wall without any wiring behind it. She believed just the presence of a camera would keep her employees honest. The camera at the front door has been giving me trouble. I think Jan pushes it around with a broom while trying to get rid of the nesting birds."

Sherrie was fully invested in the tutorial and asked, "Did the police—"

We all paused when the master bedroom door and the bathroom door closed. Chuck, ever the professional, waited for Sherrie to continue.

"Did the police ask for the tapes from when the guy collapsed in the alley the other night?"

Chuck spoke softly but directly. "Died. He died.The guy in the alley is dead. It's ok to say someone died." He looked at me.

I gave him half a nod. The day after I had shot and killed that guy when I was with Pete, I had a meltdown. The guy was rotten to his core, and I knew I had done the right thing, yet it was overwhelming to know I killed someone. My intent was to stop him from hurting someone else. It was not an accident, and I only had a nanosecond to think about what had to be done. It had shattered me in a million pieces, and Chuck had been there to dig me out of a hole.

Sherrie waited for Chuck to answer, and he said, "I gave the police what I had, but it didn't really show anything because only the entryways are captured on the screen unless the camera angle is moved."

"So all this equipment, and you have a partial view of a door?" I asked.

Chuck actually smiled. "Ladies, I am not spying on anyone in this town, and you do know I work for a security tech firm with clients in other states and countries. Those clients are slightly more interesting than people ordering muffins."

"I will try not to be hurt. I thought you had my back when I was bartending or working the register at Peach's. I guess it's every man for himself if they get robbed at gunpoint," Sherrie said.

"Is that what you were doing last week, were you looking for a panic button? No one cleans under the front counter like you do." Chuck was clicking a few more buttons and arranging the screen towards us.

"Ha, you do watch us!" Sherrie shifted to get a better view of the monitor.

Mallory and I locked eyes when we heard the bathroom shower stop.

Chuck called us forward so we could view the screen. "I only look periodically to make sure everything is functional, if someone triggers the alarm, or when the system tells me there has been a breach."

We heard the bathroom door open and soft steps leading to the master.

Chuck continued without acknowledging the existence of the guest. "Recently someone tried to manipulate the system, and they actually did a pretty good job of getting in."

"Wow, someone bested you? Impressive. All locations or just Peach's?" Sherrie asked.

Mallory excused herself to use the bathroom. After the bathroom door shut, a bedroom door opened, and again we heard the soft footsteps.

"They were successful at Peach's and one other spot. To be honest, the security features I had in place to watch people buy muffins were nominal, but it was the most current system out there. I have to give the guy credit for getting into my system." Chuck pointed at the screen. "This is all set up for you now. Just follow the instructions I wrote down to switch between the three cameras.

"You can go back ten days. I will be back in two and a half hours if you need anything. If you're are done before that, just leave everything as is. You know how to lock up the place. If you find something you need help with, just let me know or I'm sure Aaron can help."

Dead silence filled the room.

Sherrie took the lead, whispered while dramatically sweeping her bent hand across her throat, this time not warning of murderous slashers but of announcing my breakup. "Ixnay on the Aarona, splitsville, done and moved on, she's soon to be dating—"

"I think he got it." I should not have interrupted her. Would she have said Pete's name with grace or resentment? I couldn't believe her confession, or as she would call it, her observations were still hanging out there and we hadn't dissected it yet.

Chuck nodded. "Ok, you're all set. I gotta go."

"You're not even going to ask why or what we're looking for on the tapes?" Sherrie asked.

"You would tell me if I needed to know. Nothing you two do surprises me at this point." We heard the bathroom door clink open, and Chuck added, "Well, maybe some things surprise me."

Chuck grabbed his mug and passed Mallory in the hallway. We heard no words exchanged, and she walked in with no telling signs of any exchange with Chuck.

"Let's start from where it's cued up at midnight this morning." I started talking overly loud so everyone in earshot would know we were on task. "You can sit, Mallory, or stand over here, whatever makes you comfortable."

We heard the kitchen door shut, followed by car doors opening and Chuck's car starting. The office had blackout drapes tightly in place protecting the computers and creating a private security world. I nudged Mallory out of the way, and Sherrie followed behind.

"Claud, you take the kitchen window. I got the living room," she said.

"Be smooth, don't shuffle the drapes too much."

"Get a clue, wouldya. You think this is my first time?"

Twenty seconds later, we retreated to the office and found Mallory on her phone.

I asked, "What did you see?"

"I'm just pulling up the map now," she said without looking up.

"Map? What, oh, well, yes, in a second," I said.

"What are you talking about?" Mallory asked.

"Forget it, Claud," Sherrie said. "I don't think she cares. Let's look for Ben." She took control of the mouse and refreshed the screen.

Mallory asked, "Are you talking about Chuck's friend?"

We turned in unison, and she had our full attention.

"Split-second view. I estimate low thirties, not lacking in modesty as she only wore a T-shirt to the bathroom, probably his shirt. Pixie-style haircut. No makeup residue in the sink or on the counter."

"I got nothing from the living room. The glare from the sun blocked out any view from the windshield," Sherrie said.

I added, "All I could see was Chuck laugh as he backed out. Only his mug is in the sink. Several beer bottles in the recycling bin and two in the fridge. Not much other food. He said he would be back in two and a half hours so where does that put him. It's too far for Madison or Twin Cities or even the Minneapolis airport."

"I don't even have to do mental math. Airport round trip is three hours for people like us. For Chuck, he can do it in two and a half with stopping for coffee. I heard three car doors shut. I'm guessing the first was when she placed her overnight bag in the backseat and then the two were front doors."

"You two can be fun," Mallory said.

"We can be really fun when we don't lose kids," I said.

"The way you handle a crisis and spying is reminding me to stay on your good side." Mallory laughed.

"So, like, stop making a move on someone's boyfriend. I don't care now but . . ."

Sherrie's mouth was on the floor. No one was more surprised than I was that that came out of my mouth.

Mallory looked like I slapped her. "He—"

"Aaron would never say anything. I overheard you."

If Mallory sank any farther into the chair, she would have been sitting on the floor. She quickly adjusted her posture and tugged on her shirt. "That was not good of me. I—"

"You got that right. Just don't make up some BS story. I'm done with it. We can move on." I couldn't believe the words coming out of my mouth. I turned to the black-and-white screen but couldn't focus on any detail.

Mallory crossed her legs and regained her composure. "I had just found out I was pregnant and was slightly out of my mind. To be honest, I woulda made a move on anyone."

"Including Chuck?" That zinger came from Sherrie.

Mallory did not flinch. She posed herself like a *60 Minutes* correspondent, legs crossed, hands folded in her lap below her belly. She held her silence.

Sherrie couldn't help herself. "He's not the baby daddy, is he?" The hum of all the computer monitors echoed like drums at a concert. "The two of you have some weird vibe, and you nearly shit your pants when you realized we were coming here."

"He is not the baby's father. Can we move on?" Like a professional, she maneuvered the conversation to where she was asking questions and was in charge. "I think the piece of paper with the code on it is referring to the storage place. The last part of it was R and a number and D and a number. Row and door."

"That's pretty good. Now if you can figure out where that place is, that will be a bonus point for the win," I said.

Apparently, we had all moved on from the last conversation.

"That's the map I was trying to zone in on. Where is the paper—actually, it doesn't matter."

"What are you, a wizard now? You got it figured out?" Sherrie said.

"Just before I texted you from Meb's, I was thinking about what Ben said when we passed the gas station. He said something like that's where his and Ellie's vacation would start. Just beyond that was a storage place."

"River Bend Storage and Second Garages Incorporated," I said.

Mallory nodded. "That's the official name now. Merv Brooks is the owner. I think his nephew took over a few years ago. He rebranded Merv Brooks' Storage, MBS. If I had to guess, that key would open a lock. There could be that load of cash in there the guy in the parking lot was referring to last night."

"Those are some good conclusions and/or a lot of speculating," Sherrie said.

"It's the investigative reporter in me. Ask questions, gather information, try to draw fair, impartial conclusions without being influenced by personal opinions. Although, in this town, it's hard to be objectionable when I think I know someone. Based on the fact her brother was a dealer back when I was in high school, I'm just assuming it's drug money Ellie has been banking in that mug, and that's what's hiding in the storage unit. Start with what you know and work backwards."

"That makes sense," I said.

We all stared at the screen while we talked. Sherrie was speeding through the night footage. There were only two flashes of light, otherwise nothing from the rear door until Freddie, the pastry chef, arrived, and the morning deliveries were dropped off. The camera angle was limited to the door cubby area. There was no view of the alley.

We ran the footage, and no sign of Ben from the back door.

Sherrie switched to the register camera. We watched on triple speed until the café opened and we arrived. We all stood and watched, and I morphed my ponytail into a more thought-out style of a loose bun since I had watched us order. I noticed I did not look that different than a tween ordering at McDonald's while Mallory's ponytail was pulled low and swooped forward around her collarbone like a hip artist who had been pulled away from her easel.

Between slurps of coffee, Sherrie was clicking the mouse and slowing the footage down to normal speed. The hum of the monitors was the only noise. There was no volume to the video. On the video, Miller was the first customer in, and his exchange with Jan at the register was brief. He could have inquired about Sherrie, but that was before our arrival. Jan would have mentioned it when we ordered. We saw Ben walk past the register area and into the kitchen. This must of been when he went for marshmallows.

Mallory broke our silence in the workroom. "Claudia, I'm sorry about that move with Aaron in November."

"Thanks. I appreciate it."

We all continued to stare at the monitor, and a minute later, I said, "You know, now would be the time before he finds someone else."

Mallory cracked a laughed, and Sherrie giggled so I added, "With the size of the dating pool in River Bend, Sherrie might be the next one up?"

They both laughed again, and Sherrie bounced it right back to me. "That would definitely leave it open for you to go after . . ."

"Wait, slow it down and reverse it," Mallory said. "Does the camera angle move any more to the right?"

Sherrie adjusted the camera. "That looks like Justin. He's a regular at the bar. He knows me. Do you know him Mallory?"

"I don't think so. Believe it or not, I don't know everyone in this town. Especially if he's younger than me. He seems to be having a lengthy discussion with someone out of sight."

I jumped in. "Back up and go really slow. Look to the other side of the screen. Look who's ordering. Is that our guy, with his hood up? The one from the parking lot at the diner?"

"It could be." Sherrie put it on slow mode, and only after ordering, he turned towards the right and we got a glimpse of his face. "Not under oath but I would say that's him."

"Let's speed through the rest until we returned and then switch to the front door camera and see which way that guy went and if we can spot what direction Ben went."

The front door camera left us with not many questions answered. The view was hazy from the dirty camera lens. The best we could figure, Miller, our guy from the parking lot, Ben, and a few others went left and most everyone else stepped forward to the corner and a few went right.

"That didn't give us much," I said.

Sherrie's phone beeped. It was Holton reminding her to come in and repeat her statement.

Sherrie flicked off our monitor and the first monitor on her left lit up. Four images of an unfamiliar hallway popped up on the screen. One image was so detailed we could read the name written on the paper cup. We dared not to look at the security badges the men were wearing. It was unanimous that we did not want to know where and what Chuck had his eyes on.

We knew too little about Ben, but too much information about Chuck's work wouldn't be good for any of us.

CHAPTER NINETEEN

We backed out of the room, and the printer turned on. Sherrie and I received a text from Chuck stating he pulled the report from the keypad at Peach's. It had an irregular pattern of someone entering the rear doors at unusual hours. He suggested we match time stamps to the door video.

Mallory and I waited for Sherrie to grab the paper from the printer.

"Oh god, he's screwing with me. He knows it was me when I went to check the dough racks." She saw her entry from the other night, folded up the paper, and put it in her pocket.

The three of us awkwardly stood in the tiny hallway, each of us attempting to lead the group out. I took a step backwards into the bathroom to allow Sherrie to pass and then for Mallory to go.

She stopped and said, "Sorry about—"

"Would you stop apologizing for Aaron? I said we're good. Drop it."

Seriously what did she want from me?

"That's not what I was talking about. Can we just move out of here?" Mallory said and marched past both of us.

Sherrie covered her nose, and then the smell hit me.

Without looking back, Mallory said, "That is another great side effect of pregnancy. The amount of gas I let out would make any teenage boy proud. Can we just go?"

We had the sense of humor of a teenage boy and laughed while quickly exiting the hallway. I made sure the rear kitchen door was locked, and we walked out the front door.

I said, "Three grown women with cars and not one of them working, and we are all walking."

"Don't categorize me with your heap," Sherrie answered quickly.

"Because having a car trapped in an alley in River Bend for two and a half days is half a step above a flat tire and a dead engine," I said.

"Absolutely," Sherrie declared.

Sherrie and I stood on the small cement porch, and Mallory was two steps down on the walkway. We all seemed hesitant to depart. Something sweet swept over Sherrie and me because we let it go when Mallory said she was walking home to shower and figure out her flat tire. We did not call her out on the ruse to spend the night with us at Aaron's.

Sherrie did ask her to put the sheets in the dryer if she got there before us. I was impressed with her foresight and not surprisingly disappointed Mallory didn't just commit to making the beds and save us a trip out there. One minute, I thought she was ok, and the next minute, I realized I may never really like her.

Sherrie was on the way to the police station to give her report again and to see if Jenna had picked up any gossip at work. Jenna would also be able to give us someone to talk to about what to do with Ben since he is not technically missing. Something was not right with how he walked out on us. He had looked happy, and Ellie had used the code word *jellyroll.*

We hadn't heard from Jorge since last night when he went to check on EG's house—I mean, my home. I knew he would be at his auto mechanic shop by now, and I would walk over there and give him the keys to my car. Jorge would have to tow it out of the diner parking lot for me.

I didn't want to spend much money on it. All I needed was three more days out of Debby before I signed the paperwork on my new car. If I leaned on Sherrie, Kay, and Jenna, I might even get away with no car at all.

Sherrie suggested we all go to the storage unit together as soon as she was done at the police station. "Are you good to walk home from here?" I asked Mallory.

"I may be pregnant, but I can still walk," she said, and I actually took a step back. "Didn't mean to sound so rude just gearing up to deal with my doting mother." She turned and walked east, and we went west.

When she was clearly out of earshot, Sherrie said, "Before you ask, I had to invite her to the storage unit. The key is missing from the mug. I want to know if she has it and if she's willing to admit she took it. I don't want her there before us. We know she's short a car, but that doesn't mean she doesn't have friend that would drive her there."

"I thought you were beginning to like her," I said. "Maybe thinking about replacing me as your BFF."

"I could never replace you. Well, maybe if you eat the last of the cookie dough again, I would consider looking for someone else." Sherrie laughed.

I suddenly had a lump in my throat and had to push back tears. "It's just the way you spoke to me last night. Dumping all that on me. About me taking Aaron when you liked him and reminding you about chores and . . ."

Sherrie threw her arm around me as we walked. "That's just it. I dumped some of my thoughts on you. That was about me and my reactions and not necessarily thinking you are a poor friend. Maybe I was jealous of how easily you walked into the relationship with someone we both thought was hot. And I never like anyone telling me what I need to do when I know I have to do it. What else did I unload on you? Oh, cleaning the bathroom sink when you are done is just common curiosity."

"What? The bathroom? Is there more?"

"Didn't I mention that last night?" Sherrie still had her arm around me as we walked.

I kept my head straight while she talked. I couldn't believe there was more.

"I was kidding about the bathroom, except for the hair on the floor—you could put vacuuming the bathroom on the chore list. I'm skipping the whole Pete conversation because it is hard for me."

"I don't even think I like him like that, so why aren't you still with him?" I wasn't convinced of the first half of what I'd said but wanted Sherrie to have a claim on him if she had any doubt about their breakup.

"It's not that I want to be with him. It's just I am envious of how easily you can slide into a relationship with someone."

"Me? How many more guys did you date in college than I did?"

"I date and can get dates, but you are a relationship person. You don't date unless you are headed straight into a relationship."

I stopped walking and finally turned to her. "I envy the way you can have a few dates with a person and then move on. I end up dating losers like Jackson because I'm hoping for the best, or like Aaron because he's a good guy, and think I should be with him because nothing is wrong with him. You know right away if the person is right for you."

"Do I?" Sherrie asked. "Or do I cut and run too fast?"

"Honestly?"

"When have I expected anything less from you? Dump out your opinions on me like I did last night, and you can stop being so sensitive about everything I said."

"I think you are stopping short with some relationships because you never really got over—"

"OMG. You and Pete are thinking alike. Wouldya just go after him? Ya'll are thinking the same thoughts? Me and Hudson are just friends."

"Be friends, but just know something deeper is going on. Either you're holding on and holding back because you're too nervous to be with The One or you have to figure out if he was gone—I mean gone completely out of your life not necessarily dead—how would you feel?"

We rounded the third block and were about to go our separate ways, and Sherrie dropped her arm from my shoulder and then punched me in the arm. "Now we're even."

"Even for what?" I asked.

"You unloaded more on me than I did on you, and I did a lot less pouting." She turned and walked away with a smile on her face.

I shouted after her, "It's only been a minute. Just wait until you have to think about it."

Walking the three more blocks to Jorge's garage, I suddenly felt like skipping. Sherrie was never mad at me, and I was beginning to learn a life skill.

When people vent, it might not always be about you.

Sherrie had valid points yet meant no ill will towards me. I could learn not to recite her chores to her, and the other stuff will hopefully work itself out.

If she was right about the other stuff, did that make her and EG right about me and Pete? I didn't have time to think about anything because my world, or at least a little part of River Bend, blew up.

CHAPTER TWENTY

I was in Jorge's office at his shop, leaving my keys and a note asking him to tow my car to the junkyard. Debby's value was all sentimental, and I had to let her finally go. It was more than twenty years old and had no trade-in value that was greater than the cost to repair it just to drive it down to the dealership.

Jorge was in front of the large bay doors dealing with a lady who was clearly upset about something. He was kind, patient, and an excellent mechanic but did not believe in the the-customer-is-always-right theory when operating his business.

I was coming out of his office when we heard a strange loud yet muffled boom and then some more pops.

I scrolled through my phone, and in less than a minute, someone posted asking what just happened. Immediately, there was wild speculation and useless input from those not-in-the-know.

At some point, Jorge excused himself from the lady and was looking over my shoulder.

Someone finally posted that there was an explosion at a house. Just then, the emergency sirens started blaring.

Jorge went to the office and came out, tossing me a motorcycle helmet and instructed me to close one of the bay doors as he did the other one.

The upset customer was still standing there following Jorge around, waving papers in his face. He closed himself inside the bay, separating himself and the lady with a twenty-foot glass door.

I heard his motorcycle start up from the rear of the building. I hesitated a moment before I conceded to helmet hair and undid my now cool-looking bun.

Moments later, Jorge came around the corner, and I hopped on the back of his bike. He was probably one of the few residents of River Bend that did not believe in walking everywhere.

It took us six minutes to find the correct street. It was difficult to follow the sirens with the roar of the bike. Someone finally posted the location. The houses and yards in this area were smaller than most in River Bend. Two fire trucks and two police cars stood in front of a house with a large gaping hole in the rear.

Two officers I didn't recognize were putting yellow crime scene tape around the perimeter of the house. We dismounted the bike and heard a commotion on the far side of the truck.

Officer and friend Wyatt Baumann walked around the fire truck and pointed at me. I waved back to him.

Jorge said, "I think he wants you to come over there."

"Me?"

Wyatt pointed again at me and waved me over. I grabbed Jorge's sleeve, not for an escort but for support.

I should have been more surprised than I was that we found Sherrie sitting in the back of a patrol car. She was frantically typing on her phone.

Wyatt said, "She was running in and out of the house and refused to stay out of the way. It's lucky she is not handcuffed the way that she was acting."

My phone in my back pocket alerted to incoming messages. I knocked the patrol car window. Sherrie stopped typing and instantly started talking, but it was hard to hear her through the window.

Wyatt opened the passenger-side door and spoke to her. "You get one chance. If you make any move towards that house, you are back in that seat while I drive you to the station. You will be charged with interfering with a crime scene or, worse, become a person of interest."

Jorge and I couldn't hear what she said to Wyatt. He closed the door and turned his back to the car.

She knocked on the window and mouthed the word *fine*, and a few seconds later, *promise*.

Wyatt opened the back door, and before I knew it, Sherrie was in my space.

"Why aren't you answering your phone?" she said.

"I was on Jorge's bike and had no idea you were sending SOS messages. What is going on?"

"That's Ellie and Ben's house." She pointed to the smoldering house behind me.

Jorge and I turned from her to the house and back again.

"I was almost to the police station when I thought I saw Ben and someone walking down the street so I ran after him. When I rounded the corner, the house exploded or at least part of it did. That lady over there said it's their house. I ran in looking for Ben."

"Of course you did." Jorge shook his head.

"You would have done the same thing if you thought someone was in danger. You went through EG's house when you saw someone run out of it."

"It had not just exploded and most likely didn't have a second explosion pending," Jorge answered.

"What did you see when you went in?" I asked and looked around.

The crowd had grown as did the number of emergency vehicles, but there was no sign of Ben or Ellie.

"Not a whole lot because of the smoke. I didn't get past the front room. Tried several times but it was too bad inside. If it wasn't for that lady, I probably would be in handcuffs. It didn't look good that I was running out of the house when the first squad car pulled up. She told 'em I was trying to rescue—" Sherrie's eyes got big.

Jorge and I turned around. The EMTs were coming out of the house with someone on the stretcher.

Wyatt immediately sidled up to Sherrie, preventing her from moving forward. He had his hand over his earpiece connected to his radio. "The house is clear. No one else is inside."

Sherrie unclenched her fists, but she was still trembling.

Wyatt spoke again. "Look, I don't know what you're doing here, but I know they were expecting you this morning to give your statement again, and now you're here. Last night, I was with Jorge at EG's because someone was in the house. I hope you have some explanation."

"You know I am supposed to be at the station? I thought it was some formality that I needed to restate everything I saw. Do people think I'm involved?"

"Holton is trying so hard to make detective, he is multiplying his efforts in everything he does. He hit the jackpot the other night being the one on duty when the guy was found in the alley. He wants so desperately to contribute to the cases of the kid overdosing and the guy in the alley that he's attacking it from every angle he can without stepping on the toes of the detective in charge. He was jacked about the interview. When I asked what he had going on, he actually told me you were coming in. You would have thought it was a date." Wyatt laughed. "He is going to be so annoyed he wasn't here."

"So the guy in the alley is related to the family?" Jorge asked.

Wyatt started to speak but held back.

We watched the old lady in her track suit being questioned and pointing to Sherrie. That officer came over and asked if spare, spear, or spar meant anything to her.

Before Sherrie could answer, the lady came running over and said, "Ah, I just 'member he must be talking about their mama. Sparrow was a pretty little thing. Don't know if that was her god-given name or something folks called her. She died years ago. Maybe ten years or more. She's buried over in the old cemetery amongst the old oak trees. She had a lovely singing voice. Don't suppose you need to know all that, but there you have it."

The officer thanked her and walked away as did the lady in the track suit. She moved around the patrol car to get a better look at the house.

Jorge had made a mistake earlier by asking Wyatt a direct question. If you let him talk, he'd tell you more than he should.

The ambulance pulled away, and I said, "That must be Ellie and Ben's brother. I hope he makes it."

"Most likely, but not sure the extent of the head injuries. EMTs wanted to know if he was talking gibberish or if they needed to do another sweep through the house looking for bodies. Do yourself a favor, and don't get into more trouble here. Actually do me a favor and go talk to Holton now. Keep him away from here." Wyatt left us standing there.

"What have you two gotten yourselves into?" Jorge asked.

"We have no idea," I said.

"Seriously, not a clue," Sherrie said. "I saw a guy drop in an alley and was asked to babysit a kid."

Jorge asked, "You have no clue who could have been at EG's looking for you?"

"I'm guessing it's because of Ben and his brother, Adam. Now that Adam is probably at the hospital for the night and I don't have Ben anymore, we can go home."

"Not necessarily. You don't know if whoever ran from EG's and the two who showed up later are connected. Don't jump to conclusions. Find answers before you're back home," Jorge said.

"If we need to, can we crash at your place tonight?" I asked.

"No way."

Sherrie and I looked at each other, surprised by the immediate shutdown.

I tried to lighten the mood. "If you have a date, we can hide in the guest room."

"You two are not going anywhere near that street. You will end up turning my house into a spy zone, and I'm just about done with the remodel. I can't have you messing that up or putting yourselves in danger. Take a road trip."

My mouth dropped open, and I kicked a stone away in disappointment until Sherrie led me back to reality.

"You know he is right."

We laughed but Jorge didn't. "I meant it when I said stay away. Someone could be watching the house. Talk to Holton and tell him what's going on. They can officially have someone patrol the neighborhood. If they don't have the manpower for that, at least you know he will do it himself when he's off duty."

"Can we at least get some fresh clothes?" I asked.

"Later. Call me, and we'll go in together. I got to get back to the shop and make sure that lady didn't burn it down. Are you two good from here? Can you walk wherever you're going? I can take one of you on my bike somewhere."

"We're good. What's that lady's problem anyway? I can't see you doing shitty work."

"Her husband bought an old Thunderbird convertible as a surprise for her birthday. He managed to buy the car without her knowing but couldn't hide four hundred dollars in repairs on a credit card statement. I only have a few days of her yelling at me until he gives her the damn thing."

"You're always a saint. Taking one for the team," I said.

"Stop sucking up, Claudia, you are still not getting near my house or EG's until you guys figure it out. The police should be on your side, so let them help you." He took the helmet from me and left us standing with the other onlookers.

The air smelled like the Fourth of July and burning metal mixed together. The front of the house remained intact yet rather depressing. The white siding looked yellow, and the yard was full of dead leaves pushed up against the chain fencing on either side of the house. The grass had yet to have its first mowing of the spring season. A single-car garage sat behind the house. Its door appeared to be off the left hinge, and the middle panel was bending forward.

I looked around to the other houses. They were all about the same size, but most had been kept up a little better, minus the house three doors down that had two rusted-out cars sitting in the driveway and grass growing around the tires. Other cars in the driveways all looked to be older cars meant for transportation and not any type of status.

River Bend was not an overly wealthy community. However, I was seeing now it did have its middle class and not-so-middle class. My running had never taken me through this area of town. I'd never thought about it as an option. I wondered how Ellie and Ben lived.

I asked, "If the yard is abandoned, what could the inside look like?"

"From the outside, EG's house looks boring and sometimes lifeless as do most houses. We know EG's house is full of love and warmth because we know what's inside and look past the shell," Sherrie said.

"That's a pretty enlightening thought to have before noon."

"I am full of wisdom. Just need to listen more. To be fair and give you credit, I can't imagine what it's like for Ellie and Ben without their mom and dad being gone a lot."

"And an idiot for a big brother."

"Crap, I thought we would have a minute to ourselves so I could tell you about Miller giving me a ride here. Watch out, she is almost within earshot."

My head zipped from Sherrie to Mallory walking up behind us. That was about the fifth time in three days Sherrie had started a story and left me hanging.

CHAPTER TWENTY-ONE

Before Mallory could tell one of us that we looked good, I said, "I see none of us made it home to change. Do you live near here?"

"Not really. I was home, and my mom heard it on the police scanner and—"

"You have a police scanner?" Sherrie asked.

"My mother claims it's for our safety, but my dad and I say it's town gossip. Half the time, she doesn't understand the lingo and makes up what the calls are about. It's another wonderful oxymoron from Patrice: don't talk ill of thy neighbors, but one shall be in-the-know if the police are sent to their house.

"I said it might be something I could write a story on. I dropped my dad off at the office and came over here. The crowd said only one person was taken away in the ambulance. A guy said he thinks it was Adam. Any sign of Ben or Ellie?"

"I thought I saw Ben and raced to follow him, but no sign of him," Sherrie said.

"That doesn't make sense," I said.

"I'm a fast runner." Sherrie looked directly at me, thus shutting down any further questions about how she had gotten here and when she had seen Ben.

Mallory didn't seem to notice the silent exchange between Sherrie and me, and then she added, "One guy said something about fireworks going off or exploding all at once. Several rear windows were shot out, and the back porch is blown to pieces. I am probably telling you guys stuff you already know."

We just shook our heads like everything she had just said was common knowledge and kept her talking.

"I don't think we're going to get any more information from anyone here. Should we check out the storage unit? I parked over one block. Where are you parked?"

"We have not acquired any car yet so we need a lift."

We walked quietly over to a burgundy-colored four-door sedan. Sherrie and I quietly jockeyed for the back seat. I thankfully won.

Mallory was slow to drop into the driver's seat and said, "If you're wondering what that smell is, it's foot powder and Old Spice. It's my dad's car. Open the window and it goes away."

"What is that?" Sherrie asked, pointing to a box sitting on the dash.

"Heaven," Mallory said. She started the car, grabbed whatever was in the box, popped it in her mouth, and handed Sherrie the box. "Have some."

"This is a treat," Sherrie squealed. "And they were frozen! The only way to have them."

"What are you talking about?" I was whining like a little kid in the back seat. I couldn't help myself. I lurched forward over the center console.

Sherrie was holding a rectangular box wrapped in aluminum foil in a gallon-size Ziploc bag.

Mallory fidgeted with the seat belt before she pulled away from the curb. "My father buys Girl Scout cookies from the neighbor kids. Wraps them like one of my mother's casseroles and puts them in the chest freezer in the garage. He and I live off them throughout the year."

We passed the occasional car, quietly munching on the chocolate peanut butter cookies. The ride to Merv's was much shorter than I'd expected. Having grown up in River Bend, Mallory definitely knew the shortcuts. I really needed to change up my running routes.

We circled around the back side of the gas station to the entrance of the storage facility.

I said, "I'm guessing the only improvements Merv's nephew made was the investment in a new sign."

Spray-painted numbers on the end units told us there were ten rows, and the prospect of more units lay out of sight with building ten also having a large arrow sprayed on it. The road entered in the middle of the facility. The alleys between the rows were mostly gravel with large pockets of dirt.

"What are the numbers on the paper?" Mallory asked.

"I lost it. When I scooped everything back into the mug, I don't remember if it was in there or not. I assumed it was, but it must have fallen out. From what I remember, it was R3D4," Sherrie said.

Mallory turned right, slowly navigating around the potholes.

"Sounds about right," I said.

Mallory turned left down row three, but we stopped short and she backed out. The row only had three units. Then she did something that got on my nerves and did exactly what I would have done. She looked at rows one and two, verifying the number of doors before moving on to row four. The first three rows were identical with three doors each. The space beyond the storage facility opened up to a wooded area on the right.

The fourth row had six units. Mallory parked between three and four, and we all got out with Sherrie and me at twice the speed of Mallory, with Sherrie still holding the cookies. We gathered in front of the door, and all three of us flinched when a pickup truck pulled in. Luckily, it turned when went several rows down.

Sherrie verbalized what everyone was thinking. "I don't know if I'm relieved or disappointed there is no lock on either of these doors."

I shifted the metal lever out of the socket and pulled on the handle to door three. The enormous door rolled up with ease, revealing an empty space large enough for a boat or motor home. Mallory took the cookies from Sherrie when she rolled up the second door revealing an identical empty space. We closed the doors in defeat and listened to the metal doors rattle with the wind.

The door numbers were clearly marked and had been on the metal siding as long as I had been alive or longer. There had been no reason to alter the door number.

Suddenly, it hit me. "I got it. Get back in the car. Drive over three rows."

"Watch out, Mallory, when Claudia starts giving orders without an explanation, she is onto something. Don't ask questions, or you will interrupt her train of thought and she'll have to start over."

"Whatever" was the only comeback I had for Sherrie.

"You said three more rows?" Mallory asked.

Sherrie answered quickly, "Yes she did. I said no questions."

The first row was void of any tenants. The pickup truck was in the second row with the driver loading windowpanes into the bed of the truck.

Mallory started turning the car into the row when I told her to wait and jumped out.

I heard Sherrie say, "I told you the questions would confuse her. Just follow whatever she says."

I did more counting before I walked down the row and stopped between doors three and four and waved them forward. Mallory drove with the back door open and stopped short of me.

When they got out, I explained, "We were thinking like logical people. Not someone using a coded system or a like a pothead. The entry point to the units starts in almost the middle of the property. If someone comes in at night, they can't see the spray-painted row numbers. They are just going to start counting from the road."

"That's brilliant." Sherrie said proudly. "Maybe some of that weed smoking back on campus is paying off now."

Our joy was temporary when we looked at the lock. It was a lock with a numeric code and a key option.

"Are you two prepared for what you might find?" Mallory asked.

"What do you mean?" I answered.

"We are here out of curiosity—"

Sherrie cut her off. "I'm here to make sure Ben is ok."

"Listen to me." Mallory gestured to herself. "I don't how not to be condescending when I say things so just hear me out."

We stood there quietly while we listened to Mallory.

"When I was reporting in Chicago, I have been in many situations where I was going to talk to someone in apparently nice apartments, and when I walked in, I was not sure I was getting out alive. I have also asked seemly harmless questions about someone's background only to be told horrific stories that disturb me years later. Things you can not unsee or unhear that haunt me at random moments.

"With everything we have witnessed, you don't know what you're going to find. The marked bills, Ben's talk about some so-called vacation in this place, his house being blown up, Ellie not responding, you being wanted at the police station about a guy that died in the alley. Should I continue?"

Again, we didn't say anything.

"Let me add one more thing," Mallory said. "Legally, we are in the wrong. Even if the intentions are solid, this is trouble."

"We get it," I said. "All of that is moot unless you have the key."

"Me? How do I have the key?" Mallory asked.

"It's missing along with the piece of paper," Sherrie said.

"And you think I took it? I snuck upstairs while you were sleeping and put the key and paper in my bra and crawled back downstairs and waited for an invite to come to the storage unit with you?" Mallory never raised her voice. It was sharp and cracked once in the middle.

She could have been a good actor, but I thought she was telling the truth.

Sherrie on the other hand laid it all out. "You lied about asking your cousin to help with the car last night. So why not this?"

Mallory's face gave no tell of what she was thinking. She remained still as did Sherrie.

Mallory broke the silence first. "How did I lie?"

Sherrie had to navigate this carefully. "Last night when you fell asleep, your phone dropped. When I went to pick it up for you, the screen was open to text messages. The messages jumped hours between receiving messages. Don't go crazy, I didn't go through your phone."

Mallory still showed no emotion on her face. She put the cookie box under her arm, hit a few keys on her phone, and moved closer to us. "I erase the message thread between me and Brody as they happen. He is always sending crude messages I don't need showing up on my screen. Look at this one he sent when we were driving over here. He has managed to arrange sausage links, eggs, and syrup in such a way that will make you not want to eat breakfast again. Brody just can't say 'I'm leaving in ten to fix your tire.' "

"Brody is your cousin?" Sherrie asked.

Mallory nodded. "You can't swing a dead cat in this town without hitting a Douglas. He is a second or third cousin. Close enough to show up for the family summer grill out but definitely not invited to Thanksgiving or Christmas."

"I know him. When I worked at Bumbles, he would come in and annoy the crap out of me. I didn't mean to spy, I just saw the text gap."

"Understandable. Now what are we going to do about the lock?"

The shift away from the phone-spying conversation was professional and respectable but not 100 percent convincing us of Mallory's innocence.

"We can't break a code with that many numbers for a storage unit that may or may not be the one we are looking for," I said.

"I have an idea, but you'll have to trust me," Mallory said.

Sherrie and I looked at each other, then turned to her, saying nothing. We had no options at this point, and she was in the power position since she had the only idea.

She took our silence as an agreeable understanding of trust. "Wait here. It should only be a minute."

Mallory shut the back door of the car, walked around to the driver's side, and slowly backed out of the row, leaving us waving away the dust the tires kicked up. She was true to her promise. She was gone only a minute. The pickup truck with the windowpanes followed behind her. Mallory got out and asked us to roll up the door to the unit next to the one of interest.

Mallory and the gentleman talked in hushed tones. We heard him say two, and she seemed adamant the answer was one.

She took his business card and pointed to the wall the storage units shared and walked over to us. "The other unit door you opened I could see the walls don't match the ceiling height. There is probably an eighteen-inch gap. We can at least see if this is possibly the unit. We only have a minute before Matt has to take off. He prefers cherry but will take anything, and as long as it's there within a week, he won't report us."

"Cherry?" I asked.

She handed Sherrie the card. "He wants one of Ms. Clara's pies. Not one from Peach's but Clara herself. Hurry up and get on the ladder, or he will want another pie."

I had forgotten the art of negotiation in River Bend. Ms. Clara, the original owner of Peach's, Aaron and Chuck's grandmother, had moved to St. Paul and still baked. She sends her pies with Lesley, their mother or with the boys themselves when they visit her. Ms. Clara's pies fetch anything from a ride to the airport, cleaning of gutters, and apparently, the use of a ladder for something possibly illegal.

Matt placed the ladder against the metal siding and extended it.

Without hesitation, Sherrie climbed up. After reaching the top, she hesitated for only a second, then looked over the top of the wall. It felt like an hour but was probably only a minute before she turned and gave a very slight head nod. She climbed down and went to talk to Matt, buying me time to see for myself.

I was not sure which item made me believe it was Ellie's unit, but I had no doubt we'd found it.

CHAPTER TWENTY-TWO

I descended the ladder, then Matt efficiently dropped it and hoisted it into the bed of the truck with the windowpanes. He was gone forty seconds later but not without saying *cherry* and *one week* before he drove out of the unit and down the row towards the exit.

I turned to Sherrie and said, "You know getting that pie is up to you. I will deliver if you don't want that part of the deal."

"Why me?"

"You are adorable, but sometimes you're a little dense. You know I'm not asking Aaron. We can assume that brunette over there with her head in her phone is not asking Aaron, much less Chuck."

"Oh, I know that. I was just making sure you are dutifully holding up your role as ex-girlfriend and not being lazy."

"What are you saying?" Mallory finally looked up from her phone.

"I was just telling Sherrie neither you nor I will be asking Aaron or Chuck for a pie."

I didn't think she even realized that she took a step back before she spurted out, "Ah, yeah, I think Sherrie should do it." She paused a beat before continuing. "Are you sure that's the unit? We weren't sure of the numbers."

Sherrie answered, "Unfortunately, all the other units have locks on them so we can't check them out, but probably. Let's get out of here. Can you take us to the police station? I still need to give my statement. I held off Holton long enough."

"While you do that, I'll talk to Jenna and see if she heard anything interesting since this morning," I said.

We climbed in the car, and Mallory slowly drove us out off the property. "Are you going to tell me what was in the unit that made you think it belongs to Ellie?"

Sherrie answered, "No boxes labeled 'Ellie' if that is what you're asking."

Mallory didn't take Sherrie's sarcastic bait and let her continue.

"There were a couple of lawn chairs, blankets, some brown paper grocery store size bags."

"Was it neatly kept or spread out like a junkyard?"

"It was pretty condensed to one area. One blanket was folded and the other was on top of it. It did not appear to be one of those units you see on TV where they auction off the ones that haven't been touched in years and are behind on payments," Sherrie said.

"How well do you know Merv or his nephew that runs that facility? Do you think they would be willing to share whose name is on the unit?" I asked.

"I thought about that as well," Mallory said. "Merv's mind went years ago. I'm not sure if the nephew lives in the area. Maybe try calling the number on the sign and talk to whoever answers about renting a unit. Get that person talking or go as far as setting up a time to rent a unit and see what kind of bookkeeping they have."

"That is some pretty solid advice although it might take some time, and I hope to know where Ben went soon," Sherrie said.

"Start the process now, and if you don't need the information tomorrow, you can cancel, but at least you got that angle working for you."

"I can see the investigative reporter in you," Sherrie said.

"Digging for information I can do. It's putting—" Mallory stopped short.

"It's what?" I asked.

"Oh, I'm just rambling about my career. How about I drop you guys off here at the main entrance, and then I might have another idea where they could be. Let me work on it while you're inside."

We walked into the Justice Center, which sounded more impressive than it was. The police station was in the same building as the courthouse. EG had told us the fancy name had helped win the voters' approval for the tax increase needed to fund the new building.

Sherrie turned left, and I went right and found a bench to sit and text Jenna I was in the building.

I wondered what Mallory had in mind for us. Sitting there I couldn't quite place my feelings for her. She'd apologized for hitting on Aaron and had seemed sincere. She was driving us around and seemed to want to help understand what happened to Ben. Was she using us just so she didn't have to go back to her stifling childhood home? She could be an asset to us as she knew almost everyone in town.

All the plusses and minuses would probably break even, but something is not sitting right with me.

The storage unit had given us some answers. There were two phone cords pulled into the socket but no phones. The blankets and pillows gave me the impression people could be sleeping there. The juice box, empty soda cans, and Styrofoam food containers told me people could be living there.

A tear ran down my face. Now more than ever, we needed to make sure Ben was safe and not just for the night.

CHAPTER TWENTY-THREE

Jenna texted that she was deep into work and had not heard anything. I went to the bathroom to throw cold water on my face. The bags under my eyes were big, but my hair had survived the helmet, and I recreated my fun, floppy bun that did little to lift my mood.

Sherrie texted asking where I was, and I met her outside the bathroom. Holton had gotten called to help direct traffic around Ellie's neighborhood. We stood in the hallway, both acknowledging we were slow to join Mallory.

"I don't understand her game?" I said.

"Me neither. Right now, she is our only mode of transportation. Let's see what this great idea of hers is, then hopefully I can get my car out of the alley and we can lose her."

Our voices were soft, and then barely above a whisper, Sherrie said, "I think someone may be sleeping in the storage unit."

"Same." That was the only word I could squeak out without melting down.

We found Mallory typing away on her phone parked two rows back.

I didn't know what the day held and knew I had to be prepared. "Can your plan wait a few minutes? I was hoping to swing home and throw on some fresh clothes."

During the short ride, we honestly filled in Mallory about the trip to the Justice Center being a bust.

She explained her idea of talking to the neighbors to get a better understanding of the family and maybe find a friend of Ellie's. "I don't know anyone on the street but that next-door neighbor might be the best chance of any information. She seems the type to see things. The lady was talking to the police for a while."

"Right now, it's our only angle. We'll only be a few minutes changing, but please come in," I said.

Mallory parked in the driveway, and the three of us entered through the front porch.

Sherrie was right on my heels, slamming into me and pushing me into the door. "What the hell, Claud. Open the door."

"It's locked." I might as well have said it in Greek because Sherrie didn't understand.

"Don't you have a key?" Mallory asked.

"You don't understand, we never lock the door," Sherrie answered. Her eyes were as wide as saucers.

"Jorge must have locked it after he searched the house last night. My house key is with my car keys I left with him at the garage," I said.

Sherrie held up a finger. "Hold on, let me dig mine out."

Mallory looked really uncomfortable. "Can you hurry? I have to use the bathroom again."

Sherrie found the key, and we walked into the living room.

Mallory turned right for EG's room and bathroom. It irked me she had been here before, and I couldn't help myself.

"Use the upstairs bathroom. We have invaded her house enough so we keep the downstairs bathroom just for EG."

Mallory went up the stairs, and Sherrie tugged on my arm preventing me from following. "We got a problem."

"No shit."

"Someone was here last night. I am not even going to wait for another 'no shit' from you. Jorge said he saw someone run out of the kitchen back door. He said two guys came to the front door but left when he came down the stairs. The blankets on the couch on the patio are moved. I was the last one on the couch, and I know how I left them. There is no reason for Jorge to be messing with the blankets and pillows when going through the house. Someone was here waiting for us."

I was not fully convinced of Sherrie's theory based on the placement of blankets, but I was not going to risk being wrong. We ran upstairs to change and met Mallory in the hallway. I sent her downstairs to wait for us. There was no need for her to hang out upstairs.

Fresh clothes and answering a few texts from work made me less anxious. Sherrie was on her bed typing away. Jan from the café sent a message saying Maggie's husband was doing better but would be in the hospital a few days. He was having heart issues. Almost everyone was taking turns picking up her shifts. Sherrie noticed Ellie was not one of them.

My phone flashed a new message.

Just when I thought nothing could surprise me after the morning I'd already had, this certainly did.

Sherrie asked what I was reading.

"I think Justin is asking me out or maybe you. He wants to meet us this afternoon?"

"Justin? From the other night? He is kinda cute, you should go for it," Sherrie said.

"He is asking both of us? Did you get a message? Is Aaron broadcasting our breakup?"

"No messages on my phone."

"I don't get asking us both out. That is kinda weird. I'll do the kind thing and just ignore him."

Sherrie got up from her bed and tripped on the strap of her backpack. "Crap, I nearly forgot I got class in an hour. I really can't miss it."

"Can't or don't want to because Miller is there?" I asked as we walked down the stairs.

"Can't. I'm struggling in the class, and the lectures help me decipher the mandatory readings. Plus, I already saw Miller today. He's the one that gave me a ride on his motorcycle. I thought I saw Ellie drive past and started stupidly running after her. I stopped to catch my breath when he rode up and said hello. We heard the blast, and he offered me a ride to check it out. I have no idea where he went when I ran in the house."

"Seriously, how many times are you going to bury the lead story?" I asked.

"I wasn't really thinking about our game."

"Neither am I. It's just he pops up at the oddest times. Like he is stalking you and me."

"You guys have a stalker?" Mallory asked.

"Do you know Miller? He's a grad student and some assistant coach at the high school?" Sherrie said.

"Tall, brown hair, spider tattoo on his neck?"

We nodded.

She continued. "And *hot*."

Sherrie and I answered together, "Yup."

"I have seen him around. He's not local, or least back in my day, he was not around here. Tell me, where have you seen him? Got any pervy vibes from him, like a Peeping Tom?"

Sherrie shook her head. "Not creepy like that. Just odd hours of the night, and he happened to be around before Ben disappeared. He gave me a ride to their house this morning, and suddenly disappeared."

"You think he's connected to Adam, the dead guy in the alley or whoever came after you in the parking lot?"

"Sure, no, maybe, could be, not a clue. It could all be wrong time, wrong place," Sherrie said.

"Any cyber-snooping?" Mallory asked.

Sherrie and I looked at each other and felt like two little schoolgirls getting caught walking past a cute boy's house. Telling Jenna and Kay about our game, I would have sought approval for the point system put in place, but with Mallory, I felt like a gawky teenager. I finally broke down and told her about our game and our mission to find out anything personal about him.

"So Sherrie is up in points with the ride. Nice job. Should we go talk to that neighbor now?" I said.

"Let's get my car, and then I have to split for ninety minutes. Totally spaced I got class today. You guys can go."

We left the house and locked the door behind us. Sherrie and I stopped and looked at the couch on the screened-in porch.

The couch was not speaking to us, but Sherrie shivered like a ghost had run through her. "Let's get out of here."

The ride to rescue Sherrie's car was full of combinations of what was the connection to Sherrie and what was going on in town. Why would someone come looking for Sherrie and take off when Jorge spotted them? No one had anything close to a logical answer.

"I wish EG was in town. She would have some logical spin on things," I said.

After four days, Sherrie finally got her car extracted from the alley. We planned to meet up after her class and would let her know where we were.

Mallory and I drove to Ellie's in a comfortable silence. The road was not blocked off, but the yellow police tape was still wrapped around the property. The large crowd had dropped to a few lookie-loos, and a few new curious people had showed up.

The neighbor was not in the crowd so we knocked on the door. The white-haired, five-foot, track-suit-wearing woman answered the door with gusto. "I am done answering questions. Now get off my property."

"I am not a reporter. My friend was the one that ran into the house to help find Ben and Ellie," I said.

"That young pretty Black girl is your friend?"

"Actually. She's my roommate. I'm Claudia and this is Mallory."

"That girl has guts. Not so much for brains running into a house with smoke coming out of it. Is she all right?"

"Yes, nothing fazes her much. I was hoping you could tell us something about Ben and Ellie," I said.

The woman was looking at us, deciding our fate, and Mallory did what she did best these days: "If its not too much trouble, can I at least use your restroom?" She rubbed her belly and pushed it out another foot. "It seems like that's all I do these days."

"C'mon in, honey. Just like my Beth. By the time she had her third, she couldn't laugh without a little pee coming out." She stepped back and let us in. "The bathroom is the first door on the right."

We stepped into a living room straight from the late seventies. Everything was polished with a high shine, and brass photo frames of her children and grandchildren filled every table.

Mallory and Sherrie were the ones good with small talk with strangers.

I just had the direct approach. "We are concerned about Ben and Ellie. Have you seen either one of them?"

"People come and go all the time from that house. I hear that boy is a smart one at school. I don't know how as I don't always see him leaving in the morning. Can't help but wonder how those kids make it without their mama and Curt, the dad, is gone for weeks on end."

"Did you see them today? Before or after the explosion?" I asked.

The white-haired lady was choosing her words and waited before she spoke.

"We just want to make sure they're ok."

"I try to help Ellie when I can. She won't take money, but every now and then, she and the boy will come here for dinner. Me and Stan love the company. Having those two over is a treat compared to my grandkids."

"Did you see them today?"

Mallory joined us in the living room, and the lady was slower with her answer. "I think they are fine. The police would have found them if they were in the house."

"If they come back, would you tell Ellie that Claudia and Sherrie are looking for them."

"What's the name again, darling?"

"I am Claudia, my roommate is Sherrie, who you met earlier when the police were asking questions, and this is Mallory."

The lady opened the front door, telling us it was time to go. Mallory led the way and stepped down the two front porch steps.

I was in the doorway when I asked the lady for a tissue, giving me a reason to step back into the room so I could ask one question out of earshot of Mallory.

I was out of the house, and Mallory knew the tissue was a ploy. "What did the lady say to you she wouldn't say in front of me?"

"Her words not mine, 'A lady with a belly and no ring should not have time for questions about others,' " I lied.

CHAPTER TWENTY-FOUR

"That was a bust," Mallory said when we walked back to her car. She looked up and down the street.

I was just trying to figure out if I knew anyone in these houses. In this area of River Bend, the houses didn't turn over much. I didn't think we were going to get much out of anyone here that we hadn't already known about the family."

Mallory climbed in the car, and I dropped into the passenger seat. "Can you drop me at Bumbles?"

"Bumbles?" Mallory asked.

"I just want to sit and worry in a dark corner," I answered honestly.

"You might want to go to Meb's Juice and Java. The white walls and neon fruit posters make you shrink inside. Just have your phone out, and no one will bother you. The food is better. The tomato soup has so much heavy cream in it you could probably milk it. Pair it with the grilled cheese, and your blues will be washed away for a week."

"You sold me on it. Meb's it is." Then I said something I sincerely meant if only as a silent apology for my earlier lie. "Join me? I wouldn't mind the company."

Mallory didn't have much of a poker face this time, and the surprise invitation seemed to touch her. "I really appreciate it, but I got to meet my cousin before he blows me off. I need my car back."

We got to Meb's, and I was standing outside the car, about to shut the door, when I had to atone for my big lie. "You handled the comment that lady made about single motherhood rather nicely. I think I would have ranted on about—"

"I have learned to live with people talking about me for a long time. Some of it I deserve, and some I don't. My father taught me long ago that someone's opinion is that person's problem, not mine."

"Your father sounds like a decent guy. We'll be in touch."

She was right about Meb's. There was a single row of bar seats at a slender table facing the sidewalk, but the area beyond the ordering station was full of small tables and dual-seated high-back booths. The booth was the perfect place to cocoon into my thoughts.

The soup and sandwich was everything Mallory had promised it was. They warmed my soul with each slurp and gooey bite. I couldn't bring myself to order the green drink I had seen her with, but I ended up with a purplish concoction in which I couldn't identify one ingredient. It was so good I took a photo of the receipt so I would know what to order next time.

Fifteen minutes had passed, and my mood had switched from the blues to antsy. I needed to be doing something. Sherrie was tied up for another hour, and I wanted to give her some peace when she was done with class. I needed help—well, I needed transportation and some tools and knew one person who would be willing to help.

Twenty-four hours ago, I would not have hesitated to make the call, but something felt strange after the conversation with Sherrie. I put all that aside and said I was making the call in the best interest of Ellie and Ben.

Twenty minutes later, Pete was sitting curbside outside Meb's. I hopped in and told him to head out of town, but he didn't move.

"I said I would help, but you never really clarified why I need the bolt cutters. So tell me what we're doing is legal."

"Just start driving. The first part is all on the up-and-up. My car may be officially dead, and Sherrie needed hers."

"So I'm just a chauffeur. I thought my day couldn't get weirder."

"Weirder? I didn't even tell you that we're headed to the cemetery yet. Tell me how your day started. Head out to the old town cemetery," I said.

Pete pulled the truck away from the curb. "I'm supposed to be opening the bar but—"

"This should be good. You playing hooky or you got fired? I can't see you skipping work or doing something that got Aaron to fire you."

"Not fired but sent home. Now tell me why we're headed to the cemetery."

"No way, you go first. Finish the story."

"I don't need to tell you my story, but you need me to drive you places so I get to say you go first."

"Power-play move. Not bad." I told him pretty much everything except some conversations between me and Sherrie.

"Let me get this straight. You're friends with Dougie?"

"That's your take away from all that? I talk about a missing kid and sister, a weird storage unit, someone sneaking out of EG's house, someone looking for Sherrie, and you focus on Mallory. We

240

call her Mallory. We can't handle the Dougie nickname."

"You and Sherrie gave everyone nicknames, but you're snobbish if you don't make the names."

"We don't do nicknames. We do code names, and that's a big difference."

"What's my name?" Pete laughed.

"You never got a name. Not everyone does."

"I don't know if I'm relieved or insulted. Not even after Sherrie and I stopped seeing each other?"

"You guys had two and a half dates. It wasn't a traumatic event. Have you started seeing anyone else?" My hands got sweaty. I was worried what the answer was going to be. What did that mean? I didn't get this weirded out when we knew Chuck had a lady in the house, so why now?

"Not really."

"That 'not really' is not an answer, and yes, I'm using air quotes."

"Tell me if this is strange. I asked someone out for dinner and a movie. I go pick her up and her friend tags along. There was never mention of a double date."

"Who paid? Not sure why that matters."

"I paid for dinner. When we were eating, they started to rethink the movie choice. I realized then, I was on a date, but she was out with friends. I suggested a drink at Draft Bar before the movie, and I bailed after the first round."

"Yikes," I said.

"I am clueless when it comes to dating."

"You and me both. I am so bad, I am starting to take advice from—" I caught myself midsentence.

"Advice from?"

Thank god we were near the cemetery.

"Is there a back way in? I don't want to be seen walking in, and Ellie taking off. The neighbor lady said she sees Ellie on the bench near her mom's gravestone."

"It depends. What exactly did she say? Any clue as to where the grave is located?"

"The lady said 'I would see her and that boy playing in the woods and picnicking on a bench near her mama each Sunday. My Stan put up a swing for him. Didn't ever tell her it was us that put it up, but she probably well knows. She is a smart one. And that boy too, smart.'"

Pete did a U-turn, drove around the gas station, and drove into Merv's Storage, turning right into the first row of units. "I'm only guessing this is a good spot. From what I can remember, the woods line up on one side and cornfields cover the backside and out to the south."

"You have family buried here?" I asked.

"No. Back in high school, we would park here, behind the storage units and go drinking in the woods. Some would always go to the river, but that was an easy place to get busted."

We got out of the truck, and I followed Pete. The pebble lot ended five feet beyond the last unit and dropped down a large step onto a mossy bog, and twenty feet beyond that was a wooded area. Pete found a narrow trail, and I followed behind until we could be side by side walking through the woods.

"Nobody got spooked by the cemetery back in your high school days?"

Pete laughed. "Some did. It was mostly about sitting in the woods and not getting caught with the beer. We would occasionally walk through it. Seager would try to tell ghost stories so the girls would be scared and he could play hero. It never worked out for him."

"And you? Ever get lucky in the cemetery?"

"I got bad karma coming from this place. I would occasionally take a leak on this one headstone because I thought that it was the grandparent of a math teacher I hated. Later, I found out there was no relation. But what did I know back then, I was seventeen, drinking warm beer listening to Seager hitting on girls."

"Maybe you weren't the right person to bring here," I said.

"What about you? What bad karma do you have coming your way?" Pete asked.

"I was a saint in high school. Pretty much a wallflower, studying every weekend."

"You feel comfortable lying like that in a holy place?"

"Woods are not holy. Cemeteries have their opportunities for peace, reflection, and spiritual connection. I don't buy into the idea that the dirt and grass here is any more holy than what's in my backyard."

"Intriguing premise."

"Having said that, I wouldn't go peeing on headstones."

Pete raised his right arm and I thought he was going to make the sign of the cross like I had seen my Catholic friends do, but instead he gently shoved me to the side. I stumbled, trying to right myself. Pete reached out to help. Our hands got locked together when I tried to rebuff his attempt to keep me upright. He, me, we, I don't know who held on longer than necessary, and it was fine. We both hesitated for a second before we turned to continue walking side by side.

Ever since Sherrie and maybe EG had put the thoughts of me and Pete in my head, something had been stirring. Why couldn't they give me the winning lottery numbers?

We had walked fifty yards through the woods and stopped short of the homemade swing.

We could see a portion of the cemetery and several benches dotted along the headstones.

Pete walked over to the swing and started untying one of the knots under the single board seat.

I told him, "We are not here to take anything."

The kindest thing he could do at that moment was not respond to me and just let me figure it out. He retied four knots and shifted the rope two feet closer to the trunk of the tree.

"Were you a Boy Scout? How did you learn knots?"

"I am always a Boy Scout, always doing the right thing."

"Does that include when you were peeing on a headstone?"

"You are not going to let that drop are you? I never did the scout thing. The knots I learned from boating and the one summer I did a little sailing. The swing should last longer now. Did you notice the little huts?"

"What are you talking about?"

"Don't tell me you were watching my ass the whole time I was fixing the swing. Look over here." Pete walked over to a long dead log with other sticks lying over it, and pointed to a few others just like it. "Someone was building little forts."

I walked over to the one closest to the swing and bent down to get a better view inside it and jumped back.

"Got an animal in there?" Pete asked.

I got on my knees and pulled out a long fuzzy sock with reindeer on them. "They were here this morning."

We looked under five more piles and came up with a couple of green plastic army men and two bandannas. We left everything in place. The trees were a mix of maple, oak, and a few pine trees.

The first leaves of the season were almost in full bloom, and some sunlight peeked through the branches. Pete walked over to some bushes and rooted around with a stick.

"I don't think they're hiding in there."

"Thank you, Ms. Captain Obvious. I was just checking if anyone was stashing dollar beers in there anymore."

"No luck?"

"Maybe, maybe not. I may not want to share warm, cheap, expired beer with someone who can't recognize a good hiding spot."

"I am not even slightly offended by that remark." We laughed together, and I added, "A drink doesn't sound so bad right now, but I will skip the beer meant for underage high schoolers."

"I bet it won't be at BAR." Pete laughed.

"Nice shot. How about I pick you and your roommate up, and you can call it a date."

"Touché."

"Speaking of BAR. You never said why you're not working your shift right now."

"I told some guys to fuck off, and Aaron was not happy with my attitude. Don't think I'm fired, but he told me I should leave for the day."

"It's a Monday opening shift. What kind of trouble were some guys causing at that hour?"

"What makes you think it was some guys? You know women can be just as much trouble."

"Oh, did your last date bring in her other roommate and wanted to see if you wanted to go paint some pottery?" I laughed and got a half a smile out of Pete. He could definitely take a joke. "You actually said the word *guys*."

We left the wooded area, and the sun felt good. There was no fence or stone wall marking the cemetery lot line. The springtime blend of yellow grass with green roots encompassed the area of the cemetery. Several crab apple trees dotted the area. In several weeks, this area would be blooming with pretty pink flowers on the trees.

The birds singing and the occasional car off in the distance were the only noises as we walked among the headstones reading names and dates. It told us families of River Bend have been buried there for over a hundred years. Small stone plaques covered in moss were mixed with shining behemoth stones.

We took our time around the first bench. It was there we saw "Sparrow Ellison Hughes March 4, 1975 – May 2, 2014" on a simple stone marker clear of any moss. In front of the stone lay a palm-size glass angel figurine and about a half-dozen shining stones.

"I didn't expect them to be here, but I just had to look. Thank you for bringing me here. We can go," I said.

Pete didn't move until I started walking, and he followed.

I asked, "Can we make one more stop?"

"Sure" was the last thing Pete said until we were at his truck.

I directed him to the storage unit we believed to belong to Ellie.

"I am starting to guess why you want the bolt cutters, but do you know how much trouble you can be in? Even if it is the right unit. Tell me what more you hope to find out that you didn't already see looking over the top from the other unit."

When I lifted my hand to point to the correct unit, I left a sweaty handprint on my pants. "I don't know what I hope to find. I think I'm more nervous now than before. Tell me a story to make me laugh. Sherrie or I always crack an inappropriate joke to

248

lighten the mood. Better yet, tell me the story you have yet to finish about Aaron sending you home."

I had my hand on the door handle, hoping to listen and cut the lock at the same time, but when Pete didn't move, I got more nervous.

"Some guy came in the bar asking for Sherrie's number and then yours. I told him I wasn't giving out any phone numbers if I had them or not. He wouldn't leave his name or number. He was acting all twitchy."

"Well, that pretty much covers it. Someone is stalking Sherrie."

I looked out the truck window but couldn't tell you what I saw. My mind went into a vortex. Snapshots of the last three days twisted around with Sherrie having no connection besides being asked to babysit Ben.

Pete interrupted my spiral of dark thoughts when he turned, nudged my shoulder, and looked me in the eye. "And you. Someone is looking for both of you."

I didn't know if it was his concern for me or his deep-brown eyes that rocked my core.

Thankfully, he kept talking. "The guy wouldn't leave so Aaron walked in when I told him what he could do in a not so customer-friendly manner. Aaron was already in a pissy mood this morning, and I didn't feel like explaining it to him. I happily took the morning off. Also, I didn't know if you wanted him to know about guys asking for your number. I would have called the cops if I knew someone was in your house."

"Thank you for watching out for us."

"Last summer, you didn't leave me when I was knocked out cold and there was a gunfight going on two feet away from you. And you don't mock my half-coke, half-diet coke drink. And you covered my ass big-time when I busted the beer tap. It's the least I could do to not give your number out. So now it looks like we're even."

I had no other choice but to punch him in the arm. "Maybe we will be even after you cut the lock."

"What if Ellie and Ben come back and find the broken lock? They won't feel safe. It's a shitty place to stay, but it is relatively safe."

"Crap, I hadn't thought about that. I guess go buy a new lock and leave her a note saying it was me. If you haven't figured this out yet, I am pretty much winging this part of the plan."

We hopped out of the truck, and I asked, "Did you recognize him, the guy asking about Sherrie and me? Local or a Jameson student?"

"I'd seen him before, but I don't know when. I'm not great at remembering people." Pete reached over into the bed of the truck and came up with some bolt cutters."

"Did the guy have a scar on his neck or amazing blue eyes?"

Pete stopped in his tracks. "You wanna know if the psycho is hot?"

I had to laugh. "Of course not, but remember when I said a guy confronted Sherrie and Ben in the diner parking lot? I was curious if it was the same dude. Psychos can be hot. Look at serial killer Ted Bundy and all the women he attracted."

"So we know your type. Angry bar owners and psychos. I wonder what your dating app profile says."

"You better watch what you say, or I will have to tell you what—"

"I am just trying to lighten the mood as you requested. Despite not knowing how to ask a girl out, I can come up with witty, inappropriate conversation topics as you requested a minute ago. Sorry, I interrupted you. You were saying, you will have to tell me something."

We now were standing side by side in front of the locked rolling door talking to avoid what we came here to do.

I was so nervous I just blurted it out, "Don't worry about my dating app profile, worry that Sherrie and EG think we should be the ones dating."

Nothing.

I got nothing from Pete. It was like seeing the dots moving when you text someone and you are waiting for the response and then the dots just stop and you are left to wonder.

Pete took a step towards the door and dropped the bolt cutters. He held the lock in his hands and asked me to repeat what was on the tombstone.

This is the weirdest rejection ever. I didn't even ask him out. The lack of snappy comeback made me feel invisible.

Not like Ben and Ellie invisible but lost in my own emotions.

CHAPTER TWENTY-FIVE

Pete repeated, "Sparrow Ellison Hughes March 4, 1975 – May 2, 2014 several times. "Do you see this lock? You can use a key, which you guys lost, or a four-digit code."

A breeze kicked up and rattled the metal doors. The doors bounced with my beating heart, which finally started slowing down. Pete was spinning numbers, pulling the lock, reciting numbers, while ignoring what Sherrie and EG had suggested and I had verbalized.

He yanked the lock, and this time it sprang open. "This is a little less invasive than the bold cutters. If we play this right, no one will know we were here."

"How did you know the combination?" I asked.

"I love spy movies." He handed me the lock and slid the lever over. "It is Sparrow's date of death 5214. Most people don't try too hard with passwords when left to figure out one on their own. Birthdays, pet names, and 12345 should not be allowed. Are you sure you want to do this?"

A head nod was all I had, and then I finally said, "It should be easier now that we can lock it again, but I'm nervous. We have to figure this out. Maybe there's another hint where Ben and Ellie could be. Maybe there is something about Sherrie's connection in there."

"And you. You keep forgetting you're connected to this too. Someone was in your home where you and Sherrie both live. It was next to your car in the diner parking lot, and some guy was asking about you and Sherrie. You two are never far apart."

Pete is never going to date me. He thinks of me as Sherrie's sidekick. He would never separate the two of us. Had there ever been a successful transition to dating the roommate?

Well, now that that was settled, I had to focus on what was in front of me. "Roll it up."

The room was as we had seen it before. We were careful not to touch anything. Pete pointed to the car tracks. The unit was just deep enough to fit a car.

I bent over a duffel bag.

Pete pulled me back. At some point, he had picked up the bolt cutters. He used the long-handled cutters and batted the duffel bag. Nothing moved or exploded. "Don't you watch any movies?"

"You think whacking the bag was any safer?" I laughed and crouched down.

Next to the bag was a blue highlighter. It matched the blue marks on the bills from the travel mug. The duffel revealed cash and pills. Some bills neatly bundled and others freely tossed in the bag. A second bag showed the same thing. We decided not to lift the blankets and disturb anything else in the unit.

We stood near the door and looked around, hoping something would jump out and tell us something new.

The only thing new was the panic that rose up in me when I heard a car turn onto the storage facility's gravel lot and quickly getting louder. I pushed Pete to the side and tugged on the rope pull, slamming the rolling door shut.

He held up the lock, and I shrugged.

In a whisper, I said, "Haven't you figured out by now I don't know what I'm doing." I grabbed the lock like a lifeline, but it had no answers.

The car approached and stopped. Pete grabbed an empty old cooler and stood on it.

Extending his arms as far as they could go, he jammed the bolt cutter handle with the rubber grip into the roll mechanism, essentially locking the rolling door from the inside.

"What if it's Ellie?" Pete asked.

"We open the door and ask where she and Ben have been hiding and why is someone after Sherrie?"

And you, Pete mouthed.

We heard a car door open and a motorcycle turn off.

"Whose truck is that?" Man One said.

The voice sounded familiar, but I couldn't hear that well with the metal door between them and us and their walking on the gravel. Someone pounded on the hood of the car.

Man Two: "Ah, I don't know. People leave crap here all the time. Probably belongs to that guy three doors down that has some other work truck. Pop the lock two doors down, and you can score a decent ride on a four-wheeler. We can call it even."

Man One: "Not even close. This is not a barter system. Give me the damn cash you were supposed to give my boss."

Man Two: "We are here, oh . . ."

There was a brief exchange we couldn't hear.

Man One: "You said this was it. There's no lock on it. Got the right unit? Are you a dumbass that leaves it open? Everything better be in there."

OMG. I placed that voice. Pete was holding steady on the cooler with his arms stretched up. He wobbled when one of the guys slammed the door. I tugged on his jeans and mouthed the words *I know him.*

Man Two: "This is the unit. I don't screw up numbers."

Man One: "I think you been breaking the number one rule. Yer dippin' in your own supply."

Man One—or as Sherrie and I know him, AMMO—and how everyone else knows him: Miller.

Why are all hot dudes a mess?

Miller continued, "Good thing you spent an hour getting the lock cutters. There's not even a lock on this thing. Your buddy write down the wrong unit? Let me roll this bitch up and get out of here."

I stood behind Pete putting my hands on his thighs like I was holding a ladder. We heard feet shuffling around on the gravel, and Pete flexed his arm. A hand hit the rolling garage door near the handle and then the entire metal door shook. Pete was holding steady, but I didn't know how long he could last.

There were several more pulls and a kick to the door when my phone beeped with a message. When I released my grip on his legs, Pete shifted and the bolt cutter hit the door.

I silenced my phone in a nanosecond and prayed the rattling door blocked our stupidity.

Miller said, "The owner of the place must have pinned it somewhere we can't see." Someone pounded on the door. "You skip on rent? We are standing in front an empty locker. I want the supply back. You can't be selling with one stiff and someone living on air being pumped through his body. How many times do I have to tell you we have to move it all out of here? I'm not as stupid as your partner, I won't drop you like a fly in the alley until I get my supply back."

"I don't have it."

"You keep saying that. Is that why your friend was laid out in the alley? Should I check his personal stuff at the hospital, see if he has it stuffed in his pockets? Is that why our other colleague is still hanging out here. You and him need to come up with something for me to take back to Chicago. Supply or cash. The two of you have until five."

"It's not my problem you have issues with who they send up. They are your colleagues."

"You are the problem. Figure out if you are riding out of here with partner one or sharing a room with partner two and your father at the hospital."

I met Pete's eyes and mouthed *Father?* and *Adam?*

Pete's arms were beginning to shake.

Adam: "Come on, just give me one more day. I need one more day."

Miller mimicked Adam: "One more day, one more day. You whining shit. Tell me you are not dumb enough to be pushing what's left of the last drop? The cops are going to catch up to you. Hold the stuff somewhere safe, or is that what you blew up this morning?"

Adam: "We need more time. We will get it all."

Miller: "You want another day. Sure, why not, missy. We had a nice little operation going on at that school until now. Nice little stunt blowing up the house this morning. Should we meet back here and you can blow this door? I will personally add you to that list for Chicago if you don't come up with something for me. Five p.m. at the spot, or you better run—and I mean run. That piece-of-shit car is not getting you out of this town."

We heard some muffled sounds as they walked on the gravel. A motorcycle roared to life, and stones kicked against the garage doors. The thunder of the bike slowly faded out.

Adam: "Ellie, answer your phone. This is the last time. I am done. I promise, I mean it this time. You've gotta help. Where is the supply? Is it in the unit? I'm going to ram the car into the door!"

Pete and I looked at each other, and neither of us had answers for the other.

A car door opened and closed, and the car started up. My legs were shaking. The stones kicked up again outside, and we didn't need to see it to know Adam backed out of the row at top speed. Gravel ricocheting off the metal doors finally faded when Adam turned out of the storage place.

Pete dropped the bolt cutters and then dropped himself to sitting on the cooler. I hadn't realized I sweated through half my top from nerves until I put my hand on Pete's shoulder. He placed his hand on mine and held it while we caught our breath.

He used my hand to pull himself up while muttering, "Damn, my arms are done. Done."

"I thought we were done," I said and took Pete's seat on the cooler while he paced. I finally looked at the message from Sherrie.

She said Miller was not in class, and she would be off campus in ten minutes. I had my head buried in my phone relaying our findings.

Pete asked, "What are you doing? Looking on dating apps for Miller? Since hot psycho dudes are your thing now."

I looked around for something to throw at Pete and found a pebble. When he ducked, it pinged the metal wall behind him, the sound echoing.

I said, "So you agree Miller is hot too? Maybe we should update your dating profile. You are in luck, he doesn't have a roommate so you're already ahead of the game."

"He's not my type. I like the real gym lunkheads."

Pete laughed and sat down next to me. We each had one butt cheek hanging off the cooler.

He kept talking. "I better stop joking like that, or you might start to believe I'm into guys. I already have trouble dating in this town, so I don't need any rumors floating out there."

"You never have to worry about that with me. Anything I would say about you would have a thousand girls after you."

"Let's get out of here." He stood up and grabbed my hand to help me up.

We were face-to-face, inches apart, and I was keenly aware of the sweat all over my body.

Pete broke the silence. "As I was saying, we need to get out of here. You have a lot of ladies to talk to about me. Get the right word out."

"What if I don't want to?" I had no idea what had come over me.

"Too busy going for the bad boys?"

As Pete talked, I could feel his breath and his chest rising. Our hands touched, and then without surprise, we both jumped back when our phones rattled.

My hands trembled as I reached for my phone.

It was Sherrie giving Pete and me updates. Holton had called her to come back to the station, and he and the detective would wait for her. When they were talking, she had told him about Ben running away and Ellie's message that he is ok. I had missed the earlier message from Jenna that the River Bend PD was on the lookout for Ellie.

Pete replied that Sherrie should talk to her mom before going in to see Holton. See if she has any advice. He sent another text asking to leave out the part where he and I broke into the storage unit when talking to her mom.

Sherrie's mom, Evie, was a lawyer. A real estate lawyer and one of the smartest women I knew, and it was good advice on Pete's part. Minus our little fiasco here, we had done nothing wrong, and it was time to get on record that someone was watching Sherrie and me.

I was about to take pictures of what I saw, but Pete stopped me.

"We don't need any more traces of us being here."

I moved the cooler back to the original spot, and Pete rolled up the door. The fresh air was a blast of relief. The sunlight also highlighted my sweat stains, which made me feel sluggish, yet on Pete, they made him look like a rugged mountain man.

Sherrie and I got a text from Mallory asking to meet. Pete saw me roll my eyes and asked what was up. I suggested the diner, and Mallory suggested something more private so we could talk more openly. Pete volunteered his place.

"Are you saying your place just to watch Mallory and me be in the same room?"

"Earlier you asked for an inappropriate joke to lighten the mood. Maybe I need something to keep me amused and my mind off what just happened here."

"Amen," I echoed.

Pete slowed his step and turned to me. "Although I don't want to—"

We froze in place when we heard a car hit the gravel. It did not appear to get any closer. We could see dust flying up.

Pete said, "Some guy is probably turning around in the gas station lot. The diesel pumps are at an odd angle if you come in off State Road 45."

Sure enough the car drove off, and the dust settled. Another half minute passed before we moved. Pete turned, grabbed the rope, and yanked the rolling door down, extending his hand. I gave him an awkward sideways high five. His gentle laughter hit me sweetly inside.

He said, "I need the lock."

I dug in my pocket and handed it to him. "Before we heard that car, you started to say something like you don't want to ... want to what?"

Pete kept his head down like he was reading the fine print on the lock or finding a way not to answer me. I picked up the bolt cutters and tossed them in the bed of the truck.

I decided to push it one more time. "We don't have to meet at your house. We can meet at Jorge's garage. I got to pay him for towing my car anyways. I shouldn't have gotten you involved. I seem to ask too much of people."

"You think that's what I'm saying?" He walked past again without looking at me. He opened the driver's-side door, and I heard some rumblings of something like "Was she screwing with me?"

I had no clue as to what he was mumbling. "What are you rambling about?"

Pete climbed into the driver's seat.

I took three steps forward and put my back to the open door. I couldn't let this go. "I can hold this door for a long time. Sherrie will be a while before she meets us, and I don't care how long Mallory waits."

He didn't say anything for a solid minute.

I wish I could say the birds were singing a pretty song, but all I heard was my heart pounding. Time was up, and so was my patience. "Well, I guess you win. We can protect each other in life-and-death situations, but you won't repeat a simple thought for me."

"Timing. This is bad timing." Pete slammed his hand on the steering wheel.

"Now we got it straight that it's bad timing for me calling you to help. I will work on that in the future," I said and walked away from his open door.

He got out of the truck and quickly walked up behind me. "Wait."

He didn't say anything else, and I didn't turn around until he finally touched my shoulder. "You want the inappropriate conversation because you need to laugh to break the tension. Let me tell you something. The entire time the two idiot dealers were on the other side of that tin door with at least one of them packing a gun, my mind kept racing at the thought of you standing next to me, and I wondered what it would take for you to—"

"To what?" I asked.

"For you not to push back," Pete said.

"Push back what? Now I'm lost." I stomped my foot on the ground and had my hands on my hips.

Pete stepped forward. He looked at me this time when he spoke. "There might never be the right time, and this is probably the wrong time, but timing for me has not worked out before."

My body tingled, and I got lightheaded. I put my hand on his chest, and his hands found my hips. He held me still for a moment before he stepped six inches closer to meet my beating chest. I flexed my ankles to raise up to meet his kiss.

When we kissed, I folded myself into his arms to ground me. The kiss was slow and light yet it electrified my body. My insides were swirling like a lava pit.

He released his hands and took half a step back, but I stepped forward for more. This kiss sent electricity to my toes. His hands found my hips again before moving around to my backside. I wanted . . .

I wanted the sharp alarm echoing between us to stop. We jumped back a foot and both grabbed our phones.

An Amber Alert had gone out for Ben. I couldn't believe how fast Sherrie had gotten to the police station and explained the story about watching Ben and his sudden disappearance.

"We got to go," Pete said.

Neither one of us moved.

I said, "That was inappropriate timing."

"Oh . . . ah, sorry. I just . . ." Pete said.

"I meant the Amber Alert," I said.

Pete gave a sweet chuckle.

I thought for a second and said, "Although is there ever a good time for Amber Alerts?"

We hesitated before we took a step backwards, then we both ran into the truck. What we should have known was Miller was watching us from the cornfields.

CHAPTER TWENTY-SIX

Pete drove slowly out of the Merv's Storage lot. Jenna texted Sherrie and me the Amber Alert was initiated when Curt, Ellie's dad, was taken to the hospital. He was the one they hauled away from their house. Curt's sister, Dawn, was adamant that Ellie had runaway and kidnapped Ben.

"Things are never what you think. I just assumed it was dumbass Adam on the stretcher. What do you know about Adam?" I asked Pete.

"He was a year or two older. I played baseball and football in high school and don't remember him being on a varsity squad ahead of me. Coulda done something else, and I would have no clue. Don't remember the mom dying. I know him as a local face around town. He's been in the bar on occasion, but he's not a regular. I was gone for undergrad at Madison and a year of work and another year of traveling before coming back for grad school, so what he did in those years, I have no clue. Don't think he ever tried college or left River Bend. Maybe jail."

"So we can figure he's the local dope dealer and not a very good one," I said.

"Didn't you just say things are never what you think?" Pete asked but didn't wait for a response. "I'm just kidding. It's a pretty good assumption."

"Would you mind driving me to the police station? I want to be there with Sherrie."

"Not a problem. Hang on." Pete slowed his truck onto the side of the county road and continued into a wide U-turn. I held on tight as not to go flying into the windshield.

"I have to change up my running routes. I don't know half these shortcuts."

"I don't suggest running on these back roads with cars whipping past you doing fifty. Are you going to tell the police what we just heard?" Pete asked.

"Oh, crap. I guess we should but . . ."

Pete slowed the truck again and did another U-turn.

"One more of those turns and I will need a bucket or an open window because my lunch will come up."

"We have to think about this. Do you know a lawyer besides Sherrie's mom? Someone local you can talk to. We're going to my place first. We know they don't have Ben, so let's figure this out."

"Fine." My half-thought-out plan was defeated, so I texted Sherrie telling her to come to Pete's. "Shit, I just sent Mallory the message instead of Sherrie."

Pete chuckled. "Confusing Mallory for Sherrie, even if it's only via text, proves you are not in the right mind to tell the police about breaking into a storage unit."

"Maybe you're right." I properly texted Sherrie asking where she was.

I could see the dots telling me she was typing, so I called her and put her on speakerphone.

She was already out of the station. The police had the video of Ben leaving Peach's on his own. The laundromat across from Peach's verified Ben had gone left but didn't know if he had gone down the alley or continued down the street. Sherrie showed the police the messages from Ellie.

We told her to come to Pete's, and we'd figure out what to say about our little stint in the unit. I also texted EG asking for a recommendation on a lawyer. She immediately called me, and I sent it to voice mail. I sent a follow-up text. *Don't worry.*

Just want to run a 'what if' scenario past a lawyer. All is fine.

We had pulled up to Pete's house that he rented with two other grad students to find Mallory sitting in her own car with a brand-new tire.

I was so busy talking and texting I hadn't had time to comprehend what happened at the storage unit. Was it a one-time thing? Kiss the boss's ex-girlfriend? Kiss the roommate?

Is there more? Do I want more?

Yes was the first answer that came to mind.

Mallory jumped out of the car as soon as Pete parked behind her. I was so lost in my thoughts about wanting another kiss, I was slow to get out. Pete was already halfway to the door with Mallory when she turned and asked if I was ok.

My face immediately flushed hot. "Pete's driving leaves something to be desired. A few U-turns made me feel like I was at the St. Francis Church fair and did several go-rounds on the Tilt-a-Whirl."

"U-turns? Getting lost in River Bend, really, Pete?" Mallory asked.

"We had some indecision about going to the police," he explained.

I had never been to his house before. It was a powder-blue two-story house. We entered into the family room, which was set up with one long couch and two mini couches surrounding the

272

enormous television. The wall held two large canvases with abstract art, both featuring every shade of orange. I assumed they had been painted by Cici, one of the two roommates. I had talked to her at BAR occasionally, and each week she was experimenting with a new medium. Two weeks ago, she had come in covered in clay.

"We have the place to ourselves. Cici is on campus all day, and I have no idea where Trager is. I'll be back in a few." Pete went up the stairs on the right.

Mallory headed for the bathroom. I went to the kitchen as much for a glass of water as it was to scope out the place. The bedroom off the kitchen held a bed, dresser, and not much else if you didn't count the laundry pile on the floor.

The sink was clear of dirty dishes. Two people cooking in the kitchen would be a challenge to find enough prep space. There was enough room for a table for four. Unfortunately, I found the glass cabinet on my first try, unable to snoop any further. I got some water from the sink and pounded it down.

I think it was just then I realized how close we were to stupid when we had been in that storage unit.

Mallory came out of the bathroom and took a seat at the small table. I jumped into the bathroom, throwing cold water on my face. It was so refreshing, I tossed off my top and rinsed my arms, pits, and chest. I kept the mess to a minimum on the floor. I was not about to use unknown towels, so I air-dried and put my clammy shirt back on.

Mallory listened without interrupting. I nearly told her about the trip to the gravestone, but she would have asked how we knew to go there as it was not something to easily stumble upon. It would make me divulge the neighbor lady had told me something other than the lie I had relayed earlier. I insinuated Pete used the bolt cutters, and thankfully and weirdly, there were no follow-up questions.

Pete came down the stairs freshly showered and in a new T-shirt and jeans. His shirt had a tennis shoe brand logo spread across his chest, and all I could think was how I wanted to trace the lettering with my hand.

He crossed the kitchen and opened the back door, allowing a breeze to sweep through the small room. We heard a quick rap on the front screen door, and Pete waved Sherrie in.

"Let's go in the front room where we'll have more room," Pete said.

"I was just telling Mallory everything about when Pete picked me up and we went to the storage unit." I only hoped those two understood to leave out any cemetery talk.

Sherrie and I took seats next to each other on the large couch and Mallory on the far smaller couch. I kicked over an ottoman, and she quickly put up her feet. Pete stood in the open space between the couch and the staircase and in the middle of the breeze shooting through the house. Any other day, I might have gone and stood with him for the fresh air, but now that felt too intimate.

Mallory asked, "So let me get this straight, you guys are trying to figure out if you should tell the police some drug deal is going down or at least an exchange of cash. You think you know the players involved, but you did not see them and you don't know the location."

"When you put it in common sense form, I feel a little foolish," I said.

"How about I call my contact at the station and give them a brief summary and they can use the information as they want?" Mallory said.

"Why you?" I asked. "Sorry, if that came out snarky."

"I can use my press privilege and protect my source. It will be something like *Someone overheard this conversation and do with it what you want.*"

"That's not bad," Pete said. "Who are you going to call?"

"They don't know your name, and you don't get to know who I talk to."

"Fair," Pete answered.

We spent several minutes reviewing what Mallory was going to say, but she seemed to have already made up her mind. She excused herself and retreated to the backyard to make her call.

Sherrie and I were sunk into the couch like we had just run a marathon, but it was only three p.m. on a Monday afternoon. All our energy was drained out of us.

Pete had finally taken a seat on the couch closest to the front door.

I snapped at Sherrie, "Would you stop humming that song or at least pick a new one? You have been on that same tune for a week."

"I have been replaying the last few days over and over and over again. I had been singing the Beyoncé album all week when I was riding my bike. It's only been since I was watching Ben. It's a catchy tune, and I can't shake—" Sherrie sprung off the couch so fast I thought something bit her butt. She stood there looking dizzy.

I got up to hold her, but she brushed me off.

"I think I know—wait, where is my phone?" She got her phone from her back pocket.

Pete and I exchanged a knowing look that we didn't know what we were witnessing.

"Aaron, call me back immediately." She texted him the same message and asked us to call him too.

"He's not taking either one of our calls," I said.

"Pete?"

"Claudia is right. I'm on his shit list today."

Sherrie paused only a half a second to figure out her next move. I saw her send a text to Chuck.

"What's going on? Clue us in," I said.

Sherrie's phone rang, and Chuck's name popped up. She swiped to answer, and within three steps, walked to the front door, and pivoted towards the kitchen at the pace of a greyhound chasing a rabbit. There was no intent to block us from the conversation; it was just her wheels spinning as she put the pieces together.

We heard the words "explain the layout of . . ." before she disappeared into the kitchen. I took two steps forward at the same time Pete stood up. We ran into each other and did an awkward dance, trying to let the other person go first. If this had been two days ago, I would have put my hands on Pete and pushed him forward. Now the sudden thought of putting my hands on him took me someplace else.

Sherrie had plunged back into the front room twice before Pete and I disengaged from our dance. She sailed out the front door for the final time, yelling, "I got it. Claud. Come with me and, Pete, grab the other one."

"I'm assuming she means Mallory. I'll text you from the car." I was out the door before I finished speaking.

Sherrie had the car started and was backing up before my door was shut.

"Peach's. Tell Pete Peach's. That back corridor connects all the stores. Ben kept asking to go to *the* room not *his* room. It's the song. That damn song. It's on rotation at Peach's. I heard it when Ben grabbed my phone and was talking to Ellie. The other night when I saw the light."

"The light?"

"When I went to check on the dough racks. You didn't believe me about the light."

"It's not that I didn't believe you. I just didn't understand drunk-Sherrie story logic."

"I will let that pass. You should always be following what I say."

"Two nights in a row, I came to your rescue in the middle of the night. Now explain to me where Ben is, and would you mind at least stopping at one of these stop signs. You might find Ben at the cost of your driver's license."

"You know the empty store next to Peach's."

"Where the travel agency and video rental place used to be?"

My parents had been potential investors when Jan wanted to expand Peach's kitchen and bakery operation. After months of indecision, Jan had finally decided not to expand.

I said, "The front windows are covered with that brown paper except that corner angle window. You can see it's empty. Are they in there?"

We were two blocks away when she finally slowed down. She went into the same alley across the street from Peach's where her car had previously sat for several days.

I got a text from Pete. *We're leaving the house now.*

"I see we beat Chuck here. I would never have bet we'd get anywhere before him."

"Back up," I snapped.

"Why? What do you see? You see 'em?"

"You can't park where the guy dropped. That is bad juju."

"I'm looking for a missing kid, and you're talking parking spots!" Sherrie threw her old VW Bug into reverse and backed into a slanted parking spot in one swift move.

I barely knew what happened.

She said, "Inappropriate talk and action at a time like this. Luv it, give it up."

We fist-bumped as we got out of the car.

"I tried teaching Pete the artful skill of the inappropriate talking to break the tension."

Sherrie was a foot in front of me; otherwise, she would have seen me blush when she asked, "Well, what did he do that was inappropriate?"

"Where are we going? Are they in the empty building?"

"Hang on. Let me see if I can figure this out," Sherrie said.

We crossed the street and walked into the C-shaped vestibule around Peach's back door. This created a wind and rain block around the delivery door. The café had been closed for about an hour at this point. I had been through the back several times but had never stopped to take a close look at anything.

The left side wall was a windbreak wall, and even I could tell it had been added on in recent years as the wood was several shades off in color. Everything was a black brown with the exception of the metal door handle that took you inside Peach's kitchen and the beige keypad that lit when the numbers were punched. The right side wall was the same as the others, but if you looked down, there was a brown metal plate and midway up was a six-inch black metal plate with a small key lock.

"I got that key!" Sherrie took off running to her car.

I stood in the vestibule confused as I was when she'd first called Chuck.

She was back a minute later huffing and puffing. "You know how we thought we lost the key and piece of paper from the mug?"

"I actually thought Mallory had them."

"Me too," Sherrie said as she dug in her backpack.

"I'm on the fence about her. One minute annoying. One minute helpful. One minute annoying. One minute doing something nice."

"Totally agree. Damn, this swings her more in the favor we should be nice to her since she didn't steal anything," Sherrie said. "My mind has been a mess ever since seeing that guy drop in the alley the other night."

Sherrie handed me her laptop before she dumped everything on the ground. "Don't tell me I lost it again." She half mumbled while crouching when she flipped through her book and notepads.

"You have been a little lost. You keep telling me half stories. You left out some portion of Miller watching the guy drop in the alley. Then at breakfast Friday, you wanted to ask me a question that we never got to. Friday night, you confessed you never told the police everything. Saturday, when I was nearly home from car shopping, you said you did something stupid. I took that to mean you agreed to babysit, but that is not stupid just a little crazy."

Sherrie was listening and staring at me while she squatted like a folded-up lawn chair. Finally, she rolled back onto her butt. She stopped rifling through her stuff, looking for the key. "I thought I knew you better. Wait, I do know you better than you know yourself, but you have the better memory. Well, maybe just a better memory because you have been more sober this weekend than I have."

Her eyes got big and she jumped up. "Let me tell you about . . ."

She started putting everything back into her backpack and tried to grab the laptop from me, but I wouldn't let go.

"You did it again. You start a sentence and don't finish it. I am holding this until you tell me your last thought."

"I was just screwing with you on that last hanging thought. I remembered I put the key in a pocket for safekeeping and was embarrassed I forgot so I thought I should redirect you."

She returned the laptop to the backpack and dug out some lip balm and a key. She inserted the key, and we heard a click of the dead bolt turn.

Pete, Mallory, and Chuck all showed up together.

From behind Sherrie, Chuck flexed his long arm and held Sherrie's hand on the key and lock.

"You asked your questions, and now let me. We are here because of what?"

Sherrie gave him a thirty-second update about Ben and Ellie going missing. He traded places with Sherrie and moved her and me out of the vestibule as he pushed opened the door. He didn't hold us back, and we filed in like mice following the piper.

CHAPTER TWENTY-SEVEN

Disappointment swept over us. This windowless forty-foot hallway I assumed connected to the empty storefront to the identical-looking door at the other end.

Besides the two sleeping bags, one cot, and air mattresses, there was a brown paper grocery bag with animal crackers, oranges, apple juice, and chewy fruit snacks.

There were over thirty pictures drawn by a child taped to the wall. One picture hit me in the heart. It was an outline of two hands touching with a heart drawn between them. One hand larger than the other and framing the hands were about three-dozen buzzing bees alternating letters on the wings, BE & ES. Bees for Ben and Ellie. One bee had an *M* with a heart in its tiny belly.

We were lined up in the eight-foot-wide hallway and stood like we were on a museum tour gone wrong.

I even whispered when I spoke. "Do we call the police?"

I looked to my left and down the line from Sherrie, Mallory, and Pete. No one answered my question. Behind me, Chuck opened the far door, but I couldn't follow. I didn't want to leave the room, their room, their hiding spot.

"The store is empty. They probably used the bathroom because there is a supply of toilet paper and soap," Chuck said when he stepped back in and closed the door behind him. "Don't touch anything. Let's talk outside."

I turned and smacked into Sherrie.

"Sorry, I gotta tie my shoe, go around me." She dropped her backpack and bent down.

I scooted around her and stumbled a bit when she knocked my leg.

"Chuck, can you make sure she walks straight out of here?" Sherrie said with a low forced laugh.

The cool, fresh air was a treat, but the wind cut through me. Pete stood with his hands on his hips, and Mallory again was typing on her phone. I turned around inside the vestibule and took the door from Chuck. I moved him into the alley, leaving Sherrie alone inside to do whatever she needed to do. I know the shoelace, false laugh, and directing Chuck to leave the room was code for something.

"This is the camera we were looking at earlier. The angle of it is clearly on Peach's, but if I swing this door open, would it cause the shadows we saw on the video playback?"

Chuck answered. "Possibly. We can do some tests and I can queue it up and look, but we pretty much know they have been spending time in there."

I swung the door open and saw Sherrie zipping up her pack.

"Don't lock me in here!" she yelled, holding up one finger, asking for another minute.

"Sometimes I feel like I'm the one babysitting. Tie your other shoe." I hoped that bought her more time.

Sherrie exited the hidden storage area and locked the dead bolt behind her.

"Where did that key come from?" Pete asked.

"This was the key in the mug all along. It dropped into Sherrie's bag when Ben grabbed her phone."

Sherrie said, "To answer your question, Claud, I don't know if we need to call the police. They clearly are not here, but I don't know if I feel like not calling them because I feel like I'm in this deeper than I really am."

I was thankful Chuck jumped in before I had to make a decision.

"You guys head home, and I'll call it in. It's more feasible if Jan or I discovered this hiding spot that might be a link with the Amber Alert. I will do that based on the condition you tell me everything, and you guys are not involved."

"That works for us," Sherrie said.

"I mean *everything*," Chuck said. He was a foot taller, but it felt like ten feet when his eyes and blank expression tore through me.

The four of us walked towards Sherrie's car, and Chuck's words echoed in my head. *Everything.*

My mind zipped through the day. "I feel like we're one step behind them."

"I know what you mean," Sherrie said. "So we know they've slept here, the storage unit, and can assume home, but there must be another place."

"I got it," I blurted it out. "The old lady. She's the type to talk, but she couldn't get rid of us any sooner. Let's go."

"My car is on fumes. Pete do you mind driving?" Sherrie said.

"Seriously, you get your car back after four days and you can only drive it for five minutes this afternoon, and it's back in the same alley!" I said.

Sherrie rolled her eyes. "Don't complain. It got us this far and this much closer to finding them."

Logical order of us walking up to the truck had Sherrie riding behind Pete with Mallory and me walking around to the passenger side. It struck me in a particular way that at a time when Ben and Ellie were missing I was worried about sitting next to the guy I had just been kissing.

Mallory stopped walking.

"Everything ok?" I asked.

She gave me a half a smile. "The baby is kicking up a storm with all this excitement."

I didn't like her using the word *excitement* around a missing child, but then again, I was worried about riding shotgun next to a boy I liked. I flashed her a smile back and said, "Is the front seat more comfortable for you or the back so you can spread out more?"

"At this point, it doesn't matter. Just getting myself up into the truck is an accomplishment."

I pulled open the front door for her, and she heaved herself up. She was short-winded, but she looked graceful.

"You think they're hiding out next to their own house?" Pete asked.

"It's just a guess. I'm not sure she will even let us in, but it's worth asking."

"Should I hang back?" Pete asked. "How will it be if four of us go charging up?"

"Good point. Claudia and I will talk to her," Sherrie said.

Mallory pulled herself forward so she could turn and look at us. "Can I say something without meaning to offend?"

Sherrie and I looked at each other, and I said a soft, "Go ahead."

"So when I go to interview someone or several of us are working on a feature for the paper, we figure out who will best connect with the interviewee. After what the lady said about me and my present condition, I don't want to assume her worldviews and other ideals, but she might take to Claudia and Pete more than . . ."

"I get it. She might not take to a Black girl who's not from River Bend. Claudia and Pete should talk to her."

There was a long pause.

"I could be wrong, and I hope I am," Mallory said.

"We all hope for better. Don't apologize for the others. You have a point about Pete and Claudia. Do you have any idea of her name?"

"I didn't recognize her and only got a glimpse of the photos on the wall when I went to the bathroom. I suspect we are aged between her kids and grandkids," Mallory said.

290

Pete drove down the block. Several strands of yellow police tape hanging on bushes, flickering in the wind, were the only signs of damage from the front of the house.

"I'm assuming I shouldn't park in front of the house like we're on a stakeout," Pete said.

"Head down one block," I said. "On second thought, I think Sherrie should come with me. If Ben and Ellie are there, they or at least Ben will respond better to Sherrie."

"Glad you agree with what I was thinking because I am not sitting and waiting," Sherrie said.

She popped the door open. "Can you at least wait until I put it in park?" Pete said. "Do we want to think this thing out? What are you going to say if she doesn't let you in?"

"I, no, agh, we are better at winging it than having a plan. Don't worry, we only think they're hiding there. We're not going to investigate a large cache of weapons or hit a drug house," I said.

Sherrie added, "What kind of trouble can we get in?"

We were out of the truck, and Pete rolled down his window. "Right there is the problem with you two. You never see the problem when you're in the middle of it."

We waved him off and walked slowly towards the house.

I said, "I feel really bad about lying to Mallory. Making up that comment about unwed mothers when she was looking out for how you might get treated."

"Let it all go," Sherrie said.

The two houses came into view. The rear porch roof on Ellie and Ben's house was collapsing, and the screen windows were shredded. There was still a hint of smoke in the air. The lady's front window drapes were closed.

We crossed the street, and I said, "We are better when we don't have a plan, right?"

Sherrie raised her hand, and we bumped fists. Together we said, "Amen."

We climbed the small cement porch. I rang the doorbell. The drapes to the right of us shuffled, and then the lady with the white hair opened the door.

I couldn't wait for a rejection. "Hello, again. I was here earlier."

"I remember you. And this one," the lady said, pointing to Sherrie. "Running into the house like that takes some gusto, not brains but gusto."

"I'm Sherrie, and this is Claudia. She's EG's niece." I knew Sherrie was throwing EG's name out because most everyone who knows her loves her, and that might get us in the door.

"So you are a Graham. Should have seen it in the face. They call me Pearl on account of my hair. Been white more years than it hasn't been white. What can I do you for?"

We had nothing to lose at this point.

"We want to talk to Ellie," I said.

"What does that have to do with me? You can see that home ain't for the living in it now."

"We think she's here. We just need to know she and Ben are ok," Sherrie said.

"Why?" Pearl asked.

"They are missing, and we're worried," I said.

"I ain't done nothing to them. My Stan's hasn't been home since he left for his shift at six."

"We don't think you did anything. We know you care for them and have been taking care of them. That's why you told me about the swing. You care too." I was running out of steam.

I looked at Sherrie, who had her phone in her hand, and I elbowed her. She turned the phone, but I couldn't see what her texts read.

She yelled, "Jellyroll."

The noise surprised Pearl too. She gripped the doorknob and the doorframe, getting ready to swing it shut.

Sherrie yelled again, "Jellyroll!"

Pearl didn't move until we heard a voice.

"It's ok, Pearl. Better let them in."

"Are you sure, girl? I know how to run off those not wanted."

"I have no choice at this time," Ellie said.

Sherrie pushed the door from Pearl's grip, and I followed her into the living room.

"Pearl, would you mind giving us a moment," I said.

Pearl walked over, whispered something to Ellie, then went toward the kitchen. A back screen door opened and closed.

"Where is Ben?" Sherrie said and took several steps forward and looked around the small house. "Bedroom, downstairs?"

"He's not here. Please stop yelling," Ellie said.

"Where is he?" I asked.

"Somewhere safe. Thank you for watching him, but we're fine. Please go. I don't want to upset Pearl."

"Pearl can handle herself. You do know there is an alert out for you and Ben?" Sherrie said.

"I didn't plan it, and I can't help that," Ellie said. "Please just go."

"Tell me why we shouldn't tell the police you're here?" I said.

"No." Ellie's answers where sharp, but she cracked when she said, "Please. I need to finish a few things, and then I will."

"Why do I have people chasing me?" Sherrie asked.

Ellie truly looked surprised. "I have no idea. That has nothing to do with us. Ben said he had a great time with you. He was missing some items in his pack. Are they at your house? Can we get them?"

"Missing stuff?" Sherrie said. We looked at each other, and Sherrie turned towards Ellie. "You mean a key?"

Ellie's eye's got wide. "You have my key."

"I did."

Ellie was holding it together until Sherrie told her she no longer held the key to their hideout. She dropped on the couch and started crying. "I need to get in there. Please tell me you didn't take anything." She sniffed, wiped away tears, and bit her already chewed-down nails.

"You want your laptop?" Sherrie said.

Ellie sprang up. "I need it. Give it to me." She was so fast I hardly saw her grab Sherrie and spin her around.

Sherrie flailed her arms, nearly knocking down little Ellie. "I think it's obvious I am not carrying the damn thing."

"I need it. Where is it?" Ellie's voice was shaking.

"Where is Ben?" Sherrie asked.

"Safe. You should know I always keep him safe. This is all for him." Tears rolled down her cheeks. "Please, where is it? Bring it here, and I'll tell you where Ben is."

I didn't know who took a deeper breath, me or Sherrie.

"I will bring you the laptop, but you need to tell me about Ben and the guys after us."

"Us?" Ellie said.

"We are not completely sure if someone is after just me, Claudia, or both of us."

"I will tell you everything. I just need that computer." Ellie collapsed on the couch, bent forward, and began rocking.

Sherrie texted Pete to bring the backpack. Ellie stood up and went in the kitchen. I didn't hear any water running, fridge opening, or even a sniffle. Something didn't feel right.

I whispered to Sherrie, "Something is off."

"What should we do?" Sherrie asked.

It was only half a beat before we both said, "Chuck."

Sherrie went out to the front porch and texted Chuck, and I stood in the doorway. We watched Pete carrying the backpack down the street.

We reviewed everything Sherrie had done the last few days to try and figure out who was following her. We never thought about me. I had picked up the travel mug.

Someone must have seen me. They knew the key was in there.

Ellie came back into the living room, and she slipped a phone into her pocket. She must have been telling someone that she had the computer. I felt like an ambush was about to happen.

"Ellie, what's happening? You can trust us. You *have* trusted us," I pleaded and moved to the center of the living room.

Sherrie walked in carrying the backpack with Pete behind her. He stood in the doorway, and Sherrie took three steps inside, putting the backpack on the floral-print chair near the window and unzipping it.

Ellie pulled out a phone. An old flip phone. It hit me that it was one of those burner phones. Was Ellie dealing drugs with her brother?

I didn't know what was beating faster, my heart or the pounding in my temples. I was desperate to connect all the dots.

"Wait!" I said and put my hand on Sherrie's arm as she held the laptop.

Ellie pushed me down and wrestled the computer away from Sherrie. In the commotion, Sherrie's bag spilled out on the floor. A notebook and a folder with several papers sprayed across the carpet. A nanosecond later, Pete stepped forward with his arm stretched forward to help Sherrie maintain control of the computer.

Out of nowhere, he was instantly knocked back with a sucker punch to the face. He lost his balance as he tumbled into Sherrie.

She lost control of the computer. I lunged to help both of them stay upright, but my attempt was mediocre at best. I ended up kneeling next to Sherrie with Pete on top of her.

Ellie and Miller were out the back door before we knew what happened. Pete was dripping blood on Sherrie's top. Without thinking, I jumped up and ran after them, but Pearl stood at the back door blocking me. She shuffled me back into the house, holding the back of my shirt, manhandling like a puppet. We went to the living room and then back into the kitchen where she released my shirt.

She handed me an ice pack while she looked for a dish towel. Pearl nudged me into the living room, taking the ice pack from me and gave it and the dish towel to Pete, who had rolled off Sherrie and was now lying on his back. Sherrie was shoving her stuff back into her pack.

Pearl perfectly executed getting Pete up and held Sherrie's elbow, then pushed them towards me and all of us out the front door before we knew what happened. We heard the dead bolt slide into place.

"What the hell just happened?" Pete said.

No one had an answer.

We sat on Pearl's step and gathered our thoughts.

Pete leaned against the decades-old slim metal rail that I thought might bend under his weight. "Talk about a sucker punch. I didn't even see who hit me much less do anything to stop it. It wasn't one of you, was it?"

I punched him in the arm.

Sherrie said, "Miller came out of nowhere. You kept your cool when you fell on me. I will give you that. Let's get out of here."

We slowly stood up.

Pete said, "Problem."

Sherrie and I both went to his side thinking he was going to drop again when he said, "Not me. My truck is gone."

Sherrie and I sang our anthem, "Hell's bells."

We all sat down again. Pete and I listened as Sherrie explained to Chuck that we didn't go home. I didn't even bother texting Mallory. When I called her, it rang until voice mail kicked on.

"Did Mallory really take off in your truck? Is she chasing them?"

The sun had faded behind clouds as did our spirits.

"We at least know Ellie is alive, and if we are to believe her, Ben is ok," I said.

"Can you repeat that? I can't seem to hear anything over the lump on my face." Pete laughed, wincing as he touched his nose.

"Broken?" Sherrie asked.

"Only my man card. A sucker punch and losing my truck," Pete said.

"If your dog dies, you got yourself a hell of a country song in the making," I said. "You will probably have a black eye. I'd keep the ice on it. I don't think Pearl is opening her door to us anytime soon, and you need a new rag."

"I'm almost done knitting one, but I was saving it for a real emergency," Pete said.

I walked between the two houses and pulled off my sweatshirt and T-shirt because modesty was so important during a situation like this. I weighed the options between the two but decided the shirt should be enough for now. I walked back around and tossed him the shirt.

"Appreciate it," Pete said.

"No problem. It's Sherrie's."

"Are my eyes blurry, or is that Mallory walking towards us?"

Sherrie and I pivoted to see the mirage that was Mallory with a water bottle in one hand and her phone in the other.

"What the hell?" Pete snapped.

This was the closest to mad I had ever seen him.

"I got out of the truck when you went to give 'em the backpack. I was stretching my back out, and before I knew, Miller had Ellie by the arm running from the backyard. They nearly knocked me down when he threw her in the truck and took off."

"So the keys were in it?" Sherrie looked at Pete.

"One better. I left it running so the air would be on and no one would have to get out of it for some cool air." Pete gritted through his teeth with a perfect balance of sarcasm, disbelief, and anguish.

"Sorry, I didn't wait for you guys to call police," Mallory said.

"Wait for us?"

"You seem to do everything by committee. Half the time, you don't even verbalize your thoughts and still manage to have a full conversation," Mallory said.

Pete laughed, siding with Mallory. "Sometimes it's like you share one head. So it's bizarre when one doesn't know something."

Sherrie looked at me at said, "What don't I know?"

"What about me? What am I missing?" I said.

Pete stood there dabbing his nose and holding a melting ice pack. "Really, now is the time to do this? Evaluate everything you two do and say? Not to make this about me but look at the bloody shirt I'm holding or the empty parking spot. How about we talk about Ellie and the police." He turned to Mallory and said, "What did you say?"

"Me?" She looked shocked at the attention being pointed at her.

"Women. God help me," Pete mumbled. "To the police, what did you say when you called 9-1-1."

"The same thing as Mrs. Burndel in the house where I just came from. She saw the whole thing and was on the phone before I was dialing. Those two running from behind that white house and jumping into the truck and taking off."

Chuck pulled up and right behind him was a squad car with its lights flashing. Wyatt turned off the lights when he exited the vehicle.

"What's up? Fancy meeting you here," Sherrie said with a smile.

"You look like hell," Wyatt said.

Pete rightfully was the one to answer. "But I feel great."

"I need you guys to go home. Don't talk to anyone. Don't do anything. And sure as hell stay away from everything," Wyatt said.

I tried asking, "What's—"

"Nothing is *what's*. This is not a request. Go home and stay there until you are told to leave. If there is any deviation to you going home, you will be in trouble. That includes you Pete. Someone will be there later to talk to you."

"Can we—" This time, it was Sherrie that got cut off.

"One more time. Go home. And right now the only thing you get to say is 'Thank you for not taking me to the police station,' " Wyatt said.

From what I had been told about his high school days in River Bend, Wyatt was voted most likely to get lost in his own home. He was always kind and willing to help anyone at any time. His only fault was maybe telling you too much about what was going on in the police department. The person standing before us was someone I had not met before.

Wyatt retreated to his squad car and only got in when we walked to Chuck's Jeep and drove away.

Pete, holding two bloody rags and a melting ice pack, held open the front door for Mallory. She lost two shades of color in her face. If I had to guess, it would have to be sitting so close to Chuck that made her uncomfortable.

"You take the front. I'm fine in back. I can actually walk back to Pete's and get my car," Mallory said.

"Wyatt said we all stay together so we stay together, and I will need you for the police report for my truck," Pete said.

There was no reply from Mallory.

I took the center seat between Mallory and Sherrie in the back. "What I don't understand is why no one is talking to Pearl or asking us for our statements?"

"Tell me everything from the beginning, and don't edit out information you don't think I need," Chuck said.

Sherrie gave him the play-by-play, and I filled him in on mine and Pete's detour to the unit and how we ended up here. Before I knew it, we were at EG's all gathered on the porch like kids waiting for the recess bell to ring.

Sherrie opened the backpack again. "Sorry, we usually never lock the door. It will be a minute."

"I don't have patience for this. I'll get us in." I shifted Chuck to the side and stepped to the couch, pushing the back cushion away for better window access. One easy pull and the screen popped off, and I froze in place.

Sherrie's excitement broke my thoughts. "I got it."

She opened the door and declared she was going downstairs to the laundry room to soak her blood-soaked shirt thanks to Pete. Mallory was headed upstairs to the bathroom.

I gave her a pass. "Mallory you must be tired. You can use EG's bathroom if you don't want to climb the stairs."

I followed Pete into the kitchen and let him throw out the bloody towel and shirt. While he washed his hands and face, I poured myself some water and offered the boys some, but they declined. Chuck took a seat at the island.

I could see his mind racing. "Can you wait for the other one before you start with the questions?"

Mallory came in, got some water, and took the farthest spot in the kitchen from Chuck.

"Do you need more ice?" I asked Pete.

"At this point, only time will help."

Sherrie came up from downstairs in one of the most wrinkled T-shirts I had ever seen. "Got it from dryer. At least it's blood-free."

"Sorry about that. Wasn't expecting the left hook from behind the hallway," Pete said.

"Either the guy had poor aim, or you ducked just enough. Another half inch and it could have been broken," Chuck said. "Now, what's your problem, Sherrie?"

She had been looking over Chuck's shoulder into the family room. When we had walked in, Sherrie had put her open backpack on the table. "We may have a bigger problem than Pete's black eye." She held the stage.

Chuck stood up, and the rest of us watched Sherrie walk over to retrieve her pack. "This is not my computer. In all the commotion, I didn't realize I pulled out the wrong one."

She stood there with her arm stretched out, holding the computer. We all stared at it like it was the plague. You could have heard a needle drop in that kitchen, but instead we heard someone upstairs.

CHAPTER TWENTY-EIGHT

"Stay here unless I yell, then it's out the back door." Chuck looked at me and Sherrie.

Pete followed him into the living room. We watched their quiet exchange. Pete reached for his back pocket, and I saw *Shit* roll off his lips.

Sherrie, Mallory, and I were lined up between the island and the sink. I would have been offended if I wasn't given an assignment by Chuck until I saw him unlock his phone and hand it to Pete, who was instructed to stay at the bottom of the stairs.

I lost count the number of times I sweated through the T-shirt I had given Pete. Now I stood there starting on pit stains in the sweatshirt I was wearing.

Chuck was six foot, solid muscle, and not one of the old wooden steps creaked, squeaked, or bounced. I was more and more curious about Chuck's military experience.

Nine hours or ninety seconds later, Chuck came back down stairs. Pete handed him his phone and followed him into the kitchen.

"It's better if you approach the mystery guest. I might be a little scary for a kid."

"Ben?" Sherrie asked.

"I saw two little legs under the blanket. The far bedroom, closet, and bathroom are clear. Come up with me and I will clear the far closet, but I think he's alone."

Mallory and Pete stayed in the kitchen while Sherrie and I followed Chuck to the staircase.

Sherrie said, "Wait. I go first, and I will tell you when to come in. When you come in, your name is Chuck and Jellyroll."

Chuck was not going to let Sherrie up the stairs, and I would have given anything to see the look she gave him that got him to change his mind.

"Ben. It's Sherrie and Claudia. We're coming up," she said.

We hurried up the stairs and found Ben on the pullout couch under the blankets. Sherrie sat down next to him.

He peeked his head out and looked at her and then me. He sat upright and nearly on top of her. "I did exactly as Ellie said. I stayed up here, making no noise."

"You did fine. I do see you like your crackers in bed. Are you hungry?"

Ben didn't say anything.

"We have food in the house and can make something fun. It's ok but first I want you to meet a special friend."

I waved Chuck in, and he sat on the floor facing Sherrie and Ben. His legs stretched out almost as long as the bed. "I'm Chuck."

Sherrie coughed.

Chuck continued. "Some call me Jellyroll. You did a good job here by yourself. Do you know how to fist-bump?"

Ben dropped the blanket he was holding and pressed his fist together.

Chuck said, "I like giving fist bumps to people that help me. Like Sherrie and Claudia. They helped me find things. They helped me come to the house." He held out his fist, and I gave it a bump. "They also helped tie my shoes." He and Sherrie bumped fists. "I think you did a good job up here. You did as you were told. Do you think I can give you a fist bump?"

Ben held out his fist to Chuck's. Ben even cracked a smile.

Chuck continued, "Is there anyone else you want to bump fists with here?" Ben turned to

Sherrie and then to me. "I bet you want to fist-bump Ellie."

Ben nodded and squeezed his eyes.

"It's ok, buddy," Chuck said and gently placed his hand on Ben's knee. "Until she gets here is there anyone else?"

Ben tilted his head sideways.

"I'm going to get up and stretch. Do you think you can help me?" Chuck asked.

Ben didn't move.

"If I put my hand out to you, will you pull with all your might? You can ask Sherrie to help, but I bet you don't need it. You're a big boy."

Chuck put out his arm, and Ben tugged. It was amazing watching Chuck in action and winning over the affection of a seven-year-old boy. It seriously made me wonder what kind of negotiation skills Chuck had learned in the military. Within seconds, Chuck was up, and Ben was bouncing on the bed.

I hardly noticed that Chuck had opened Sherrie's closet door, ensuring we were alone in the house. He picked up Ben and threw him over his shoulder like a flour sack. He carried him downstairs and tossed him on the couch. Ben wanted to play more with Chuck but had to settle for Sherrie and the television remote.

Chuck went into the kitchen and out the back door. Pete was pacing in the kitchen, and Mallory again was typing away on her phone.

I spied Chuck on his phone outside and told Pete and Mallory about Ben being alone in the house. "I think there's sandwich stuff in the fridge. I gotta make something for Ben, and I can make something for you guys if you want something."

Pete said, "Do you have a computer I can use? My phone is in the truck, and I can track the phone's location and see if they ditched the truck or if it's halfway to Mexico by now."

"Sure, let me get it. Mallory. Yo. Mallory." I had to wait for her to look up. "Can you start on sandwiches or something for Ben? Pete, let me introduce you to him. You have to say the safe word, Jellyroll."

I left everyone downstairs and found my laptop in one of my overnight bags. I sniggered at the thought that my life used to revolve around one of these when I was in school, and now it was just an afterthought.

When I stood up, I got a glimpse of myself in the mirror and realized my hair and my complete look needed attention but thought I'd better give Pete the computer without looking too vain. We had spent the day like this, so he knew the bad and the good.

Downstairs, I found Mallory asking Ben if he wanted the crusts cut off his bread. She had to remake the ham sandwich because she put "funny white stuff" on the bread. Sherrie helped negotiate the sandwich, which came down to ham, butter, bread with crust and no mayo.

Chuck was at sitting at the island typing away at Ellie's computer. "Damn." Before I could ask, he mumbled, "She's good."

Pete was sitting next to him, munching on chips Mallory had found. "Let me power this up. What's got Chuck all worked up?"

"Beats me," Pete said.

I sat at the short side of the island next to him and let Chuck do his thing. Our knees knocked, and it sent me back to our kiss. My face flushed. Pete shifted two inches to his left, leaving me feeling wide-open. Maybe he just wanted the kiss, and he didn't feel anything like I did.

"You ok?" Mallory asked me.

I hadn't even heard her come back into the kitchen.

"Ah, oh. I was just wondering what the police said when Chuck called. Just waiting for him to take his eyes of that screen for a second so I can ask."

"Ask what you want," Chuck said without shifting his focus from the computer, his fingers typing away.

"Is someone coming for Ben? I'm assuming that you called and told them we have him safe."

"They will send someone to confirm." Chuck was lost in his work. He said, "She is good" more than once.

I was not so adept at talking and typing. It took me three tries to get my password correct. Mallory took a seat at the long dining table between the kitchen and living room. She sat by herself and was typing away on her phone again, looking like a person without a country.

My laptop fired up, and I slid it over to Pete. Sherrie finally extracted herself from Ben and joined us in the kitchen. We quietly busied ourselves making sandwiches. Mallory had stopped short after making one for Ben and herself.

"It's nearly five. I wonder if Adam is able to do what he was supposed to do?" I asked.

"Do you think the police are onto him, and that's why Wyatt sent us here and not the station? I told the police someone may be watching the house, but he must think it's safe if he sent us back here."

"Maybe under the supervision of Rambo over there, they deemed us safe," I said, with no smart comment back from Rambo, I mean, Chuck.

Sherrie whispered, "Is Ellie a bargaining tool? How much danger can she be in? To think, we were just in his apartment."

With his head down, still typing away on my computer, Pete asked, "What do you mean in his apartment?"

I froze. It had only been three nights ago I had left Aaron's and was in Miller's loft for what I only now realized I had done because of curiosity and a reaction from my split.

Bile rose in my throat. Guilt washed over me as I stood next to Pete. We were not even dating, and I felt like I owed him an apology.

Suddenly, I smirked. I had dated Aaron for eight months and felt no guilt about going to another man's place or even kissing someone else. There was no whiplash for me and Aaron, and that was nice. Although there was also no me and Pete. Did he even want something with me?

Hell, he has not even made any gesture or half gesture that he wants something since our kiss. Maybe he settled his curiosity and has moved on.

Lost in my own thoughts, I missed Sherrie explaining how we had searched his apartment. I had already forgotten about our little fiasco.

My train of thought was interrupted when Chuck said, "How are you two still alive?"

Pete just mumbled something under his breath, and seconds later, he slid my computer towards Chuck. "Found my phone."

"They ditch the truck, or running to the border with it?" I asked and got no reply.

Pete stood up, and Chuck finally turned his focus away from Ellie's computer.

Chuck shifted from hunched over to standing straighter than a ruler, and with a calm and definitive voice, said, "Sherrie take Ben and the other one to Jorge's and don't come out, prefer you go in the basement." His contempt for Mallory was so high he could not even say her name. "Claudia, is there anything besides this computer someone might want from this house."

"I-I, ah, I don't think so," I kinda mumbled.

"Now is not the time to be coy." Chuck looked at me seriously. "You've said someone has been here and watching you guys."

Sherrie took Ben's hand and pulled him from the sofa. The movie had his attention, but he was no match for Sherrie. They walked past Mallory, who had not responded in any manner to Chuck's instructions and was typing away on her phone.

Sherrie tapped her on the shoulder and said, in a voice reminiscent of an army general, "Grab the blanket on the couch and follow us."

Chuck asked again, "Why are you guys of interest to someone?"

I just shrugged, watched Mallory walk out the kitchen back door, and then I saw my computer screen and a tiny image moving. The map had a phone icon moving and getting closer to the house.

Miller and Ellie must have realized we have her computer, and they were coming here to get it.

"Claudia, answer me," Chuck said.

Pete answered, "If she said she doesn't know, then she doesn't know."

It should have been a romantic gesture defending me, but it put me back to how we were bonded. We had each other's back in a crisis. We would always be buddies. A pit grew inside my stomach. We hadn't even been together as a couple, and I was mourning this relationship more than any other. Maybe it was just a case of romanticizing the unknown.

Both men were looking for me to answer. "We have been honest from the start."

"You just leave out convenient details," Chuck said, and I had no argument opposing it.

"Everybody out," Chuck said, and grabbed Ellie's laptop, dialing his phone.

Pete grabbed my computer, and we left through the back door. I was surprised at how quiet Chuck's conversation was until I realized he was not behind us nor could I hear any noise in the house.

I was more confused when I found Jorge's back door locked.

We heard our names being called. Pete and I turned around to see Sherrie waving at us from behind Jorge's garage. We ran over and found the three of them snuggled between the garage and back fence.

Pete walked over to the side door of the garage.

"Don't you think I tried that already?" Sherrie said to him.

He turned the knob, shimmied the door with all his strength, and either the hip check or the shoulder slam popped open the door. We quietly all walked in. The garage was void of cars but full of sawdust and large power tools from Jorge's remodeling of his house.

Sherrie tried moving from the back, but Ben wouldn't drop her hand. Pete handed me my laptop and then pulled two old aluminum-framed lawn chairs off the top shelf.

We put Ben in one with the blanket wrapped around him. He still didn't want to let go of Sherrie's hand, so she sat next to him and pulled out her phone, trying to distract him. I walked to the front corner of the garage and found camp chairs made in this century.

"At least what I found doesn't have layers of sawdust all over them," Pete said, and he took a seat on a large black bin that was probably the case to one of the machines in the garage that did something cool. I shook off the cobwebs and sawdust for Mallory while Pete opened the laptop again.

"Put in your password," Pete whispered.

I pushed it back to him and said, "I p p i s s i s s i m 1."

He pushed it back again to me, and I said, "It's 1Miississippi backwards."

Pete let out a loud laugh and quickly covered his mouth. "That is your security?" He asked and started typing, and I could tell there were several attempts.

"Next time no judgment please. It's not so easy. Give it to me before we are locked out." And then I sang to myself, "I pee pee I see saw I see sea I me 1," and then handed him back the computer.

I moved the chair next to Pete, and Mallory sat behind us, looking over our shoulders. We watched the map, the phone slowly getting closer. At least they weren't breaking any road laws getting to us.

My heart started beating faster. "Can they track my computer?"

All Pete did was give me a sideways glance to tell me no.

I looked at Sherrie, who was watching us from the back side of the garage. I knew she wanted answers but couldn't text her with Ben holding her phone.

"We stay in here until we hear otherwise. You got it?" Pete looked at Mallory and me.

Mallory, who had been mostly quiet since Chuck arrived, finally spoke, "Don't worry about me. Unless it's a bathroom, I have no energy for anything else."

Pete waited for me to agree, and I finally nodded. I wasn't sure where he thought I would be going at this point and didn't want to ask. There was no need or want on my part to play the role of hero.

Sherrie was finally able to leave Ben's side for a minute and came over to us. She asked, "What are you seeing on the computer?"

We couldn't answer because we heard some faint cries for Ben. The calling stopped, and then we heard some pounding.

"I think someone is trying to get in EG's garage," I whispered.

We heard another shout for Ben.

Pete jumped up and tried handing me the laptop. I tried pushing past him, and Sherrie tried to sneak around a tabletop saw. I thought Mallory was just trying to get out of the camp chair, and somehow we, minus Mallory, all ended up two feet farther back than when we started. I grabbed the laptop teetering between Pete and me and jammed it at Mallory, keeping her in the chair.

I remembered what Chuck had said just a few minutes ago about surviving certain situations. I kinda had to agree with the fact that I don't know how we had survived some things when we couldn't even take two steps without tripping on each other.

We were too slow to stop Ben who had managed to untangle himself from the blanket cocoon and was out the door before we could get to him. Sherrie was the first out the door, followed by me and Pete.

Sherrie and I turned the corner in time to see Ellie break away from Miller and run towards Ben and gobble him up in her arms. Miller took two giant steps towards Ellie before Pete rounded the corner. I didn't see the running lead or the first half of the leap that Pete took catapulting himself, but I had a front-row view of him body-slamming Miller to the ground.

Sherrie went to Ellie, who was kneeling and holding Ben in a bear hug. Sherrie was trying to shuffle them away from the melee on the ground, but they refused to move. Chuck had flown out of the house and went to help Pete—or not.

CHAPTER TWENTY-NINE

Mallory and I stood side by side, watching everything go down. I couldn't understand Chuck's actions as he seemed to be pulling at Pete. Ellie had released Ben from her embrace but held his face while she talked to him. She ignored all efforts to be escorted away.

After several moves, Chuck found his balance and extracted Pete from Miller. He flipped him onto his back a foot away and gingerly put his foot on Pete's shoulder, saying, "Take it easy."

All three men where huffing and puffing, and the rest of us were hardly breathing or moving.

It was only when Miller sat up that we saw a badge drop from around his neck. I couldn't read it, but I understood Pete had just attacked some type of federal agent.

Sherrie and I chorused a slow guttural, "*Shit.*"

All the men looked at us, and from behind us, Ben said, "Pit."

The seven-year-old boy captured everyone's attention when he repeated "Shit pit."

Ellie, who was holding his hand, gave it a tug and said a gentle "Shh."

Ben replied, "It's ok. It rhymes. Shit pit. That's what they taught me." Ben pointed to Sherrie and me. "I kept learning when you were away."

Laughter broke out from everyone.

Pete was now sitting up, holding his chest and accepted the hand from Miller who helped him up.

Miller gave Pete his truck keys and said, "I had to take your truck. Hoping to slow you guys down. I couldn't afford you guys following Ellie anymore than you did."

We should not have been surprised when EG's back door opened and Wyatt walked out, asking us all to come in.

Sherrie asked Chuck, "Anyone else in the clown car or any more surprises?"

"This is your circus not mine," Chuck replied, and those two walked inside.

Miller walked over to Ellie and Ben, and he addressed her, "You ok?"

Ellie nodded and squeezed Ben.

"You have some place you can go for a few days?"

Ellie nodded yes again.

"You were great. Not just today." Miller paused. "It will get harder, but you will be ok. No visiting Adam without your lawyer."

"Understood."

"Buddy, you did great too," Miller said to Ben.

Ben hid his face behind Ellie.

Ellie pulled him in front of her and said to him, "Say thank you to Mr. Miller."

Ben didn't move.

Ellie said to him, "It's because of him you and I can stay together."

Miller said, "I think Ellie is wrong."

Ben gripped Ellie so hard I thought she might bleed.

Miller continued. "It's because of her, her work, and you, big guy, that you'll be together forever. I was happy to assist."

"Thank you," Ellie said as a tear fell.

"I probably won't see you again. Maybe if they all go to trial. Agent Lindsey Abersole will be in touch for the next step."

Miller turned and walked up to Pete. I couldn't hear their exchange, but I saw them shake hands.

Pete held the back door open for Ellie, Ben, and Mallory. He waited for us, but Miller gave him a nod and Pete obliged and followed everyone inside.

The only thing moving for Sherrie and me was our hearts beating a hundred miles an hour.

Miller came over to us. "You two sure know how to step into some shit."

"We do that sometimes," Sherrie said.

"We can't help ourselves," I added.

"You got quite a reputation there, Ebony and Ivory."

Sherrie and I looked at each other to decipher Miller's words.

I said, "Jackson."

Last fall, my college boyfriend had accidentally gotten mixed up in something and pulled us into the mess. Federal agents raided EG's house looking for evidence we didn't have. At some point, we were given the code names Ebony and Ivory.

Sherrie repeated, "Jackson." And we both laughed.

"It was actually entertaining and infuriating having to dance around both of you," Miller said.

"We try our best," Sherrie answered.

We laughed again. Miller did not laugh. He turned and stepped away, and Sherrie and I took a step towards the house.

Miller reached back, touched my arm, and softly said, "Next time, the beer invite will have nothing to do with a case."

He walked away, and I barely registered his proposition. Four days ago, I would have been over the moon at this very idea, and now, I just found it weirdly inappropriate. To be honest, maybe slightly flattered but with zero interest.

Pete was at the kitchen island finishing the sandwich Sherrie had made him earlier, rubbing his shoulder and chest. Mallory laid my laptop on the island, and I assumed went to use EG's bathroom.

We found Chuck leaning against the bookshelf in the living room. Wyatt was talking in hushed tones, kneeling in front of Ellie and Ben who sat on the couch. Ellie was doing a lot of nodding.

Wyatt stood up and looked at Sherrie and me standing in the large entryway between the kitchen and living room. "I really don't know what to say to you two except I see way too much of you while I'm at work."

He left through the screened-in porch and got in his vehicle, which was parked behind Pete's truck. Miller was waiting in the passenger seat.

Ellie asked for crayons or any type of markers and some paper for Ben. Sherrie went through the kitchen junk drawer and I went through a couple of bookcase drawers, and together we came up with a half-dozen markers, three crayons, and a fair amount of paper.

It was Chuck who suggested Ellie take Ben upstairs to Sherrie's room, and the duo trotted up the stairs.

Pete went to his truck to finally retrieve his phone, and Mallory took a seat on the sofa. I took a seat at the head of the table.

We were silent while we waited for Pete, who came in carrying his phone and keys. He sat at the other end of the dining table.

Ellie came down the stairs. She stood on the landing, pulling on her sleeves, and not looking at anyone. She held our attention.

"I-I, sorry, I got . . . thank you for helping Ben. He is very fond of you, and he trusts you." Tears rolled down her cheeks.

Sherrie jumped up from the chair and pulled Ellie off the last step, wrapping her arms around her. It took probably twenty seconds for Ellie to either accept the hug or have the ability to move her arm because of Sherrie's tight embrace, but Ellie finally hugged her back.

Sherrie led her to the couch, and I got up and found the tissue box for Ellie.

She sat flat-footed and hunched over, clutching the tissues like a lifeline. "I never meant for you to be involved. Ben was supposed to stay with Maggie."

"You don't have to apologize," Sherrie said. "We're glad you two are safe."

Ellie nodded and didn't really look at us.

"Would you mind explaining what all happened? Are you safe? Is it over?" Sherrie asked.

Ellie nodded again. "I don't have much time until Ben calls me. Whenever something happens, I have him draw it out. It's our way of talking about the bad stuff without saying bad stuff."

"That's smart," Chuck said. "You have a real nice handle on how to deal with stuff."

Ellie just shrugged.

Usually, Sherrie was the master at getting people to talk, but it was Chuck that navigated the information from Ellie.

He said, "Wyatt gave me a brief rundown. How you helped the DEA. He said you were brilliant."

"Not so much." Ellie half laughed and sniffled before she sat back. "I had been keeping track of who was coming and going, license plate numbers, and if I saw pills or other stuff. I kept losing the little USB drives. I didn't want it on my school computer. That almost ruined everything and was why it took so long and why I ended up with the laptop. Mr. Miller figured I couldn't misplace that."

"Boy, was he wrong on that," Sherrie said, and the entire room broke out laughing.

Ellie sat back and folded up her knees to her chest while she spoke. "Everything was supposed to be done Thursday, but they were going to do a raid in Chicago. They wanted everything to happen all at the same time as not to tip anyone off. We needed to stall the final drop. I hid the pills. My brother Adam had been dealing for years. I think it started out with weed, but then pills came into the picture. We had people coming to the house and . . . not good people. I begged him to stop. He was making good money, and he thought nothing could stop him, not even nine months of jail. Our dad was gone for weeks at a time, working wherever and anywhere. I tried getting rid of the supply once, and Adam caught me so he hid it somewhere else. I started keeping track of who was coming and going. These men would show up and . . ." Ellie had a hard time finding her voice.

Sherrie spoke for the group. "You don't have to say anything that makes you uncomfortable."

"I know. I just owe you guys."

"No you don't. We just want you to be safe," I said.

"I was worried about Ben and being taken away. I was not even sure—" Tears were streaming down Ellie's cheeks. This was the longest minute of silence I'd sat through, before she spoke again, "I was not even sure Ben was family."

Sherrie, Pete, Mallory, and I all exchanged looks. Chuck never took his eyes away from Ellie.

"Six years ago, Adam's old girlfriend showed up with Ben. She said he belonged to Adam. She stayed around for six days before taking off and never coming back. We never really knew if she was telling the truth." Tears freely flowed now. "I was too scared to do one of those DNA tests in case it came back that he was not my nephew. People just assumed he was my brother."

"Regardless of any test results, you are that boy's family," Sherrie said.

"Tell that to the law," Ellie said. "Later, some people came to the house and—"

Ellie stopped talking, and Sherrie offered her some water. While we waited for Sherrie, we let silence hold the room. I didn't need to hear the words nor did Ellie have to tell us what the man did to her or Ben. That was her story, her privacy.

Ellie drank some water and, with her shaking hand, put the cup on the side table. "I needed a plan. I really started watching everything and recorded who was coming and going. I can be invisible, and they were too stupid and said things they shouldn't. After that man ... I went to the police. Then, one day, one of the guys that came to do the exchange I realized was a police officer."

I wasn't sure who echoed my gasp, but the room was in shock.

Ellie continued, "I hated River Bend and everyone in it. All that mattered was getting me and Ben out. I wanted revenge so I contacted the FBI after I turned eighteen so I could fight to take custody from Adam when he would be arrested.

"I didn't know it, but Mr. Miller was already here undercover. All the agencies confused me, or they did that to keep me confused. I just know the ATF was looking at drugs in the high school and someone was looking into the connection to the police. When the kid overdosed, everything went crazy and Mr. Miller wanted the operation shut down or at least to pull me out of it. I couldn't stop until I knew I had Ben. I am so happy Mr. Miller never stopped watching me and Ben." She shredded the tissues in her hand and let them drop on her lap. "That night in the alley, he saved me. I don't know where he came from, but those men were after me because they thought I took the pills. Mr. Miller hit the one man and chased after the other one."

"That was Thursday," Sherrie said.

Ellie nodded.

"I was just seconds behind it all. I watched that guy stagger and fall."

"I would never tell Mr. Miller where we would hide. He was not happy with that." Ellie took more water. "Freddie was so nice. He knew I was in some kind of trouble."

"From Peach's, grumpy baker Freddie?" Sherrie asked.

Ellie didn't even flinch and looked directly at Chuck. "Don't be getting him in trouble. All he did was give me a key to the unused space."

I noticed when Ellie defended Freddie and talked or acted on behalf of Ben, she was strong, decisive, and willing to march to war for people, but the second she talked about herself, she retreated into a turtle shell.

"Freddie is fine in my book, " Chuck said.

"Adam told me he was getting out, but I didn't believe him. He liked the money. There was supposed to be another exchange on Monday because of the failed one on Thursday. They did supply drops and money pick up on different days, and different people would do it. They had no idea when I was around or listening. I am good at sneaking around.

"Adam was supposed to hand everything over to Orange. They used code names like that stupid movie. Should've known better, everyone died in that movie. Orange was the guy in the alley, and he was freaked out because of the kid overdosing at school. He thought the police would be all over this town, and he wanted it Friday, but we had to stall until they were ready in Chicago.

They didn't tell me much. Mr. Miller is nice, but he did not always tell me much. Adam had to show up empty-handed. Blue, he is the one with the scar by his ear, showed up at our house when Adam realized it was me that took the pills and cash. I took off, and Blue saw me."

Ellie was losing me on the date and order of events, but I clearly understood this was tough and she had been through some tough shit.

"How do you get around town?" Chuck asked.

"I gotta car, but it doesn't always go so well. I bike. A lot of walking," Ellie answered.

Ben called Ellie, and before he even finished her name, she was off the couch and yelling, "I'm on my way."

She stepped onto the stair landing and turn to go up but pivoted to us. "Maggie's amazing. Always taking Ben when things were bad or I knew a drop would happen. I never meant for her to give you trouble, bringing Ben here." She didn't wait for a reply; her attention was on Ben.

"Ellie," I called after her.

We heard her shout to Ben, and she appeared on the stair landing seconds later.

"Did you come here Sunday night?" I asked. "Check on Ben?"

"Or spend the night on the patio?" Sherrie asked.

"I wanted Ben to know I was ok." She looked at her feet when she spoke.

"The door was locked," Sherrie said.

"The window from the porch was open, and the screen popped out easily. I knew you guys weren't home. I was hoping to find his backpack and put a green army man in it so he would know I was watching over him. I couldn't find the bag, so I put it in the tent that I assumed you'd made for him. I closed the window because I didn't want anyone else getting in."

Pete chuckled at the irony.

"I saw you pick up the mug and need the key. I needed the laptop," Ellie confessed.

"Were two guys following you?" I asked.

"I'm always pretty careful. I try to be. I didn't see anyone that night and even came back and slept on the porch."

"Where did you go in between?" Sherrie asked.

Ellie just turned and went up to Ben.

"At least some of the mystery is solved?" I said.

"Is that why you were acting strange on the patio when we came in?" Chuck said.

"Nothing gets past you. We keep a paint can opener on the windowsill between the screen and glass so if we need to get in, we don't break a nail pushing the window up. She must have pushed it in when she crawled in and didn't know to put it back."

Chuck just shook his head.

I answered his silent dismay. "We do just fine." I kicked Sherrie's foot. She was suddenly busy on her phone. "Hey, get your head out of your phone and help me defend our key procedures."

"I'm ordering pizza. Just assuming everyone is as hungry as I am," Sherrie answered.

"Ted's Pizza not Pizza Guru," Pete said.

"Definitely Ted's for delivery. Before you object or take off, Chuck, I got you the protein-packed salad and I added fries for Mallory."

Chuck acknowledged Sherrie with a head nod.

Mallory was watching him out of the corner of her eye, despite having a direct view. She didn't respond to Sherrie. It seemed as if it was too soon to answer after Chuck.

"Food is ordered. We know who has been sneaking out of EG's house. Are we assuming Adam is arrested or with police? Miller is or was undercover. Did you know all along, Chuck?"

"It wasn't until I started looking at her laptop after we got here that I figured something was up. The way the system was set up was familiar. Oh, and when those two drove up in Pete's truck, Agent Miller had his badge hanging around his neck. Nice tackle by the way, Pete."

"Glad it looked good, but I think I jammed my shoulder. Didn't even see the badge. I just saw her trying to run from him."

I noticed Pete rubbing his chest again and couldn't help but wonder if the badge had sliced into him.

"Who do you think it was coming here after Ellie left when Jorge was searching the house? Miller, Adam, or what did she call them—Blue and Orange?" Sherrie said.

"From Jorge's description, it doesn't sound like Miller. Could Blue get from here to the diner so fast? It was only Blue in the parking lot," I said.

"Hey, Chuck, what did Wyatt say when he was here?" Sherrie asked.

"He was here only a minute," he answered.

Sherrie shook her head. "That is not an answer."

I jumped in. "When he met us outside Pearl's house and sent us home, it was a personal record for him not disclosing information. Give it up. We will know sooner than later. Plus, Ellie knows who the dirty cop is because he showed up at her house."

"Cole," Chuck said.

No one had any response, and Chuck needed to be prompted so Sherrie gave him some help. "Read the room, big fella. We don't know who that is."

"Cole Gundersen. Been around about six months," Chuck answered.

"Dark hair, crew cut, about the same size as Pete?" I asked.

"Sounds about right," Chuck said.

"He was there Thursday night blocking off the alley when I went to pick up Sherrie. He saw me pick up that travel mug," I said.

Chuck shook his head. "I don't have many more answers just that the police knew they had issues inside the department. Everyone was under scrutiny, but it turns out it was just him."

"That doesn't necessarily mean it was him and a sidekick Sunday evening. Why come here not in uniform and take off when Jorge spotted him, or them?" I said.

"Do we know what happened to the guy in the alley? The one that dropped and EMS took away?" Sherrie asked.

"I told you everything I know," Chuck said.

"Doubt that, but I believe that's all you're going to tell us," I said, managing to get a smirk from Chuck.

Ellie came down the step, Ben following her with his backpack.

"We're going now. We put you through enough stuff," Ellie said.

Sherrie and I stood up together. I felt lost with the thought of them leaving.

Sherrie spoke first. "Go where? You can't leave."

I threw in, "Sherrie ordered pizza for everyone."

Ellie shook her head. "We can't."

"It's on us," Sherrie said.

"You've done enough. We can't ask for more."

"You didn't ask. We're offering," Sherrie said.

"Please, I want some pizza," Ben begged.

"I don't think the girls are going to let you leave," Chuck said.

Ellie nodded. "Ok, ok, we can stay."

Ben bounced up and down.

"Ben, are you able to draw each of us a picture, like a place mat at a restaurant?" Sherrie said.

Ben nodded. He looked at Ellie, and she shooed him back upstairs and then sat down on the landing.

"Where are you going tonight?" I asked.

"Maggie's."

"You two can stay here tonight in Sherrie's room," I said.

"Absolutely. He's comfortable here," Sherrie echoed.

Ellie smiled. "That he is."

"Do you know how your dad is doing?" I asked. "Have you been able to see him?"

She shook her head. "Maggie saw him. She was there with Don because of his heart. They say Dad might have lost some hearing and weren't sure about his vision because he was so close to the blast."

"What happened?" I asked. "You were there and then hid at Pearl's?"

"God, you guys are good. My dad was home, and he wasn't supposed to be. As usual, he and Adam were fighting about something. I tried breaking up the fight. Adam took off through the front. I didn't want to be there, so I went out the back. I saw my dad drop his cigarette on the back porch, and he thought he snubbed it out but he must have kicked it back. It lit an old box of fireworks and a propane tank. One set off the other one and then hit the electrical panel."

"So your dad and brother saw you," I asked. Ellie nodded.

My mind flashed to the pictures on the wall in their hiding spot. The BE + ES. "This might be an odd question."

Ellie just rolled her shoulders like nothing could bother her now.

"What are your middle names?"

"Ben Edward, and I am actually Sparrow Ellison."

"You are named after your mom?" I said.

"Yup, she was Sparrow Ellison, and I am Sparrow Ellison Hughes." She was playing with the hem of her jeans looking down as she spoke. "I look exactly like her, and it just kills my dad to look at me sometimes. It was after my mom died I wanted to be called Ellie. I didn't want to hear her name every day because it hurt too much."

My heart broke listening to her.

The pieces shattered when she said, "Do you know what it feels like when you're six and see your name on a tombstone?"

Sherrie went to sit next to her on the step and leaned her shoulder into Ellie's. It was the warmest non-hug she could give. Ellie didn't pull away, and that seemed to be the most she could give back to Sherrie at the time.

"Where is your car now?" Chuck asked.

Leave it up to him to be the practical one.

Ellie continued to tug at a loose string.

I said, "Chuck is going to find out one way or another so you might as well tell him."

"Jameson College. The yellow lot."

"Do you know what will happen to your brother?" I asked.

"It depends on how much he helps them. I may have hurt him by supplying all the information I tracked and recorded. There's not much for him to bargain with."

Chuck crossed his arms. "You didn't put him in that situation. Adam caused his own problems."

"Believe me I know that," Ellie said.

A car door slamming out front turned our attention away from Ellie but towards something I was not ready for but should have expected.

CHAPTER THIRTY

Car doors slamming made us all jump, except of course Chuck.

"Food?" Mallory said. She had been so quiet I had almost forgotten she was here.

"Problem," Pete said.

Ellie was on her feet within half a second and Sherrie right after her.

Chuck was at the front door before Pete could finish explaining, "The passenger, that's the guy I kicked out of the bar when he was asking about you guys."

Chuck instructed all of us upstairs. Ellie probably would have been at Ben's side already if Sherrie hadn't been blocking her way.

It was fortunate that for the first time in years Ellie was not able to slip away. She said,

"That's Lucas who was driving. He's all right. I can't see the other one."

"The driver is Justin," Sherrie said. "The guy with the hat."

"I know that's Lucas. He's two years ahead of me. He lives a block away from me," Ellie said.

"He was with me in the alley that night the guy dropped," Sherrie said.

Just then, a second car pulled up with a box light on top.

Chuck was out the front door and Pete behind him. Mallory was at the window first followed by me, then Sherrie. I assumed Ellie too, but she was out the front door before we could stop her.

The first guy delivering the pizza took one look at Chuck striding towards him, turned, and practically threw our food to the two other guys before running to his car.

Chuck grabbed him by the collar and patted him down while the other two stood there stunned. He then escorted our deliveryman to the porch and told the others to follow.

Mallory had kneeled on the couch, looking through the living room window, and I helped her stand up. We got on the porch in time to see the three guys sitting on the couch, Chuck standing over them, tossing their wallets back to them. Pete was holding the food with Sherrie and Ellie next to him, leaving just enough room for Mallory and me on the porch.

"Talk," Chuck said.

He could have great compassion, like he did getting Ben to talk, and then he could install fear with one word or a look.

The three guys sat there frozen.

Ellie inserted herself in front of Chuck. Proving again you always want Ellie on your side. Chuck just let Ellie do her thing.

"Lucas, you better start talking. You hurt anyone of them here, I will personally cut off your balls and feed them to your brother and idiot number two."

"I didn't do anything," said the guy on the left.

"Justin, were you guys here the other night?" Sherrie asked the guy that ten seconds ago Ellie had called Lucas.

The guy in the middle elbowed the guy on the right. "I think she's talking to you."

"We were here the other night." The guy on the right answered Ellie, who was still just a foot away from them.

She was a hundred pounds less and at least a foot shorter than Chuck, but she had instilled as much fear in the boys as he had.

"We just needed to talk to Sherrie."

"Why?" Ellie demanded.

The guys looked at each other.

Ellie said, "You and Adam were friends. Don't tell me you're as stupid as him. You taking the shit he was selling? Dumbass."

"Not dumb enough to blow up my own house." The guy on the right cracked up.

Ellie lunged for him, and it was because of Chuck the guy was safe.

"But just dumb enough to be sitting here," she snapped.

"I would start talking if I were you, or I will let her go," Chuck said.

The guy on the left finally spoke up and looked at Sherrie. "We just wanted to make sure we had our stories straight."

"We didn't do anything wrong," Sherrie said. "Vince called the police, and you nearly passed out from the blood."

The guys just sat there. I was losing my patience, and the smell of hot pizza was overwhelming.

The guy closest to us stood up and came closer, standing near the door, almost to distance himself. "Just fess up. They're not cops, and at this point, no one cares."

"I was the one there Thursday night," said the guy with the hat on, who Ellie had called Lucas.

"We established that fact," Sherrie said.

"Yes, but I'm Lucas, and that's my brother Justin. I'm twenty and he's—"

"No, no, no," Sherrie stammered. "I am good with IDs when I'm at the bar."

"Not so much," said the guy with the hat who now managed to find some humor. "Plus, I thought you knew. You called me Lou."

"Your buddy called you that, and I thought it was like lieutenant because you called him captain."

"We call everyone captain. The Lou was a slip. He caught himself before he said Lucas."

"So you needed me to say Justin, Vince, and I saw what happened in the alley when I gave my statement. Of course I would say Justin because that was your name as I knew it." Sherrie turned to the guy standing. "You're the third one that took off. I never told the cops about you. I thought that was a big deal, leaving out the name of the witness."

Pete asked, "Why did you take off that night?"

The guy standing didn't say anything.

Sherrie said, "Let me guess, you're fourteen."

That got a laugh from the peanut gallery sitting on the couch. "I'm twenty-one." He left us hanging.

Ellie pieced it together. "You recognized who was on the ground. You've been buying from him or Adam."

"Just once. But I know a stupid situation and when to get out, so I took off."

"So, in the bar this morning, why were you being coy?" Pete asked.

"I was asking for Sherrie's number so that one of us wouldn't get busted for underage drinking again, and I was . . . sorry about that."

"We cool," Pete said.

I looked at him and saw he was now short one box of food. Mallory stood in the corner munching on the fries, but at least she didn't have her head in her phone.

"We thought we had the wrong house the other night when we saw some guys inside. When he saw your name come up for delivery, he gave us a heads-up that you were finally home so we thought we would talk to you."

"You guys work out what you're going to say on your own. My statement just has the names Vince and Justin with no mention of the guy that took off. Just know if you guys are using or do something stupid, my memory is long and I won't be shy to correct myself," Sherrie said.

"Honest." The kid raised his hand like he was taking an oath. "I'm not into that shit anymore."

Justin—I mean, Lucas asked, "So are we good?"

"Sure," Sherrie said.

"How about we celebrate with a few beers and that pizza," Lucas said.

"Why don't you spend some time working on your sense of humor before you turn twenty-one. And no you're not invited in."

The three guys filed out of the porch, and the screen door slammed shut.

Lucas turned back to Ellie. "Sorry to hear about your house. You ok? Ma went to check if you and the kid were around. I'm supposed to tell you Shelby is home, and you can crash with her in her room if you need."

"We're ok. Tell your mom thanks." Ellie turned in a flash and ran up to Ben.

The rest of us staggered inside.

"Pete throw the food on the table, and I will get us paper plates. Beer anyone?" I asked.

Sherrie and Pete took me up on the beer. Ellie came down with Ben, who passed out pictures to everyone.

"Ben, would you like chocolate milk?" I said.

He looked at Ellie, who gave him a head nod before he said, "Yes, please."

Ellie added, "Can you make that two?"

Mallory popped up with "Make it three."

There was little talking while I was gathering the beverages, and everyone was munching away. A few minutes later, we were all sitting around the table filling our bellies and silently reflecting on the day, each taking turns talking with Ben about the pictures he had drawn for us.

Chuck brought us back to reality. "Ellie, was that you a couple months ago looking into the camera system at Peach's?"

"After Freddie gave me the key, I just wanted to see the view of the back door. Sorry," she said.

"Impressive. It's not top-level security, but you did a decent job of covering your tracks."

I was waiting for a thank-you from Ellie. I was quite surprised when she leveled up with Chuck.

"I wouldn't recommend using the same PC for three functions."

She said other stuff, but it was nothing I could understand. Before we knew it, they were in a tech talk.

Mallory was on her phone. Ben was sitting next to me, tracing my hand on a paper plate.

Sherrie was grilling Pete about a few other bar regulars, making sure they were of age. "How about we not tell Aaron about my little mishap. I am trying to get my job back."

It was a simple statement that under other conditions would have been a throwaway comment and everyone would have moved on. However, tossing Aaron's name in the air was a louder blast than the propane tank exploding at Ellie's house.

Mallory kept her head down, but the typing slowed.

I could feel Pete looking at me, and I looked at Chuck, who was playing it off as if he hadn't heard. We knew he heard all.

He kept his focus on Ellie and asked, "You planning on staying here?"

"I think at least for now. Ben has to get through the school year, and I guess I have to see how my dad is doing." She paused and thought she was reading our minds. "I don't care what people say about me or my family. I learned to ignore it. Don't have enough money to go far enough away where people won't hear about the Hughes family. I'd rather people face me when I know they're talking about me. I want to show them we are bigger and stronger than stupid words."

"Would a job help?" Chuck asked.

"I'm working at Peach's," Ellie said.

Chuck shook his head. "How about real money. Come work for me. I need about twenty-five to thirty hours a week to start. Flexible with hours. If it works and you know as much as I think you do, we can turn the job into more if you're interested."

"Absolutely but my time with school and Ben . . ." Ellie said with almost a full smile.

"We can work around all that," Chuck replied.

No one was more surprised than Chuck when Ellie plunged over and gave him a hug. "Ben, did you hear that. I got a job."

"Making coffee," Ben said.

"Not anymore. I will be punching buttons," Ellie said.

"You like punching letters on your computer."

She walked around the large table and hugged Ben. Chuck went to the kitchen with his Styrofoam container. I heard him place it in the garbage and his fork in the dishwasher.

Ellie followed him, and I couldn't understand their exchange. We were surprised when Ellie raised her voice, and Chuck responded, "It's a condition of the job."

"Then no deal. You can't blackmail my employment every time you think you're right. I will just stay at Peach's," Ellie said.

We froze around the table. The highs and lows of the day were too much at this point.

Chuck replied, "But am I wrong?"

"Fine. You win this one."

"Great. See you on Thursday at ten." Chuck came back to the dining table. "Pete, can you give me a hand? We'll be back in less than an hour."

"Sure, man." Pete got up and looked at each of us. "I guess I'll be back in an hour." He turned to leave but hesitated for a minute.

I was hoping for something more from him, at least more than the others got in the way of a goodbye, even knowing it would be highly awkward and I would be seeing him later. But we all heard the same thing from Pete.

"Can you all manage just to stay here and keep the trouble to a minimum?"

"There is no sense in telling them anything," Chuck said as he walked out.

It was too dark out to see them once they left the porch, but we could hear them get in Chuck's Jeep and leave.

I turned to Ellie. "You must be pretty good at computer stuff to impress Chuck. Understand that it's no pity offer. He doesn't do pity."

"It's always been interesting to me. I spent many hours at the library growing up so I wouldn't be home. There was a guy there that showed me how to do stuff, and it kinda stuck."

"You probably haven't had to process most everything yet, but where can you stay until your house is ready? You have an Aunt Dawn, the one on the news?" Sherrie asked.

Ellie let out a little laugh. "That was her fifteen minutes of fame. Not once has she contacted me directly. I don't think now after all these years she is going to offer help."

"What about Maggie's? She's been helpful. Can you stay there?"

"Probably. If not, we have our places we can go."

The storage unit and the hallway behind Peach's flashed in my mind. An overwhelming sadness flushed through me. There was a need for me to fix things. Things that weren't my problem but caused heartache.

I took a big leap in my suggestion with putting two people in an awkward situation or providing an ingenious idea.

"Hey, Ellie and Mallory, I am going to say something, and I don't want either one of you to answer. I don't have time or energy to corner both of you separately to feel you out before I say it."

Ellie stood up and took Ben's hand. Sherrie, who had stood up with the empty pizza boxes, sat back down, and Mallory actually looked up from her phone.

"Sherrie, can you take Ben upstairs?"

Sherrie's lower lip stuck out, and I knew she was disappointed to not be one in my puzzle, but she followed along and took Ben upstairs.

Ellie slowly sat down and kept her eyes on me before fixating on a spot on the table, and Mallory surprisingly kept her phone down.

"I was just thinking. Mallory is moving into a house soon and will need help. Ellie and Ben need a place to stay for a bit. I don't know how big or where the house is or if either one of you like each other, but I think you could be good for each other."

Mallory kept her porcelain face still while she processed the information, and Ellie hadn't moved.

"Like I said both of you think about it."

Mallory surprised me when she spoke. "It's two bedrooms, but we can fix up the basement for more space. It's one block from the Rivers Elementary School."

"Why?" Ellie didn't look up, and her voice was shaking. "Why would you want to do that? Look at the trouble we caused today."

"Claudia's right. I need help. I hardly know the first thing about babies, and I will need to research and write for work. I'm not sure how much I can count on Claudia and Sherrie to help babysit."

I let out a big laugh.

Ellie looked up, and her eyes were swollen.

Mallory kept up with the sales pitch. "We'll even get some cute guys to cut the grass."

Ellie dropped her head into her hands and started crying. Through the sobs, she said, "Why? Why are you all doing this?"

"Helping you?" I asked.

She rocked back and forth, never looking up.

I went over to her and rubbed her back. "That's easy. Because you would do the same for someone else. When we were on the porch with the guys, you were ready to tear them apart because we thought they were after us, not after you but after Sherrie and me. You jumped in front of Chuck, and nobody does that."

Ellie looked up and smiled. "Ok."

I was feeling good about coming up with this idea, and them both liking it energized me. "You guys have some stuff to talk about, and I will be cleaning up in the kitchen."

Sherrie came downstairs and said, "Ben's getting tired, and I didn't know if I should let him fall asleep."

"I need to get up there," Ellie said, "but when he falls asleep I'll be back down."

"If you want to shower or bathe Ben, there are fresh towels in the closet in the bathroom," Sherrie said.

Ellie just nodded in agreement before she went upstairs.

CHAPTER THIRTY-ONE

"What did I miss?" Sherrie asked.

I looked at Mallory. "I didn't mean to put you on the spot. It just popped in my head."

"She is obviously great with Ben, and it'll be nice to have someone around to help," Mallory said. "Honestly, the fact that it will irritate my mother that she won't have free run of my house is just an added bonus. My mother means well but doesn't know when to stop."

"I suggested Mallory and Ellie and Ben live together for a while," I said, finally answering Sherrie's question.

"Aw, look at that. You had the idea of the week! It's only Monday, so the rest of the week might fall apart," Sherrie said.

I chucked a piece of pizza crust at her, and she batted it back to me.

"Mallory, I guess you have to wait for Pete to return to give you a ride. Do you need anything?" I asked.

"I'm just going to get myself some water if that's ok."

"Go crazy in the kitchen. I'll take a glass too," I said, and then I stacked the pizza boxes.

Mallory extracted herself from the dining room chair, and I couldn't help wonder about her real due date again. I had no idea about how big her belly should have been, but she seemed further along than five or six months.

Sherrie was collecting the pictures Ben had made for everyone. She moved Mallory's phone off the picture of a race car. The screen was lit up, and Sherrie was looking for a clean spot to put it down when something caught her eye. She scrolled up on the phone, and her eyebrows went up, her back stiffened, and her right leg started to swing like a nutcracker.

Something serious was on Mallory's phone. So serious that Sherrie didn't even have a snide remark. I had to buy Sherrie more time so I asked Mallory for a glass of water.

Sherrie walked into the kitchen, pulled a pot out of the cabinet, and filled it with water. Mallory stepped around Sherrie, who was in a trancelike state at this point, and handed me the glass of water that I nearly forgot I had asked for thirty seconds ago.

Sherrie put the pot of water on the stove and turned on the burner. From the corner of my eye, I saw Mallory looking for her phone. She pushed the pizza boxes to the side and felt the pockets of her pants several times.

"I have it in here," Sherrie announced from the kitchen.

Mallory looked at me. I gave no reaction, but my insides were flipping. She walked into the kitchen.

Sherrie was holding the phone over the pot on the stove.

I was mesmerized by the scene. It was like watching a thriller movie when the murderer was about to be revealed. I stepped sideways into the kitchen since Mallory was blocking most of the doorway.

I took a seat at the island, like I was in the movie and had no speaking parts, just part of the scenery.

Sherrie was holding the phone with two fingers like she was getting ready to drop a chicken leg into the fryer. "We told you from the start. No story. No articles. Give me one reason why I shouldn't drop your phone into the water."

"Everything is backed up to the cloud. I won't lose what I wrote." There was no despair and no crack in Mallory's voice. I should remember never to play poker with her.

"That's not a reason not to drop your phone. It still will cost you big-time."

"Nothing had been published or sent to my editor. You know the papers and television are reporting the house being blown up, a drug bust, and a bad cop. There is no mention of Ben."

"Most decent media outlets won't report a child's name so you have to do better than that."

I was watching this exchange like a statue, only my eyes were moving. Mallory was right that most likely all this was already being reported on. Not sure who knew about Gundersen being a bad cop or how fast that would get out.

Mallory said, "I would need your approval before it would go to print anywhere."

"Bullshit." Sherrie lowered her hand six inches. "Throw in *allegedly* or other fun words that will skirt around the legality, and you are off the hook and we are plastered all over."

"We?" I didn't even know I said that out loud until Sherrie answered me.

"Yes, *we*. This one here has been writing a story about us."

"Us? Why? Did you miss the bigger story about the undercover agent and drug bust in our lovely town? You got issues if you can't spot the story."

Sherrie's arm must have been getting tired because she tried switching hands. With the steam building up, she nearly lost the grip on the phone.

"Would you please move my phone away from that pot," Mallory asked.

Sherrie crossed her arms over her chest, tucking the phone out of reach and the boiling water.

"Remember in the diner when I said I was having work issues? I can write any crime story or pull information from a police report with details and facts. I've been listening to my mother's police scanner for decades, and I know facts, police shorthand, and lingo. My editor tells me I am missing the 'human interest' side of the story. I need to develop that more if I want more print space. You two are a gold mine of human interest."

"Yes, we are." Sherrie walked three steps over to me, and we high-fived.

"See, right there. I can't write that stuff. You guys are full of animation and life. You are the story I could write so I get the assignment I want. There's something going on with the governor and I think interviewing the first lady is the angle to take, but my editor says I don't have the soft touch to approach her. I need to prove her wrong and get the story.

"Sherrie, the way Ben took to you and how you always have an action plan. I was dizzy watching you at Aaron's house in the morning, doing laundry and orchestrating our exit even before I knew the time of day. Claudia, never leaving Sherrie's side and coming to her rescue each night and tracking down the video from Peach's is all amazing stuff. You should be proud."

"We are good with what we do but don't need anyone else knowing. Sherrie can TikTok the crap out of biking around and the best spots for a beer and view of the river up and down the Wisconsin coast, and I will keep posting about cute pets that check into the hotel. That's where we draw the line."

"You really can't stop me," Mallory said.

I felt like the wind got sucked out of me. Sherrie turned up the burner and raised the phone above the pot again.

Mallory pleaded, "But I am not going to. I will not take it to my editor."

"How can we trust you? We said no from the beginning, yet you've got a catalog of crap on us."

"You have to believe me. Now can I have my phone back?" Mallory said. "You can record me saying you have my word and can sue me for any profits."

"That is a bogus offer." Sherrie was gritting through her teeth. "One story without money can still lead to more work for you, and we are still sitting out there for everyone to know and be all up in our business. You can't find two people less interested in fame. Give me a real offer, or you lose your phone."

Mallory seemed to be struggling with her words and any resolution. Something suddenly popped into my head. I looked at Sherrie, and she nodded like we had the same idea: tell us who's the baby's daddy.

For the first time in a long time, Sherrie and I missed connecting our thoughts, but she nailed it. I was not prepared for what she said next.

"Tell us what's between you and Chuck."

Mallory actually took a step back and into the doorjamb, which she clutched for balance. She was weighing her options. "If I were to tell you, there is nothing you could hold over me because you wouldn't do anything with it. You're too nice."

"Don't be so sure. We're not all sugar and spice," Sherrie said. "We need to know your secret so you won't write our story."

Sherrie sat on the counter next to the stove. Mallory came forward and sat on a stool near me, closed her eyes, took a deep breath, and slowly began to talk. "You guys know that the Rhomily boys, Aaron and Chuck, are good and loyal. Loyal to the end. All that military training about loyalty and being brought up with values that run deep.

Well, I learned where that loyalty stays is a matter of who you ask first."

The story had barely started, and I was already sweating through my sweatshirt all over again. She was talking slightly louder than a whisper, and with my heart pounding, it was difficult to hear her.

"This is not easy for me to say."

We had no intention of stopping her or even giving encouraging words to continue, this was all her.

"Aaron and I had been dating. Well, I was dating, and he was planning to be in married mode. I will skip most of that. It doesn't matter so much. One day I realized I was pregnant. I freaked out. I knew there was no discussing it with him. He would have raised a child with or without me. I just couldn't at the time. I was young and had a decent start to my career. Anyway, none of that matters. I had no one I could trust with this. Not friends, definitely not my mom or even my dad. I needed not to be pregnant so I made arrangements for that."

I was so still you would have thought I was a piece of furniture. My emotions were at a zero level because absorbing all this information was way too much, and I couldn't sort the emotions out without missing everything she was saying.

"I am not proud of any of this. I was young and seemingly alone in a situation I wasn't ready for.

"The thing is, when you go to one of those places, you need to bring someone along. There was not one friend I could trust with this information. So who do you call when you need a loyal friend? I told Aaron someone at a paper in Texas was interested in my writing and I was going for an interview. I made sure it was when Aaron wasn't available. I had Chuck drive me to the airport. I had it all worked out. He dropped me at the airport, and I taxied to a hotel. The next day when he was supposed to pick me up from the airport, I gave him the new address, and he had no choice but to wait and be my person.

"Talk about seeing someone mad. The entire ride not one word was spoken. Not even when he dropped me off at my place. It turns out Aaron was there, at my place, setting up a surprise for when he thought I was to return the next day. While he was there, he had to have seen my work computer and that it was not with me on the fake work interview, and then he also saw my small overnight bag when I got out of Chuck's car.

"I assumed he jumped to the conclusion that Chuck and I cheated on him. Aaron walked out of my place without speaking to me. I don't know what happened between the two of them, but at best, Chuck was screwed no matter what he said or did. He either had to admit to a nonexistent affair or that he had just driven his brother's almost-fiancée to abort his child. Two days later, my stuff from his place was in a box outside my door, and a week later, I returned his stuff—including the ring and some champagne he'd brought over for the surprise he was setting up and had forgotten to take it when he stormed out—in a box outside his door as I drove out of town to Chicago.

"I never thought what I was doing would put a wedge between them. That was probably my only regret in the whole thing. I understand they are past it, but as you can see, Chuck is content to not have anything to do with me."

My head was swirling, ears ringing, and my stomach had dropped. I remained frozen, praying there was no more to the story.

Sherrie pushed herself off the counter. She brought three mugs, chamomile tea bags, and the boiling water over to the island. She put down Mallory's phone and said, "Can't let good water go to waste."

Mallory gave her a smile of appreciation for the peace offering.

"As I said, I am not proud of what happened between them. If you want loyal, Chuck is your guy." Mallory wrapped her hands around the steaming mug of tea. "Never before have I told anyone what I did."

"I feel like I should say something, but I don't know what," Sherrie said.

"There is not much to say after that. Don't worry, and please believe me when I say I won't write your story."

"Was the ring at least amazing?" Sherrie quipped.

Mallory was raising the mug of tea to take a sip and put it down. She lowered her head.

Had Sherrie gone too far with that semi-tacky question?

"I couldn't look at it at first. Who knows if he had even known he left it behind with the champagne and flowers. I knew what I did was bad, and I couldn't bring myself to look at it. Then, almost as a penalty to myself, I needed to see what I'd lost."

She took a drink of the tea and had a nervous chuckle when she admitted, "Is it bad not to like it? It didn't make the whole situation better, but I was more confused that he had thought I'd like the narrow pear-shaped style of the diamond. Then it hit me that it was probably a family heirloom, but that still didn't make it any prettier."

The three of us giggled mostly to let out the weight of everything Mallory just said.

The screen door slammed shut.

"Saved by the bell. Give me another minute, and who knows what else I would have told you two," Mallory said.

She passed Pete walking into the kitchen, and he took Mallory's seat.

"What'd I miss?" he asked.

Sherrie and I just let out a laugh. "Claud orchestrated a pretty good situation. Ellie and Ben are going to live with Mallory when she moves into her new house."

"Nicely done. I think," Pete said.

"What do you mean you *think*?" I asked.

"How should I know if that's a good thing?"

I nodded. "Fair point."

Sherrie's phone lit up, and she plopped herself onto the living room couch leaving Pete and me alone in the kitchen. Mallory took a seat on the smaller couch with her phone back in her hands.

Pete leaned over, and I could feel his breath. My heart did a little dance.

"I'm sorry," he said.

My heart dropped. He was backing out of when we kissed. Either the kiss or me didn't do anything for him. He wanted to know what it would be like, and apparently it didn't meet his needs. My eyes welled up, and I shut them to block out his next words, but thankfully I was wrong.

Pete whispered, "I'm sorry. I totally heard everything. It's safe."

My face was hot, and my reaction was not swift. "Shhhit."

"What's wrong?" Ellie asked as she walked in.

Pete answered, "Claudia's embarrassed because I heard her fart."

"It was the chair and you know it." I punched him in the arm.

Ellie laughed. "I'm just getting some water and going back up."

"Do you need anything, tonight or tomorrow? Can you get in your house?"

"I spoke to Pearl. She said she went in and got some clothes for me and Ben and washed them. Stan boarded up the hole in the back wall. I will let my dad figure out the house with all the electrical issues and what smells like smoke. That's his problem."

Pete chimed in, "Chuck and I got your car, and it's parked next door. Jorge is taking a look at it. He'll leave the key under the floor mat."

Ellie left us and went upstairs. Pete and I joined the others in the living room.

"I think I'm officially done for the night. I may never leave the couch," Sherrie said.

"You're not moving to the porch?" I asked.

The porch was a favorite spot among many who visited. The comfy couch on a screened-in porch with the softest blanket ever was the best version of sleeping under the stars. You couldn't see the stars, but you could hear the crickets and not worry about mosquitos. It beat a tent or a stuffy room on a summer night.

"If I manage to extract myself from this couch, I may take your bed if you want the porch," Sherrie said.

"Deal. Let me get my running clothes so I don't wake you at six. I want a sunrise river run before I have to work," I said.

"I have to figure out if I have a job," Pete said.

"Well, I have to go back home to my parents' place and field questions on what I was doing all day. How does researching house explosions and bad cops sound?" Mallory said.

"Sounds like you're inviting a lot of questions with that," I said.

Sherrie added, "I think that sounds perfect."

"Pete, would you mind giving me a ride?" Mallory asked.

"Of course." Pete looked at us. "You guys good?"

"Thanks for your help. Maybe you should stop answering when we call," Sherrie said.

"Sometimes it's not all bad," Pete answered without looking at anyone.

I didn't know how this day would end, but I hadn't expected it to be with Pete and Mallory walking out together. It was just a simple ride, but I was jealous of the alone time she would have with him.

CHAPTER THIRTY-TWO

After Pete and Mallory left, Sherrie went to use EG's bathroom, and I stood in the center of the living room trying to assess everything that had gone down in the last few days. I got a little overwhelmed, and tears streaked down my face.

The lights made me a little dizzy, and I felt out of control and didn't like it. I ran upstairs to my room to collect myself. A flappy pajama T-shirt made me feel exposed, so I threw on my running clothes as pj's. I needed something snug to hold me together.

When I went downstairs, Sherrie was in the kitchen, and I went straight for the porch. Sherrie came out with two beers.

"No tea?" I asked.

"That tea shit is for EG. I don't know how she drinks so much of it."

"I wonder what she would think about everything that happened these past few days and what we just heard in her kitchen. Can you believe Mallory?" I said.

"That was diabolical. I didn't know what she was going to say, but I never imagined that."

"Thought you were going to ask about the baby daddy."

"I figured that would come out eventually. She is going to want someone in that delivery room, and from the sounds of it, it's probably not going to be her mother."

I held up my beer bottle. "Here's to our good mothers, families, and friends."

Sherrie and I clinked our bottles, and we both took a long sip of beer.

"Do you think Pete is smart enough to understand your invitation to come back here and find you on the patio?" Sherrie asked.

"Probably not, but your offer to sleep in my bed to give us space was generous. I appreciate it. Are you seriously good with it all?"

"Absolutely. Otherwise, I wouldn't have said something to him." Sherrie smiled.

"When did you say something? Are you already taking credit? I'm not sure anything more will happen."

"More? So something happened?" Sherrie asked.

"Nice try, don't deflect. You go first, what did you say?"

"Remember when you came home from car shopping, and I said I did something dumb."

"I thought you meant any of your late-night stops in the alley or agreeing to a thirty-six-hour babysitting marathon."

"I'm ok with all that considering how it turned out. Actually, I'm ok with this too. When I met you guys for breakfast and watched you two interact, so natural and comfortable around each other, I just knew you should be together. However, I know Pete will second-guess things because of our two and a half dates and his boss being your ex so I decided to speed up things. I called him, and let's say I just gave him my blessing and a little push. I had no idea you were five feet away car shopping when I called him. He didn't say anything to you about me being obnoxious, so that means he didn't shut out the idea. Wait, you said something happened."

"We kissed when we were at the storage unit but nothing since then. Not even a hand squeeze or anything."

"Don't overthink things before they start."

"But you and I are so good at overthinking things." I laughed. "Do you think they will be ok?"

"Ellie and Ben? I'd like to believe so. That was a brilliant idea of having them live with Mallory. A home without her brother can only be an improvement. Some stability will do them both good. And with Chuck getting her on a decent career of computer hacking, spying, coding, or professional gaming, whatever they do, can only be positive."

"Did you understand one word when they were talking computer stuff?" I asked.

"Is that what that was? I was thinking it was Greek or Lithuanian," Sherrie said.

"She is really tough. I admire her."

"Absolutely," Sherrie echoed. "What was the crazy thing you did while car shopping?"

"You've got an amazing memory. I went for it. My dad scoped out several cars for me to look at, and I jumped to the end of the list."

"Snazzy convertible, country long-bed truck, gone funky with the Brit flag on a Mini Cooper—oh wait, you are following me with a VW Bug?"

"Better."

"Hmm? Don't make me guess 'cause we could be here all night. Oh, did you join that cult of duckers and get yourself a Jeep?"

"Yup. I get the keys Thursday. And no, it's not like Chuck's souped-up, off-road beast with monster tires. Just a pretty slick-looking Jeep with windows that function and all the heating vents work. I might even go all out and make sure the radio can turn on and off."

"Wow, that is a big leap from twenty-two-year-old Debby. Are you going to know how to drive something so cool?"

"You may need to show me how it's done."

"Definitely count on that. I'm off to bed. I hope you get a visitor."

I was not sure how long I lay awake. Talking to Sherrie had settled me down from the frenzy of the past few days. I never told her Pete had heard Mallory's confession, and I didn't know why. Sometimes, I thought it was because it wasn't my secret, and just talking about it in any form seemed wrong.

Pete never showed that night, and when I woke at a quarter to six, I found a note in the kitchen in Ben's handwriting that simply said, "Thank you."

I never heard them leave the house. What I had assumed was Jorge leaving at five thirty must have been them. I did see two green army men on the bookshelf next to a framed picture of Sherrie and me.

A bowl of Cheerios and a cup of coffee, and I was out for a run. I had hoped the run would funnel all the drama and emotions of the last few days into neat little compartments in my brain. No podcast or music was syncing with my run.

The air was damp, and the spring fog was rolling off the river. It was usually my favorite time to run as the day began to break, but my legs were heavy. I couldn't shake anything out. After two miles, I decided to call it quits and just walk. I'd never cut out on a run before no matter how tired I was, and I didn't like the feeling of stopping short. It was the first time a run had put me in a worse mood than when I started.

My mood lifted when I saw a black truck pull into the parking lot at the boat ramp. My legs found their stride, and I ran up to the lot. I watched Pete swing his truck backwards into a spot overlooking the river. As I approached, he got out, and I spied three large coffee cups.

"Need the caffeine do you?"

"Well, one is for me. One cup is full of five different types of sugar and creamer. I have no idea how you like your coffee."

"Straight and pure. No muss no fuss. Happy coincidence I ran into you, or are you fishing?"

Pete froze before he handed me a coffee. "Damn, I really do suck at this stuff. I thought it would be a cool move bringing you coffee, but you think I'm here to fish. I might as well have brought my roommates. Last night, you said you were going to do your favorite run along the river."

Pete walked around to the back of the truck and dropped the tailgate. He took my coffee back from me as I hopped on, letting my legs dangle over.

He held out my coffee. I grabbed his hand, not the cup, and let our eyes meet.

I held his attention and said, "I was hoping you weren't fishing, but I hate to assume things."

He hopped up and sat next to me. We watched a barge float downriver and sipped our coffee.

"I didn't mean for you to cut your run short, or did you get a real early start?"

"For the first time, it was a real struggle. Normally, I can shake things off, but something was telling me maybe I should turn around."

"You should listen to that voice more often. I was nervous I would be sitting here for an hour, and the coffee would be cold. I really didn't think this through very well."

"Maybe you shouldn't think out things too much because this worked out."

"Thinking is not my thing today. My head is still pounding from yesterday."

"Hate to tell you, but I'm sure you know that your nose and eyes are not looking too good."

"I don't think they'll turn black and blue, just this shady pea-yellow color. Just praying I don't have to sneeze. My nose is a bit tender." We both laughed, and Pete asked, "How are you doing?"

"Thinking I am ok. More tired than I thought I was, and the run didn't do anything to help."

"I really didn't mean to eavesdrop last night. I assumed you guys heard me come in. I grabbed a breadstick and waited for one of you to come in and call me out for eating more than my fair share. Before I knew it, I was listening to Mallory and didn't know what I should do."

I didn't say anything.

Pete asked again, "You ok?"

"Why do you keep asking?"

"That was a lot of information about your very recent ex, and *you have a very recent ex*."

"You know what, I'm ok. Almost relieved somehow. I know he broke it off officially Friday night, but in some ways, I think I was done much earlier and should have done it myself. I have a history of dating losers, so I thought being with a nice guy is the right relationship for me. I kinda forgot about the partnership portion of the relationship."

We sipped our coffee, and both were quiet.

"Now you're quiet," I said.

"I'm just trying to figure out my next play. I didn't think past getting coffee."

"This might be hard to hear." I jumped off the tailgate and turned to face Pete, slowly backing away. "My interest only lies in tombstone-peeing, always-got-your-back, coffee-toting dudes."

"Where are you going?" Pete smiled.

"Gonna walk home and think about the best morning run I ever had."

It was this moment and that look: his smile and sweet eyes that I have tattooed on my heart and soul. It was more a moment of hope. It was what we both knew to be more than just a moment of love—it was a lifetime of love.

It's this moment I think about, and not when we said our vows or when I held his hand as he lay dying or when I fought to clear his name after the incident.

ELLIE'S STORY

They make me believe in people again. How do people do so much for someone they don't know? I don't know if I can make things even with Claudia and Sherrie.

Paying back Maggie and Jan is pretty easy. They knew the difficulties at home and they tried different ways of slipping me cash. There is no way someone makes twenty-five dollars in cash tips for a three-hour shift at the register, but the thought of it chokes me up. At one point, I was putting my money into the tip jar just for Jan to hand it back to me at the end of the shift. I was also ringing up bogus drink orders and putting cash in the drawer to cover whatever Jan told Maggie to pay me.

Money hasn't been a problem for a while, but I couldn't let anyone know that. More on that later.

I have done more housekeeping for Maggie in the six months than she has done for herself in six years. Her time spent reading to Ben has been priceless. His teachers say he is reading two grade levels ahead.

Grumpy Freddie is another I have to figure out how to pay back. The fourth night I crashed overnight on the couch in the corner of the dining room at Peach's, he caught me. He was the only one that ever caught me sleeping where I shouldn't be. Instead of saying anything to Jan, he gave me a key to the storage hallway. Two nights later, a cot and sleeping bag showed up.

Pearl has a younger sister that might be a good match for Freddie.

The school counselors haven't done much for me or Ben, but I guess it's all about what you tell them. Since I'm eighteen, there's not much they can offer me. I will give a shout-out to Mr. Graystone for getting me those computer coding classes at Jameson. Although that isn't the teacher's job, he's looking out for students. All students, not just the high academic achievers or those in total despair. It's the C-average kid that needs the attention. Can someone in charge tap a kid on the shoulder and say we see you, you count, can we help?

As for the rest of the River Bend residents, I really don't care what you say about me or my family. Most everyone has dirty little secrets. I know Adam being the town drug dealer is one of the worst things, but we are not all Adams.

Just remember, folks, you can have all the things money can buy, but if you don't teach your kid empathy and compassion, they have nothing. Let everyone see me and Ben thrive without their help.

Also remember, folks, I know who was buying, using, and turning a blind eye to it all. From the coaches who ignore the signs to the teachers that should have known better, the parents that were using, and best of all was that dumb cop who thought he was better than that badge he wore—I know all of you.

The job offer from Chuck was a surprise. I guess it's true: keep your friends close and your enemies closer. I would never call and Chuck and myself enemies, but me accidentally getting into his network when I was trying to hack Peach's cameras was purely accidental, sorta. I didn't go looking for it, but maybe I snooped further than I should have. Either you are with him or against him. I opted to go on his side. He has a pretty impressive list of clients he does cybersecurity for, and that he is letting me into his world is a nice compliment.

Plus, the paycheck will help with the cash flow problems. It's not because I'm low on funds, but I am cash heavy. As stupid as Adam's career is, he did one smart thing. The cash he was taking in was much higher than the boys in Chicago ever knew. That's a good thing because they would have wanted a bigger piece of the action. The bad thing is—well, at least for Adam—he had no idea how much money he actually was taking in or I was taking out.

I was siphoning funds before I knew what I was doing. The first time I did it, I was around Ben's age. I marched over to Pearl's house asking to play Monopoly and said I brought my own money and did not need to use their funny-looking money. Collecting a five here or a ten there from his stacks was fun, so it turned into twenties and hundreds.

Years ago, I would mark some bills and see if any of them turned up while I was working. Then I had to mark the bills that came in from Chicago in case the police were onto Adam. Those were the ones I hid.

Long before I went to the police, I had files of information. Who was coming and going. Where the drops were located and when. I only gave the police a tidbit of information as I only wanted to stop my brother. When the police did nothing and my brother continued, my collection of data only grew. I was ready when I went to the FBI, and someone with the ATF contacted me. I told Mr. Miller I'd lost one of the USB drives and could only recover some of the information, but I had it all. I needed to wait until I was eighteen and could prove Ben was my nephew or if we would have to disappear before any arrests were made.

I figured the information I gave Mr. Miller would have to be vetted and was probably not sufficient for court, but it would give them solid leads and keep me in the clear.

My father was absent most of the last nine years, taking contract construction jobs out of town. That alone is enough to vote him the shittiest father of the year, much less, how complacent he was when he figured out what Adam was up to. Being ignored by your classmates, looked over by teachers and counselors sucks, but being invisible to your father slices through you.

Ben and I will be fine. He has a few friends at school. Sean's mother even lets Ben come to the house and play and do sleepovers despite what people say about our family. Maybe I will consider counseling for him now. I am trying my best by reading as many books as I can to understand what someone his age needs. He knows I am his aunt and there is no mama in the picture. Just because that is his normal doesn't mean he doesn't feel the emptiness of not having a mom. And now his dad will be in jail. Adam himself is to blame for that, but

Ben's reality is he has to survive without his parents. He is a smart, funny and caring kid I would do anything for and I hope I am doing it right.

I just said Ben and I will be fine. More than fine. The key is knowing when to leave town. Drug-dealing is good money with high risks. Stealing from the idiot dealer is also very good money. I have piles of cash stashed all over this town.

Not only have I slept on random lawn chairs or in a house while someone was on vacation, there is thousands of dollars stashed in different yards and around town. I figure in five years' time, if it's still there, it's mine to take back. If you have found it, consider it rent for a night or two of sleeping at your place. I never took anything from the places I stayed, just sheltered from the chaos of the men that would come to my house.

Chuck may be the answer to help uploading some of this cash into legitimate accounts. He seems smart enough to know where my money came from and how it can help Ben and me.

Pete was not the only one who had heard Mallory's story. Chuck is loyal and seems to like to help those that need the help. I just have to work hard for him and earn his trust.

If one was to do the math, it was not much each month considering how much was coming and going. One to four hundred a month was average for ten years. It was never about greed. I rarely spent any of it. Maybe it's wrong stealing from a drug dealer, but maybe if someone had noticed or noticed me, I would not have collected all that cash and those scars.

Chuck did notice me and my hacking work. He might be the answer to my cash problem. How else am I going to get twenty-thousand-plus dollars out of River Bend? I told you my brother is an idiot.

BOOK CLUB DISCUSSION QUESTIONS

Things are never what they seem. Claudia and Sherrie hear the story about Ellie shoplifting, but it was to feed her and Ben and not a cheap thrill. What was the biggest misconception you learned about someone?

When Ben disappeared and Sherrie received the text Ben was ok, should she have gone to the police despite her promise to Ellie, or was she in the clear?

How soon can you start dating someone after a breakup? Pete and Claudia have been friends and went through some stuff together, but is it too soon?

Can you date a roommate's ex? Does that ever work out? Pete and Sherrie had two and a half dates. Would it matter if they had dated longer?

ACKNOWLEDGMENTS

There are not enough thank yous I can give my beta readers —Alexis, Molly, and Mel. I know I give you rough, rough, rough drafts, and I appreciate the honest feedback.

A large shout out to Kate and Layne. I am clearly not in my twenties and you provide real life answers to my silly questions that help keep Claudia and Sherrie from sounding and acting middle aged.

Thank you to Gretchen for keeping my website going.

Thank you to my editor, Starr Baumann. The story and mistakes are mine, but Starr helped smooth out the rough edges.

Most of all, thank you to my husband, Brian, and son, Alex, for their love and support.

ABOUT THE AUTHOR

After graduating from the University of Wisconsin-Stout, TJ embarked on a career in the hospitality industry, which led to multiple moves across the country. An avid marathon runner, TJ turned to writing after her knee eventually gave out. The author lives in Kansas with her husband, son, and dog, Reba.